A MARRIAGE OF CONVENIENCE

Debra Lynn Collins

Published by: Magnolia Charm Publishing
Cover by Lynnette Bonner
Images ©BigStock-36432853 - 49288418

Printed in the United States of America

Library of Congress Cataloging-in-Publication Data
is available upon request.
ISBN-13: 978-0692276471
ISBN-10: 0692276475

Acknowledgements

Thank you, Debby Mayne, for believing in me and guiding me in the right direction. You are such a wonderful teacher, instructor, mentor, and friend.

Special thanks to, Debra Ullrick and Staci Stallings for everything you have done. Both of you have helped me turn my dream into a reality. I couldn't have done this without your constant support, encouragement, and critiques. I am so thankful to God he has blessed my life with such two amazing Godly women.

And a special thank you to my wonderful daughter, Coby, for taking the time out of your very busy schedule to be my "proof reader" and my inspiration.

Dedication

This book is dedicated to my real-life hero
and husband, Steve, who has encouraged me
every step of the way on my writing journey.

To my wonderful children,
Tiffany, Coby, Andrew, and Kara,
thanks for still loving me when I was knee-deep in edits and
missing in action at home. I love you all!

In loving memory of my daughter, Tosha,
and my mother, Doris Dover,
I love and miss you both.

CHAPTER ONE

Isn't it strange how someone's death can bring all sorts of strangers out of the woodwork like termites from an exterminated home?

Lily Meyers wondered who these other three women and two men were as they waited together in Attorney Charles Hopper's conference room for the reading of Martin Chapman's will. Not one of these people looked familiar to her. One thing she was certain of, during the past three years while she'd lived on the ranch taking care of Martin, not one of them had ever visited.

The group huddled together on the other side of the long mahogany table, whispering and chatting among themselves. They sounded like chipmunks arguing over a nut. Each one of them had a sour expression on their face, and they were as cold to her as the artificial tree tucked in the corner. They took turns pointing and glancing down the table at Lily. They weren't even trying to hide the fact that she was the topic of their conversation, and with raised eyebrows, they made it obvious they wondered who she was, too.

She definitely didn't fit in with this crowd. These people were money. They were three-piece suits and Armani while she was Wrangler jeans, boots, and plaid. In fact, she felt more out of place than a colorful hummingbird in a flock of black crows.

All five of them were dripping in jewelry and not one of them had a hair out of place. She guessed they were the type of people who had weekly standing appointments at a hair salon.

She overheard one of the women whisper loudly, "She looks like she just stepped out of an episode of…" she tapped her well-manicured nail on her temple. "What's the name of that show?"

"The Beverly Hillbillies," one of the men replied with mocking derision.

"Ellie Mae," a couple of them said simultaneously.

Laughter thundered around the room. It was so loud it vibrated Lily's eardrums, making them ring.

Now, Lily wished she hadn't pulled her long brown hair back in a ponytail. Compared to these people, she was as frumpy as she could be.

They were all quite a bit older than she was. She guessed they were probably in their late fifties or early sixties. Around these parts most people of their age were usually friendly and would greet you with a smile and a, *How are you today?* But not these people. She feared their faces might crack if they smiled.

Shifting uneasily in her chair, Lily began to look around the room to try to avoid their icy stares. The room was as dreary as a rainy and cold December day. The carpet was a deep brown that perfectly matched the table. Three different abstract paintings hung on one of the beige walls. None of them was particularly interesting, but all had probably cost more than what she'd made in the last year.

The four large windows on the outer wall were from ceiling to floor but were covered with dark shades preventing the sun from streaming in. If it hadn't been for the fear of bringing even more attention from the others, she would have asked Mr. Hopper to open at least one of the shades to brighten up this dreary room. Anything would be an improvement at this point. Nevertheless, one thing she was thankful for was the four empty leather chairs on the other side of the table. Being trapped in this room with these five people was enough for her.

She glanced up at Mr. Hopper who was sitting at the head of the table for some kind of moral support or at least a friendly face. His glasses were perched on the end of his long, straight nose as he read over some papers. Deep in thought, it was as if he were the only person in the room.

"How much longer are we going to have to wait?" The woman with the long red fingernails impatiently tapped her nails on the table. "I have dinner guests coming at six tonight. Can't you hurry this along?"

Mr. Hopper looked at his watch. "I'm sorry, but I can't begin until everyone is here."

"Meg, you know we're waiting on Bryce. He should be here any moment," the woman with the triple-strand pearl necklace replied as she wound one strand around her finger.

"Are you sure he's even coming, Sherry Ann?" Meg, the woman with the red fingernails, asked.

The door opened, and every person in the room twisted in their chairs and looked over at it.

"See I told you he'd be here. I know my son." Sherry Ann childishly stuck out her tongue at Meg.

Oh no, not another one. Lily breathed out slowly, trying to settle her frayed nerves. The knot in her stomach pulled tighter at the thought of another one like them showing up.

The man slowly reached up, pulled off his sunglasses, and slipped them into the v of his shirt.

His blue eyes sparkled like early morning dew in the sunlight. His sandy-brown hair bounced when he turned his head. This man appeared to be no stranger to the gym, from the way his biceps bulged beneath his white polo shirt. She was certain he turned heads when he walked down the street. A funny feeling thumped into the pit of her stomach.

Lily hadn't realized she'd been staring at Bryce until he looked her way. He smiled and gave her a quick nod. She diverted her eyes as heat rose into her cheeks.

"Well it's about time," Meg huffed. She leaned forward in her chair, shaking a finger.

"Hello to you, too, Aunt Meg." The man flashed the woman a crooked, impish smile.

"Do you know how long we've been waiting on you?" Meg's top lip curled up like a mare that had just smelled a foul odor as she glared at him.

"Sorry you had to be kept waiting. I know how you hate that." He bumped up his brows, making her irritation grow worse.

"Humph." She swirled her chair back around and crossed her skinny bird legs.

Mr. Hopper stood to greet the newcomer and extended his hand. "You must be Bryce Fowler?"

"Yes, Sir. Sorry I'm late." He walked over and shook Mr. Hopper's hand. Then he strode over, and dropped down into the seat next to Sherry Ann.

"Why can't you ever be on time, Bryce?" Sherry Ann whispered.

"Sorry, Mom, my flight was delayed," he said and then leaned over his mother and spoke to the man next to her. "Hello, Dad."

The man's father scoffed and mumbled something under his breath.

"Can we please get this over with? I'm bored with all this waiting, and this Alabama heat is playing havoc on my hair." Meg bumped up her overly bleached-blonde hair with one hand.

"Well, all I can say is, if we inherit the old man's place, I'm putting it on the market as soon as possible. You couldn't pay me enough to live in Al-lua-bam-mur." Bryce's father sneered as he chuckled deep in his throat.

The others laughed at his pitiful attempt of trying to imitate a southern accent.

Lily wrapped her sweaty fingers tightly around the arms of her chair and pinched her eyes shut. *Lord, give me strength to endure these dreadful people.*

"Come on, Dad, that's enough." Bryce frowned.

Bryce glanced over at Lily, and for a fleeing moment, she thought she saw an apologetic smile sweep across his face. Shaking her head almost without moving it, she knew she had to be imagining things.

Sherry Ann elbowed her husband and giggled under her breath. "Now, Russell, behave yourself. We're supposed to be serious after all, but that was funny."

The hair on the back of Lily's neck prickled. She swallowed the bitter-tasting anger rising up in the back of her throat.

Lord, who are these insufferable people? They were too young to be Martin's siblings. Were they his nieces and nephews? He'd never mention having any living relatives.

From the front of the room, Mr. Hopper loudly cleared his throat. "Now that everyone's here, we can get started on why all of you were summoned here today. Typically this kind of thing is handled in the Probate Court, but at Martin's request, it's going to be carried out exactly how he wanted it."

Lily's heart ached at the mention of Martin's name. The reading of his will made it all too real that he was gone.

She smiled when she recalled the first time they'd met. She'd come to his rescue after he'd fallen in the local market's parking lot and broken his hip. Soon he'd hired her on as his caregiver, but it didn't take long before he took on the role of a father to her and a grandfather to her son. Over the last three years, he had become her family regardless if they shared the same blood or not.

"Now, that Bryce has finally made it. Can we get started?" The man in the tweed jacket lifted his hand in the air and snapped his fingers.

The woman seated next to him, shook her head in irritation, and nudged him with her elbow. "Sid, be quiet. After all, this man was your father. Can't you show just a little respect?"

Father? Lily's breath jerked in her throat. These people were Martin's children!

She took a quick look around the room. Not only had these people never visited Martin in the past three years but not one of them had even attended his funeral a week earlier, nor did they seem upset by the fact Martin had passed away.

"Respect? That's a laugh." Meg snorted and narrowed her eyes at the woman next to Sid. "He's not going to get an ounce of respect from me, I can assure you of that."

Sid lifted his hand in the air. "I second that. Can I get a third?"

Lily's blood turned to ice in her veins as the group all laughed. She shot Mr. Hopper a glance in hopes he would intervene and put a stop to this.

As if he could read her mind, Mr. Hopper pushed his chair away from the table and stood. "Silence, please." He said as his voice climbed an octave.

"Okay, okay. Let's all settle down so Father's attorney can wrap this up as soon as possible. I know we're all ready to head back to New York and leave this place behind us. So, go ahead, please continue, Mr. Hopper." Sid leaned back in his chair and folded his arms over his chest. "You have our full attention."

Mr. Hopper took his seat again. "Martin was a man who had his own way of doing things, and he certainly didn't like to do things in a traditional manner." He flipped open a folder and pulled out a DVD. "This is Martin's own version of his will, and he'll be reading it himself through video."

"He always did have to have the last word," Sid grunted and snarled his nose in disgust.

Mr. Hopper cleared his throat once again and ignored Sid's remark. He twisted his chair around to the cart that held a TV, which was directly behind him. He pulled the remote from his shirt pocket, switched on the TV, and then slid the DVD in the player.

Tears burned in Lily's eyes when Martin's sweet face filled the TV screen. It was amazing the love she had for him. It was hard to imagine not ever seeing him again rolling around in his wheelchair or hearing him whistling a tune. Grief tugged at her heart, but she quickly blinked away the tears.

"Well, I guess if you're watching this, it means I'm no longer living in this world, and I've moved on to the next." Martin lifted one brow and grinned. "I wonder, how many of you will miss me?"

Lily refused to turn her focus to any of the people on the other side of the table because she feared all she would see would be stone-cold expressions.

"I have appointed my legal counsel and dear friend, Charles Hopper, executor of my estate, and he's already taken care of all the legal jargon. All the papers have already been drawn, signed, and filed. Therefore, everything you hear today is legal and binding, but I wanted to tell each one of my children myself, exactly what I'm leaving to each of you. I guess you could say, I'm going out with a bang."

Meg huffed, leaned back in her chair, and mumbled something under her breath that Lily couldn't quite make out.

"But, first things first." He picked up his pipe and lighter, and with trembling hands set fire to the tobacco. He pulled in a couple of puffs. Within seconds, a swirl of smoke surrounded his graying, partially bald head. Even though his face was heavily lined with wrinkles, his blue eyes still were as bright as a young man's.

Lily closed her eyes and could almost smell the familiar aroma of Captain Black tobacco.

"I guess by now you're all wondering who the cute little brunette cowgirl is. Well, everyone I'd like to introduce you to Lily Meyers."

Lily squirmed in her chair when everyone's attention turned to her. The old cliché "*if looks could kill*" came to mind.

Martin continued, "I took a nasty fall about three years ago and broke my hip. Lily's been the one who has taken care of me all this time. I certainly don't know what I'd have done without her either, especially when I had my stroke last year." He paused and patted the arms on his wheelchair. "That's what put me in this thing. Lily has made an old man's life a little brighter just by knowing her. When I could no longer manage the ranch, she stepped up to the plate. She's been my ranch supervisor for the last two and a half years. My place would have fallen apart had it not been for her." He laid his pipe in the ashtray and smiled. "I just thought all of you needed to see what a pure and loving heart really looks like. It's embodied in her."

"Ah, now I'm beginning to see." Sid's voice made Lily's skin crawl with the hate and condescension it held.

"So Father had a playmate, huh?" An evil smirk curled Meg's lips as she made a clicking sound with her tongue.

"You know, Meg, I think you're right." Russell grinned, and then winked at Lily.

Lily's breath hitched in her throat at their insinuations. She opened her mouth to speak in her defense but quickly closed it. She didn't owe any of these people an explanation. If they had been in their father's life, they would've known the relationship between her and Martin was like a father and his daughter.

Martin had always been so kind to her and her five-year-old son, Joey. It was hard for her to believe these selfish, cruel people were even his children.

She decided to let them think what they wanted. So what if they believed Martin had a girlfriend young enough to be his granddaughter? He deserved to have had someone in his life to love him like that. A sly grin tickled the corner of Lily's lips. She liked the idea of irritating these awful people.

Martin picked up a red folder and waved it in front of the camera. "I guess this is what all of you have been waiting for. Inside this folder is my legal will. Charles will supply each of you with a copy of it when you leave here today. I'm just doing this video for fun."

Lily couldn't stop herself from smiling at Martin's last comment. He was still a clever old fox even at his age.

His famous mischievous smile slowly began to grow on his face. She knew that smile all too well. *Martin Chapman, what are you up to?*

"So, here we go. I, Martin Wayne Chapman, of Trinity, Alabama, being of sound mind, body, and judgment declare this to be my will, and I revoke all prior wills and codicils that I have made. To my children Sydney, Meg, and Sherry Ann." He rubbed his chin massaging his invisible beard and gave a nod. "Charles, if you'd be so kind."

Mr. Hopper pulled out three white envelopes from a folder and slid them across the table until they were in front of each of Martin's children.

"Inside those envelopes is what I'm giving to each of you and nothing more. If you remember, when I left New York City all those years ago, I left everything I owned at the time to the three of you. I then purchased the ranch and came here with a few dollars in my pocket to start over and that's exactly what I did, with no help from my children." Martin held up his hand. "So, none of you are entitled to anything I have here. Now, I have one more thing I want all of you to hear directly from me. I have only two beneficiaries named. They will be entitled to all my assets and wealth, and those two people are… my only grandson, Bryce Fowler, and my caregiver, Miss Lily Meyers."

Lily's head jerked up. "What?"

"What?" Bryce's voice echoed from across the table.

The room erupted like a volcano. Within seconds everyone was on their feet yelling and screaming at Mr. Hopper. He rocked back in his chair completely unaffected by their rage. Only a wily smile touched his mouth.

"This is absurd! You'll be hearing from my attorney, Mr. Hopper. It's bad enough the old man thinks he's going to leave it all to Bryce, but he was insane if he thought I would stand by and let some grubby little farm girl get her hands on my father's money," Sid shouted at Mr. Hopper, and then he turned his angry face to Lily. The veins in his neck bulged.

Gripping the edge of the table, Lily pulled herself up. Her legs wobbled underneath her like a newborn colt trying to stand on its own for the first time. "I didn't know Martin was—"

"Sid." Sherry Ann grabbed Sid's arm. "Bryce is Father's grandson after all, and if it's all left to him, you know Bryce will do right by the family." She then focused her attention on Lily and narrowed her eyes. "But as for you, you knew about this all along, didn't you? That's why you've been hanging around a dying old man."

"No, I didn't know he was going to do this," Lily said, shaking her head in disbelief. "I didn't have any idea he was…"

"Let's all just calm down for a moment." Bryce waved his arms in the air and shouted above the noise.

"I figured you for a gold digger." Meg glared at Lily, ignoring Bryce. "Well, not in this family, honey." She tore into her envelope, gasped, and let out an ear-piercing scream. "This has to be some kind of joke!"

The scream shot right through Lily's eardrums causing her to flinch. She lifted her arms to cover her ears but quickly snatched them down. Meg could put tornado sirens to shame.

Sid ripped his open. "Five thousand dollars, that's it?" His nostrils flared.

"Yes, that's the only thing your father has left to you," Mr. Hopper replied.

"I'll fight this, Mr. Hopper. The old man's money rightfully belongs to us." Sid slammed his fist down on the table causing Lily to jump. She felt sweat beads gathering on her top lip.

"You might have fooled our father, but you're not fooling us." Meg took a step toward Lily, but Mr. Hopper had already rounded the table and stood between Lily and the others.

Mr. Hopper held up both hands and tried to silence the group as he walked over to the door and held it open. "I appreciate all of you coming today, but from here on out the rest of the reading only concerns Bryce and Miss Meyers."

"What? You're asking *us* to leave?" Sid's face was a glowing mask of rage.

At that moment, two security guards came up and stood in the doorway.

"Yes." Mr. Hopper dipped his head toward the door. "And so are they."

"This isn't over, Mr. Hopper, I assure you. This isn't over!" Sid reeled around on his heels and stomped out of the room.

"Sid, wait. You have to do something. You can't let him do this." Meg snatched hold of his arm as she shuffled quickly in her high heels.

"What do you expect me to do?"

"Bryce, I need to speak to you. Now!" Sherry Ann yelled just before Mr. Hopper closed the door.

Slowly pushing himself up from his chair, Bryce stood. "I guess I need to go speak with my mother."

With a nod, Mr. Hopper opened the door again. "Please don't be long, Bryce. I'd like to wrap this up as soon as possible."

"I understand. I shouldn't be long." Bryce gave a nod in Lily's direction as he ambled out of the room.

Mr. Hopper still held onto the doorknob as he turned to Lily. "I know it's all a little overwhelming, Miss Meyers, but if you can be patient with me for just a little while longer everything will be explained to you in more detail. Would you like a cup of coffee or perhaps a bottle of water while we wait for Bryce?"

"Water would be fine. Thank you." Lily's throat felt as dry as dirt hungry for rain.

"Please take your seat again. I'll be right back."

A flush of adrenaline rocketed through her body. Feeling like she'd just escaped from a pack of hungry wolves, she dropped down into her chair with a thump.

Putting her fingers to her temples, she closed her eyes in exhaustion and disbelief. "Martin, what were you thinkin'?"

A few minutes later, Mr. Hopper re-entered the room and handed her a bottle of water.

"Thank you." She twisted the cap off the bottle and took a long drink despite the shaking of her hand.

He took his place at the head of the table again, slipped off his glasses, and rubbed his eyes.

"Mr. Hopper, I just don't understand this. Martin told me once he would take care of me after he passed, but I assumed it was just for some small amount of money to see me through until I could get on my feet. I never expected anything like this. You know that family won't leave this be. Can't I just walk away?"

Before Mr. Hopper had a chance to reply, the door opened, and Bryce Fowler stepped back into the room.

CHAPTER TWO

As Bryce took a seat next to Lily, he looked over into those dazzling dark eyes again. She was a beauty. Her long brunette ponytail hung halfway down her back. Her dainty nose was the perfect size for her almond-shaped face. Delicate cheekbones. Plump, full pink lips, which didn't require any lipstick, and a flawless, sun-kissed tawny complexion.

He had dated a few models in his lifetime, and this girl could give all of them a run for their money. No wonder his grandfather had fallen for this girl. Who wouldn't like having her around?

But, was Lily Meyer a gold digger like his aunt had said? Probably. What other reason would a young woman like her want to waste her time taking care of an eighty-eight-year-old man? Besides, she never did deny being his girlfriend, did she?

"Are the two of you ready to watch the second DVD?" Mr. Hopper drew out a different disc from the back flap of the folder.

With a huff and a raised eyebrow, Bryce grunted, "A second DVD?"

"The first one was for the family; this one is only for the two of you." Mr. Hopper turned, pushed the *Open* button on the player, and slipped the disc inside.

When the video started, once again regret tugged at Bryce's heart to see how old and frail his grandfather had become, but anger quickly replaced the regret. His grandfather had chosen to walk away from his family fifteen years before and never looked back. So, why did Bryce feel guilty?

"Now that the others are gone, let's get down to business. If you're listening to this portion of the video it means, Bryce, you made it here today." Grandfather smiled but sadness filled his eyes. "You're the one I think I've let down the most. I know you don't understand why I had to leave those many years ago. I hope you can find some forgiveness in your heart for a selfish and foolish old man. I can't make up for the hurt I've caused. Therefore, I have a question for you. What do you think of Lily? She's a beauty, isn't she?"

He couldn't argue with his grandfather there. Bryce grinned when he heard Lily gasp. He glanced over at her and noticed her cheeks had taken on a nice pink tint.

"Lily girl, what do you think of my handsome grandson?" Grandfather chuckled. "Okay, enough of my teasing. So, I guess by now both of you are wondering how you can inherit the same property?"

The thought hadn't even occurred to Bryce until now. He wasn't sure what was going on, but the knot in his gut made it apparent he wasn't going to like it.

"Bryce, I want to help you make the right decisions in your life. No matter what you may think, I want you to be happy. You need to know what it feels like to be a family man with responsibilities and to work for what you want instead of everything being handed to you." Grandfather stopped speaking, held an oxygen mask over his pale face, and took several deep breaths. Removing the mask, he continued, "Lily girl, I know what a struggle it will be trying to raise that boy of yours on your own."

She has a son? Bryce looked at her out of the corner of his eye. She sat upright in her chair staring at the screen, and Bryce saw her jawline twitch a couple of times.

Grandfather continued, "You're a good woman, Lily, and you need someone in your life that will love and take care of you and Joey."

"Where is this going, Mr. Hopper?" Bryce slid to the edge of his seat. A sinking feeling stirred in his stomach.

Mr. Hopper placed his index finger to his lips and then pointed at the screen.

Grandfather grinned. "So, I have a proposition for you both. It's pretty simple, there's only one thing the two of you will have to do which will entitle both of you to your inheritance." He leaned in closer to the camera, and with a gleam in his eyes he said, "The two of you will have to get married."

♥ ♥ ♥

"What?" Lily coughed as she choked on the word.

"Is this some kind of joke?" Bryce heaved himself out of his chair, shaking his head as he shoved a hand through his hair.

Mr. Hopper hit the pause button on the player as soon as Bryce was on his feet. "Hold on a minute, Bryce."

"If this isn't a joke, I'd say my grandfather has lost his mind. Wouldn't you agree?" He whipped his head around to glare at Lily in utter disbelief and waited for her to answer.

Her body stiffened in shock as she stared in disbelief at Martin's frozen face on the screen. She tried to control her breathing as her heart slammed against her ribs. Slowly she lifted her eyes to meet Bryce's befuddled face.

"I… I…" This was bizarre, even for Martin. At times, he was somewhat eccentric, but this?

"I don't have time for this. I have a plane to catch." Bryce threw up his hands and headed toward the door.

"Bryce, wait!" Mr. Hopper demanded and rose quickly to his feet. "At least listen to the rest of your grandfather's video before you make any hasty decisions. All I'm asking for is five more minutes of your time, just five minutes. What do you have to lose?"

Bryce stood motionlessly at the door for a moment with his back to her and Mr. Hopper. A few seconds later, Lily watched Bryce's shoulders rise and fall. He raked his hand through his hair, turned, and held out his hand with all five fingers extended. "Five minutes, I'll give you five minutes."

Bryce strode back and dropped back down into his chair. The crackling of the leather rattled her nerves as she tried to slow her erratic pulse.

Mr. Hopper sat back down, twisted in his chair, and started the video again. She shivered as she closed her eyes and prayed this nightmare would be over soon. Was this a nightmare? If it was, it was definitely time to wake up.

Fighting the urge to pinch herself, she opened her eyes and stared at the TV screen until her eyes burned.

"Bryce, Lily, I know this is a strange request, but I assure you I'm doing this for both your benefits, even if you can't see it right now. I'm only going to go over the basics, but Charles will explain all the stipulations when I'm finished. Remember he is the lawyer." Martin winked, picked up a yellow folder, and held it up.

"If the two of you decide to honor my wishes and get married, here are the rules of the game." Martin's voice was low and raspy.

"Is this a game to him?" Bryce grunted under his breath.

"Beginning the day you hear this reading, I'll give the two of you three months to become more acquainted, and then after the three months the two of you will marry and remain married for at least nine full months. Bryce, I want you to live at the ranch, so you'll move into the guesthouse, and Lily, you and Joey will move into my home. I have set up a separate account that Charles is in charge of, and the monthly bills will be paid out of that account for the next year. I've also taken the liberty of setting up an account in each of your names for your own personal use."

The hammering of her heartbeat sounded like a river rushing through her ears.

"Sounds pretty simple, doesn't it? Date three months, marry, and remain husband and wife for nine more months, that's it. Simply said, if each of you abides by all the rules, at the close of the year you'll receive the inheritance you're both entitled to." He fought to pull in a shaky breath and smiled.

Even though Lily was upset with Martin and his outrageous scheme, she still fought back tears as she watched him struggle to breathe. She knew what a battle it was for him to breathe on his own without the oxygen.

"If the marriage doesn't work out when the year has ended and you decide to go your separate ways, there'll be no questions asked. Once the contract is fulfilled, both of you will return to Charles' office at the end of the year, and you'll hear the last section of my will, and at that time you will be informed of exactly what each of you will receive. And I can assure you, it's worth sacrificing one year of your lives to grant an old man's dying wish." He leaned back in his wheelchair and clasped his hands. "One year. That's all I'm asking of you is one year."

"This is ridiculous. Apparently the old man *is* insane!" Bryce leaned forward, propped his elbows on his knees, rubbed his hands together, and shook his head.

Lily licked her dry lips as she spun the empty water bottle in her hands, wishing she hadn't already drank it all. "I can't believe Martin is doing this. I'm not a part of your family, Mr. Fowler. Nor do I want to be. I'll just walk away, and you can have it all." She dropped the empty bottle into her purse and started to get up.

"Wait." Mr. Hopper stopped the video and motioned for Lily to remain seated. "Miss Meyers, it doesn't work that way, if either one of you chooses not to enter into the marriage, the entire estate will be turned over to the state. That's one of the conditions. We're almost finished. I'll address any questions you may have at the end of the video." Mr. Hopper aimed the control toward the screen one more time and hit the play button.

There was more? Lily didn't know how much more she could take. Sinking back down, she put the bag on the floor not knowing if she would have the strength to pick it up again after this.

"Bryce, I'm doing this for you. You may not see it now, but you will. Lily, think about little Joey, he needs a stable home and a father figure in his life. If you don't agree to this for your sake, at least do it for his. The decisions you make today will not only affect your life, but they will have an effect on his life and his future, too."

The image of Joey's face flashed into her mind. Lily clutched her fists in her lap until her nails dug into her palms. She swallowed back tears once again, but this time it was angry tears. How could Martin have put her in such a dilemma?

Martin beamed, and a chuckle escaped his throat. "Bryce, I know you're furious with me at the moment, but if you don't agree to this, can you live with yourself knowing you were the one responsible for a woman and her young child being left with nothing? I know I haven't seen you in years, but I don't think you want someone else to have what rightfully belongs to you either, do you? It is your inheritance after all. Wouldn't you rather share your fortune with only one other person, or would you rather receive nothing?"

Lord, is this really happening? Lily wanted to run out of the room as fast as her legs would carry her, but the overpowering love she had for her son kept her glued to the chair.

"Now there's one more thing I need to add before we go any farther. Bryce, I don't want you to think you don't have to work for your part of your inheritance. Until the day the two of you are married, you will work on the ranch just as everyone else does, as an employee. I want you to learn what it takes to run one, and you will work under Lily's supervision. In other words, she's the boss. However, after the *I do's* are said, then and only then will both of you become equal partners. Now, about the living arrangements." He scratched his scruffy chin again. "Lily, I want you and Joey to go ahead and move into the main house as soon as possible. Now remember, Bryce, you'll be living in the guesthouse. We can't have the two of you living together until you're married, can we?"

Lily's cheeks burned at Martin's remark. Closing her eyes, she begged for the floor to open up and swallow her. How could this be happening?

Bryce leaned back in his chair with a thump. "Am I the only one who thinks the old man's delusional?"

"Stop calling him old man! He has a name," Lily snapped, and then rubbed her temples trying to ease the throbbing pain in her head. Where had that come from? She was infuriated with Martin, too, wasn't she? So, why was she so quick to jump to his defense? Her mind was in shambles as were her nerves and good sense.

Martin continued, "Bryce, Lily, just remember the decisions you make today will affect the rest of your lives. Charles will inform you of all the details I haven't covered. All I want is for the two of you to be happy and to find real love in your lives. Besides, who knows, the two of you may actually fall in love with each other. Wouldn't that be a hoot?" Martin winked, and the screen went black.

Lily's dry lips tingled. Her vision blurred to hazy, and her body trembled as Mr. Hopper explained in greater detail Martin's proposal. After fifteen minutes or so, Mr. Hopper closed the folder, propped his arms on top of it, and leaned forward. "Well, you've heard the conditions of Martin's will. Do either of you have any questions?"

"How long do we have to think this over?" Lily's voice cracked.

"If you agree to this, I expect to see both of you back here at eleven o'clock tomorrow. We will finish this in my office. It's a little more private. My office is down the hall second door on the right."

"Eleven o'clock? That's not enough time." She looked from Mr. Hopper to Bryce and then back to Mr. Hopper. "We need more time."

"I'm sorry but this is the time frame Martin wanted."

Bryce raised his hand and gave Lily a momentary glance before turning his focus back to Mr. Hopper. "I have a question. What if one of us doesn't show up?"

"Then I will assume your answer is no, and as Martin's stated, both of you will lose it all. I hope that isn't the case. I want you to think long and hard about everything Martin had to say. This is a once in a lifetime opportunity, I'd recommend you don't let it slip away." Out of the folder, he pulled out two sheets of paper and slid them across the table until they stopped in front of each of them. "I think this will help each of you with your decisions. It's a copy of Martin's financial records, and everything you need to know about the Chapman's Quarter Horse Ranch."

The paper lay in front of him as Bryce sat at a local Starbucks half an hour later and sipped on a cup of steaming hot coffee. The last two hours had turned his world upside down and inside out. "You're really trying to guilt me into something I have no desire to do, aren't you, old m…" Lily's flash of anger popped back in his brain. "Grandfather?"

Marriage was something he did not intend to be a part of. His parents were living proof that people marry out of convenience. They'd lived together in the same house, but for the past ten years, they had slept in separate rooms and lived separate lives.

He had grown up listening to his parents bickering and yelling on a daily basis, and he would never want to raise a child in that kind of environment. He always questioned why his parents decided to have a child in the first place. They certainly were not Ward and June Cleaver.

Then Lily's sweet smile raced across his mind. She was a beauty with those charcoal-colored eyes, delicate cheekbones, and pouty lips. A smile tickled the corner of his mouth. He wouldn't have minded getting to know Lily Meyers a little better under different circumstances. Much different circumstances. Shoving the paper away from his sight, he jerked that thought out of his brain.

One question still plagued his mind. Was she a gold digger?

He rubbed his face with both of his hands, slid the paper back to him again, and scanned over it once more. "But this is very convincing. I'm not going to let my inheritance slip through my fingers. Okay, Grandfather, I'll play your little game. But, let's just see if Miss Lily Meyers is up to the challenge."

He looked up as the waitress returned to his table. "Can I get you anythin' else?" she asked as she batted her long make-up covered eyelashes. She smiled and bit down on her pen, leaving a red lipstick ring around the end.

He drained his cup, pulled a couple of bills out of his pocket, and handed the money to the girl. "No, thank you. But, I do need to find a hotel for the night, any suggestions?"

CHAPTER
THREE

Lily's heart was as heavy as a rain-soaked bale of hay as she sat on the top step of the porch and replayed the day's events in her mind.

"Lord, show me what to do. I have no money saved, no job, and nowhere else to go. If I were on my own, I could make it, but I have to think about Joey. How can I date and marry a man I don't even know? And this man doesn't know anything about loyalty, love, or commitment. He didn't even have enough decency to show up at his own grandfather's funeral." She rubbed her hands down her jeans, squeezed her eyes shut, and leaned her head back against the rail.

"Martin, why did you do this to me?" Her scream sliced through the humid mountain air.

Her thoughts went back to the day she first met Martin. One cold December morning, she came to the aid of an elderly man lying on the pavement in the local market's parking lot. Apparently, he'd slipped on a patch of ice, fallen, and was in excruciating pain.

She called 9-1-1, sat with him, and held his hand until the ambulance arrived. Then she followed them to the hospital and waited in the emergency room. When they allowed her to see him, she remembered their brief conversation.

"Well, hello there. I can't believe you're still here." The elderly man's face lit up when Lily slipped into his room.

"I wanted to make sure you were okay. Sir, they told me you've broken your hip and need surgery. Can I call someone for you?"

The light in his eyes dimmed. "Nah, there's no one to call. No one at all."

The same loneliness she saw in his eyes was the same loneliness she had felt in her own heart most of her life.

So she had taken to visiting him every day during his stay in the hospital, bringing flowers, reading to him, and bringing Joey along for company. When it came time for Martin's release, his doctor suggested placing Martin in the nursing home, but Martin had refused.

When he offered the job to her of being his full-time caregiver, with the agreement that she and Joey would live in the two-bedroom guesthouse behind his home, she had gladly accepted.

That was the first time since the death of her husband that Lily felt like she was part of a family again.

Now Martin was gone, and she was left with the choice of dating and marrying a man she didn't know or becoming homeless and jobless, not to mention uprooting a five-year-old little boy from the only stable home he'd ever known.

She swiped a tear away and looked down at the crumbled report in her hand. "But this would definitely secure Joey's future."

She lifted her eyes to heaven. "Lord, show me what to do."

The rumble of the school bus coming down the drive caught her attention. When it stopped and the door swung open, love flooded her heart as she watched Joey climb down the steps. When he spotted Lily, a smile stretched across his face and he began to wave.

The heaviness in her heart disappeared like vapor from a steaming pot as she watched the only person in the world who held her heart in the palm of his tiny hand, running toward her.

Martin's statement echoed in her ears. *The decisions you make today will affect his life, too.*

"You're right, Martin. I have to do whatever it takes to make sure Joey has the best life has to offer. I refuse to make him suffer because of my fears and selfishness."

She took a deep breath, grabbed a hold of the rail, and pulled herself to her feet. "I guess I'm getting married." Saying the words aloud made her stomach cringe.

"Mommy!" Joey threw his arms around her waist and looked up at her. "You look pretty, and you have on your good boots. Where ya been?"

"Come on. Let's go inside, and I'll whip you up a peanut butter and jelly sandwich. Mommy has to talk to you about somethin' very, very important."

The next morning, Lily gnawed on her bottom lip and tried to keep her legs from trembling as she sat in Mr. Hopper's office. The ticking clock on the wall sounded like a bell-tower at noon matching the rhythm of her heartbeat.

Mr. Hopper pulled up his sleeve and glanced at his watch. "I'm sure he'll be here any minute now."

Panic gripped her throat, squeezing her airway. *What if Bryce doesn't show up today? What if he doesn't want to do this? Where will I go? What about Joey?*

When the door opened, relief mingled with uncertainty washed over her, causing her stomach to churn. She closed her eyes as she pulled in a shaky breath.

"Sorry, I'm late." Bryce strolled over, sat down in the chair next to Lily, and flashed her a lopsided grin. "Good morning."

"Mornin'," Lily whispered, trying not to notice how his Polo shirt hugged his chest and shoulders.

Every nerve in her body twitched when Mr. Hopper's chair squeaked as he leaned forward. The sound echoed around the room almost as if it were bouncing off the walls. "In view of the fact that both of you are here, I assume your answers are 'yes' to Martin's request?"

"Would we be here if it wasn't?" Bryce settled back in his chair with exaggerated casualness. "How is this supposed to play out? What do we do first?"

"I guess the first thing we need to do is to set a date for the wedding." With his black-rimmed glasses perched on the end of his nose, Mr. Hopper smiled and flipped over several pages on his desk calendar.

"Let's see, three months from today that will make it August 21st. How about we mark it down for that day?" Mr. Hopper glanced at them over the rim of his glasses waiting for an answer.

"Whatever she wants is fine with me." Bryce tipped his head toward her though his gaze didn't quite follow.

Full body tremors bolted through Lily's body as she gripped the arms of the chair. Panic gripped the back of her throat, choking her, making it hard to breathe. "Wait. Wait. Wait. I don't think I can do this. I'm sorry. I thought I could, but I can't."

With another glance in her direction, Bryce turned to Mr. Hopper. "Sir, may we have a moment, please? We haven't had a chance to discuss this amongst ourselves. We only need a minute."

Nodding, Mr. Hopper rose. "I have an idea, since it's so close to lunch time, why don't I give the two of you a few minutes alone, and when you're ready, the three of us will go and have lunch? That might help settle the nerves. I'll go and bring the car around."

He rounded his desk and placed his hand on Lily's shoulder. "Lily, I encourage you to rethink your decision. I know it seems like all of this is happening quickly, but whether you believe it or not, Martin did have your best interests at heart. I'll be waiting in the lobby." He gave her shoulder a squeeze and left the room.

When Mr. Hopper was gone, Bryce stood, leaned against the corner of Mr. Hopper's desk, and crossed his arms. "What's going on?"

"I don't think I can do this," Lily said, shaking her head. Her hands throbbed from gripping the chair so tightly.

"Miss Meyers. Lily." He hesitated for a brief moment, relaxing his stance and giving her a dazzling smile. "I can assure you, this wasn't one of the things on my to-do list today either, but I've given it quite a lot of consideration over the past few hours. You read the report. How can we say no? You know I'm right, or you wouldn't be here."

Lily didn't reply. She couldn't. The words stuck in her throat, growing there until they were about to choke the air right out of her.

"One year isn't so much to ask, and then we can both walk away with a small fortune. What do we have to lose? Look, I don't appreciate my grandfather trying to have control over my life, especially in light of the fact that I haven't seen him since I was a boy, but we can't say no to this opportunity. I'm in no way ready to be a family man, and I can also promise you I'm certainly not husband material, nor do I ever want to be, but I still think this can be beneficial for the both of us."

Releasing a hesitant sigh, Lily took a gasp in because she was getting light-headed. The last thing she wanted to do was pass out on the lawyer's floor.

Bryce leaned in closer to her and looked straight into her eyes. "I have a proposal for you, if you're interested."

Her brows crinkled as she leaned back further in her chair, putting more space in between them. "What's that?"

"Let's consider this a friendly business arrangement. Then at the end of the year, we'll say our good-byes and that will be that. It will be a relationship with no strings attached, no commitments, and no obligations. This will be a financial investment only and one that will pay off big in a year. So, what do you think?"

"A financial investment, huh? You have this all figured out, don't you?" Lily folded her arms over her chest and bit down on her bottom lip.

"I believe it's a good plan. Now, be honest, you do too, don't you? Of course, we'll still jump through all the hoops to please Mr. Hopper, but we'll be the ones who will be in control, not him or my grandfather. Then after we're married, I'll be your houseguest and nothing more. We'll only be business partners."

The breath of relief felt better than she had realized it would, and, she lifted her chin and looked straight into Bryce's blue eyes. "I think I can live with that arrangement." She stood, took a step closer to him, and extended her hand. "I reckon we've reached an understandin', Mr. Fowler. So, we shouldn't keep Mr. Hopper waitin'."

He straightened, uncoiling to take her hand as if she'd been speaking a different language. "Reckon? I take it that means, yes."

Lily nodded and even managed a smile. "Yes."

He returned the nod and took hold of her hand. His fingers were cool and smooth as they touched hers. "There's just one thing I think we should take care of right now."

"What's that?" Quirking a brow, she lifted her eyes to meet his.

Still holding her hand, he tugged her closer. "Since we've just became engaged today, Lily, don't you think it's about time you call me Bryce?"

Before she could reply, the door opened. Lily jerked her hand away and took a step back as they both looked toward the door. Mr. Hopper's secretary, who was all of 35 with a body and manner that would stop a train, stood in the doorway. With one hand on the doorknob and the other on her shapely hip, a smile stretched across her face as her eyes skimmed over Bryce. "It's nice to see you again, Mr. Fowler. Mr. Hopper wanted me to let you know he's waiting for you in the lobby."

"Thank you. We were about to head that way," Bryce said, flashing the secretary a million dollar smile. "And please call me Bryce."

The secretary's bright red lips curled into a smile as she dropped her eyes demurely. "Well, if you need anything at all, don't hesitate to ask."

"I'll keep that in mind," he replied, the smile still lingering on his face. Charming. It was a great word for him though not one Lily particularly liked.

"You do that." The secretary sucked in her bottom lip and gave him a once over again before pulling the door closed behind her.

Bryce chuckled under his breath and then took hold of Lily's elbow. "Are you ready?"

What am I--invisible? The nerve of that woman, she was blatantly being flirtatious with Bryce as if Lily wasn't even in the room.

Lily looked up at Bryce, cocked her head to one side, and yanked her elbow from his grasp. "Are you serious?"

He shrugged one shoulder and gave her an innocent smile. "What?"

She huffed, rolled her eyes, and jerked her bag higher on her shoulder. "Men."

Mr. Hopper glanced at the two of them in the rearview mirror. "I was thinking of *The Yellow Crab* for lunch, is that okay?"

"That's fine with me." Bryce turned to Lily, slanted his head to one side, and popped up a brow. "Lily, how about you?"

She crossed her arms like a pretzel and released a sigh. "That's fine."

"Afterward we'll go back to my office. I have just a few more minor details we need to go over. Lily, if you would like a bridal shower or something along those lines, I'm sure my secretary can put something together."

"Oh, I just bet she could." Lily's whisper was soft, but Bryce heard it just the same.

He grinned. This lady had spunk.

"I can give her a call right now, if you'd like for me to," Mr. Hopper offered, waving his cell phone over his shoulder.

"No thank you, Mr. Hopper, that won't be necessary." Lily turned and stared out of the window, gnawing on her fingernail.

Bryce twisted sideways in his seat. "Are you sure? I thought all women loved that kind of stuff."

She turned and met his eyes. "I guess I would if I were marrying the man of my dreams, a man I was in love with, but this…" Shaking her head, she turned and stared out of the window again.

He had to agree, this wasn't your average engagement. It was time to change the topic of conversation. "So, Lily, tell me more about this little boy of yours."

"His name is Joey, and he's five-years-old." Her voice was soft as she spoke toward the window.

"Where's his father? I mean, I know the two of you must be divorced, but is he going to be a problem?"

"You have nothing to worry about." Lily turned her head and met his eyes again. Her jawbone flinched.

"Sorry my mistake, I just know how jealous people can become when an ex decides to move on. You know, it's that old scenario, I don't want you, but I don't want anyone else to have you either. I just don't want to be blindsided, that's all. You can see my point, can't you?" He cocked his head to one side and lifted a questioning eyebrow. That was one road he'd traveled before, and he didn't want to go down that same old road again.

Blowing out a breath, Lily lips tightened into a narrow slit. "If you must know, a drunk driver decided to take a joyride at the same time my husband was leaving work. The drunk driver walked away without a scratch, my husband didn't. So, like I said before, you have nothing to worry about."

Bryce felt like he had been sucker punched. He didn't know what he was expecting, but he sure wasn't expecting this. "Oh. I'm… I'm sorry for your loss. I didn't know. It must be tough on you, raising a child on your own."

"It was, until I met your grandfather. But now," she lifted one shoulder in a shrug and sighed heavily. "It looks like I'm right back where I started. I want you to know Joey is the only reason I'm doing this. I'm not doing this for myself or for the money or the ranch or anything else of Martin's. I'm doing this for Joey. He deserves the chance to have a great life, and if marrying a complete stranger is what it takes, well, that's just what I'll have to do."

With a tight chest, he could never imagine his mother ever doing anything like this for him, unless there was something in it for her. Was Lily Meyers the real deal, or was she just a splendid actress? He could usually read a woman's motives within minutes of meeting her, but not this one. He felt completely perplexed.

When it came time for her to order, Lily's appetite took a leap out the window. "I'm not very hungry. I think I'll just have a sweet tea with a lemon."

"Are you sure you don't want anything to eat?" Bryce leaned in and asked.

"To be honest, I don't think I can." The queasy feeling washed over her like a heavy downpour in the middle of a summer storm.

"Not even an appetizer?" Mr. Hopper crinkled his brows.

"I don't think so." Lily handed her menu back to her waitress. "Tea will be fine."

Although Bryce didn't look happy about her decision, the two men managed to carry on a light conversation until the food arrived.

"I haven't had lobster in quite a while. This is really good," Bryce said in between bites.

Stealing a glance at Bryce, she noticed every time he smiled, his dimples deepened. Why did he have to be so handsome? The shiver in her stomach made her queasy.

Just as Mr. Hopper polished off his last bite of fish, his cell phone rang. He pulled it out of his pocket and glanced down at the screen. "Excuse me, I need to take this." He rose from the table and walked toward the entrance.

Bryce forked a sliver of the white meat and twirled the fork in the air. "You have to try this. Do you want a bite?"

"No, thank you."

"Ah, come on. You don't know what you're missing." He whirled the fork around, his eyes teasing her. "It's so good."

"Give me that." With no warning, she jerked the fork out of his hand and took the bite. "There. Now, are you happy?"

His smile said he was. "See, that wasn't so hard, was it? Now admit it, it's good, isn't it?"

She nodded as the buttery meat tingled on her taste buds.

He reached out and took hold of the fork she still held. "We'll have to eat here on one of our dates."

Dates? A strange mixture of trepidation and excitement zipped through her body like a jolt of electricity.

"Sorry about that. I have to get back to the office. Are you two ready to go?" Mr. Hopper asked as he approached the table, motioning for the waitress. "Check please," he said when she came within earshot.

Lily and Bryce both nodded.

When the waitress returned with the black check presenter, Bryce reached for it.

"Oh no, lunch is on me today." Mr. Hopper took it from the waitress. He glanced at the ticket, pulled a couple of bills out of his wallet, and slipped them inside.

Ten minutes later, they were back in Mr. Hopper's office. Why did life feel so very out-of-control every time she stepped into the room with the huge mahogany desk?

"I have another client coming in about thirty minutes, so let's get things wrapped up here." Mr. Hopper dropped into his chair, opened the top drawer, pulled out two white envelopes, and slid them across his desk. "Here's each of your bank cards which I have already activated for you."

He then turned to Bryce. "Bryce, how long do you think it will take you to get your things moved here from New York?"

"I'd say it shouldn't take me any longer than three or four days to get all the loose ends tied up." Bryce lounged back in the leather chair looking more at ease than he had earlier. Confidence looked good on him.

"Good. I've taken the liberty of purchasing an airline ticket for you. Your flight is scheduled for eight-thirty in the morning." Mr. Hopper pulled the ticket out of his jacket pocket and handed it to Bryce. "Lily, you and your son can go ahead and start moving your things into the main house while Bryce flies back to New York and gathers his belongings."

Lily nodded although breathing was again becoming a problem.

"Now with that settled, Lily, I have a few questions for you. I need to ask you about the ranch hands."

"What about 'em?"

"Let's start with your foreman, Wade Haston. Martin has left him a sizeable amount of money as well, but there were no other details about his employment, and I know he's still been running things out there since Martin's passing. Do you plan on keeping Mr. Haston on?"

The thought never crossed her mind that Wade's job at the ranch would be in question. Why had Martin not secured Wade's position in his will?

"Yes. Yes, of course, I want to keep Wade on. He's been at the ranch for almost as long as I have. I know Martin would want me to keep Wade on. Besides, I couldn't run the ranch without him. He's indispensable."

"Bryce, do you have any objections to this?" Mr. Hopper asked.

"What?" Lily leaned forward. "Mr. Hopper, with all due respect, he hasn't even seen the ranch, and I'm sure he doesn't know the first thing about ranchin' or what it takes to run one."

"Lily, don't you think we should at least inquire his opinion on the matter? Remember, after the 21st of August he will be the co-owner of the ranch," Mr. Hopper said, and then he turned to Bryce.

The back of Lily's throat burned. She had already lost Martin, she couldn't lose Wade too. "I realize that, but we have to keep Wade on. We wouldn't be able to run the ranch without him. Martin trusted him to do it, and we should too."

Bryce slouched farther in his chair and flipped his hand in the air toward Lily. "Whatever she wants to do is fine with me."

"Okay. I'll give Mr. Haston a call, and let him know his position will remain permanent." Mr. Hopper scribbled on his notepad. "If you need to make any changes later on down the line, all you have to do is give me a call."

"I'll keep that in mind. Thanks," Bryce said before Lily got any words into her head.

Just who do they think they are? They're both crazier than a box full of hungry chickens if either one of them thinks Wade is going anywhere.

"Now, about the other employees on the ranch—"

"Mr. Hopper, if there're any other questions you have about any of the ranch hands, I think it's best to speak with Wade. He's trained them, and he knows best."

Mr. Hopper only nodded as he scribbled on his notepad again.

"I thought you were the supervisor." Bryce tilted his head to the side and lifted one brow at her. "Don't you think it's a mistake to give an employee that much authority? I'm just saying."

"I'll have you know, Wade is much more that an employee. He knows Martin's ranch inside and out, and he knows more about how to run that place than the two of us put together."

Lily closed her eyes and rubbed her forehead. What was wrong with her? She wasn't normally a snappy person, but all of this was wearing on her nerves, making her overreact to everything. Taking a slow, deep breath, she settled back in her chair and forced her fists to unclench. It wasn't easy.

CHAPTER FOUR

Exactly who was this Wade Haston person anyway? Lily thought he was indispensable. Bryce wondered if this man was his grandfather's age. He pictured Lily doing most of the work while old man Haston shuffled around behind her. Why did this man have any say when it came to the employment of a worker?

Still, Bryce held up his hands in defeat. He didn't want to upset her any more than necessary. "Sorry, I didn't mean to upset you."

He had to admit, he liked the way her lips pursed when she was angry.

"I'm not upset. But, I do want you to understand one thing. All of us work together to keep the ranch runnin'." She narrowed her eyes and gave Bryce a quick glance up and down. "And since you're going to be living on the ranch for the next year, I expect you to work as hard as the rest of us do, and I can promise you, it's not going to be a cushy, cushy job either."

He stifled the chuckle threatening to rise to the surface. He knew a laugh would only fuel her anger, and he didn't want to make a prickly situation worse, not in front of Mr. Hopper anyway.

Looking her over, now that she was going to be his wife after all, he guessed she was probably somewhere around five foot-two, maybe three inches tall, and she couldn't have weighed more than 120 pounds, but she would certainly prove to be a feisty one. If he were a betting man, he'd bet she'd match any man toe-to-toe if she was pushed into a corner. He liked the fire he saw in her eyes.

This year is going to be an interesting one.

"I think we're finished up with things on my end. Now, do either of you have any questions for me?" Mr. Hopper asked.

"No, Sir," Lily replied through pinched lips.

Bryce shook his head.

"Good. Each of you has my number." Mr. Hopper nodded and rose to his feet. He extended his hand to Bryce. "Remember to call if you have any questions at all." He shook Bryce's hand and then turned to Lily. "I wish both of you the best of luck."

Mr. Hopper walked with them to the door and held it open. "Bryce, I'll swing by the ranch around seven in the morning and give you a lift to the airport."

"What? I thought… well… You're staying at the ranch tonight?" Lily's long eyelashes fluttered as a surprised expression rolled across her face.

"If that's going to be a problem, I can go back to the hotel for the night," Bryce said.

Mr. Hopper cleared his throat and shifted his glasses. "I called Bryce this morning and suggested he go ahead and check out of the hotel, Lily. I assumed you would want him to see the ranch before he leaves. That's not going to be a problem, is it?"

Lily's jaw tightened as she narrowed her eyes. "No, I guess not. That will be fine. Joey and I will be staying in our place tonight anyway. You're welcome to stay in the main house."

"Great, and if it wouldn't be too much of an inconvenience, could I catch a ride with you to the ranch, too?"

"I guess so. You didn't think I'd make you walk, did you?" The playfulness in her voice caught him completely by surprise. But he liked it.

"I appreciate the ride, Lily." Bryce pushed open the glass door of the attorney's building, and his face contorted when they stepped out into the heat again. "Whew, this heat will take some time to get use to."

She dipped her head. "Like the lyrics in one of Bachman Turner Overdrive's old songs, 'You ain't seen nothing yet.'"

Mild fear trounced across his features. "That's reassuring."

Lily shrugged. "If you're here long enough, you'll get used to it."

"I don't know if I want to." He wiped his brow with the back of his hand. "It feels like I'm in an oven out here."

"Well, I hope you're up for a nice little walk in this heat because I had to park a block away this mornin'."

"A block? Whew."

Lily rolled her eyes and shook her head in disbelief. How could this man be Martin's grandson? Even at his age, Martin never complained about the heat, the cold, the rain, or the storms. As a matter-of-fact, she couldn't recall him complaining about anything.

Four steps and then two more, and Lily just had to know. "Can you answer a question for me?"

"What's that?"

"Mr. Hopper said you might want to see the ranch before you left town. What did he mean? Are you tellin' me you've never been to the ranch?"

"No, I've never been there." Bryce dipped one hand into the pocket of his expensive looking pants as he strode along at her side.

"What?" The disbelief hit her square in the face. "How's that possible? Martin's lived there for years."

"Lily, I haven't seen nor spoken to my grandfather in fifteen years." The words flowed so nonchalantly from his lips that it seemed like he was talking about a stranger. Someone he'd never met.

With a swing, she tossed her dark hair over her shoulder as she spun to look at him. Her brows sank tightly toward her nose. "Fifteen years? But, he was your grandfather, I don't understand."

"It's complicated."

Lily's face puckered as if she'd bitten into a lemon. "Complicated or not, he was still your grandfather."

Bryce glanced at her and smiled. "You really did care about the old man, didn't you?"

"Like a mother hen cares for her chicks." Her lips tightened. "Look, I want you to know, this thing with us is completely out of his character, and I have to admit, I can't believe he's done this, but Martin was a good man, an honorable man. A man I was proud to call a friend."

"A friend?" Sarcasm oozed through the word *friend*.

In the next heartbeat, she stopped and placed a hand in the middle of his chest, stopping him in his tracks. "Let's get something straight right now. I know what you and your family thought about me yesterday, and who and what you thought I was, but only twisted minds would think such things. I did love your grandfather, but I loved him like a father, and he loved me as if I was his daughter."

Bryce stared down into her eyes, digging there for the truth. "Really?"

"Yes, really." For reasons she didn't understand herself, it was important to her that he never have the question of that horrible lie lurking in his conscience. "He was my family, and Joey and I were his."

"I wished I had known the same man you knew, Lily. But, sadly I didn't." Bryce's chin twitched as his jawbone tensed.

That softened the take-no-prisoners stance of her spirit. "Frankly, I think it's a shame you didn't know Martin the way I did."

The flinch of his jaw tightened another notch. "And, that was his choice, not mine. He's the one who chose to walk away from his family and never look back. Not to be rude, but I'm finished with this conversation." With that and a comb of his hand through his hair, Bryce strolled ahead.

Letting her head fall, Lily had to admit that whatever happened between Bryce and his grandfather was still obviously painful for him, and she realized this was something she needed to leave alone. There was enough pain in the situation as it was; they certainly didn't need any more.

Bryce stopped and looked around the parking lot. "Which ride is yours?" he asked when she walked up beside of him.

"It's the blue pick-up." She nodded toward her truck as she fished the keys out of her bag.

"You drive a truck?" Bryce snorted and with a bob of one brow, he said with a smile, "Of course you do."

"What's that suppose to mean, and why is it so funny to you that I drive a truck?" She flicked one hand on a hip and lifted her chin.

He quickly ran his eyes up and down her. "I just pictured you in one of those girlie cars. You know a bug."

"You've got to be kiddin' me. Is there anythin' about me that would make you think I would drive one of those matchbox cars?"

"I don't know, maybe because you're a female?"

She didn't know why, but this man had a knack for rubbing her the wrong way. One minute he was sugar sweet, and the next minute he was as irritating as a bothersome gnat. "Oh, I see. I guess where you come from you think girls are just too ditsy to know how to drive a truck. Well, here in the good ole south, we girls know how to do lots of things, other than just paintin' our nails and gigglin'."

"Okay, okay. Boy, I'd hate to see you angry." He grinned and waved his hands in the air.

Was he poking fun at her?

"You're right. You would." Lily jerked open the door to the Ford Ranger she'd just paid off three months before, crawled in behind the wheel, and started the engine.

Bryce climbed in on the passenger's side, fastened his seatbelt, and then turned to her with a smile on his face. "So, where exactly is the ranch?"

Her irritation didn't seem to faze him in the least. *Let it go, Lily. Don't give him the satisfaction of knowing he's gettin' to you.* "The ranch is in Trinity. It's about twenty-five miles from here."

"Have you always lived in Trinity?"

Before she had a chance to reply, her cell phone rang. She reached across him, popped open the glove compartment, pulled out the phone, and looked at the screen. *Wade.*

"Excuse me, I need to take this."

He dismissed the pleasantry with one shrug. "Sure, go ahead."

"Hello?" Lily cleared her throat to suppress the shakiness she felt in her voice.

"Hey, girl, where are you? I've been callin' the ranch and your cell phone for over an hour. I've been worried sick. Are you okay?" Panic mixed with concern etched Wade's voice.

Lily jerked her gaze across the seat and then retrained it to the street outside. "Yes, I'm fine. I'm sorry I worried you. I had to make another trip to the lawyer's office again this mornin', and I left my phone in the truck."

"You had to go to the lawyer's office again? What on earth for?"

She wasn't about to tell him about Bryce, not right then anyway. Later. Definitely later. "Can we discuss this later? I'm exhausted and ready to get home."

"Sure. So how are you holding up?"

"I'm okay, but it feels so odd without havin' Martin around the ranch. I sure do miss him." Biting back tears, she cleared her throat again. "It just won't be the same."

Bryce moved in the seat, and Lily knew he had turned to look at her. Feeling his eyes on her face, her cheeks warmed.

"I know, but you still have me hangin' around." Wade's husky voice softened. "A team of wild mustangs couldn't drag me away."

"I appreciate it, Wade. I don't know what I'd do without havin' you around. Do you know what time you'll be back tomorrow?"

"I should be there around noon. Why?" Wade asked.

"When you get in, could you please come up to the house? There're some things I need to discuss with you."

Trepidation fluttered around in the hollow of her stomach. The nagging in the back of her mind refused to be stilled. Wade wasn't going to like this arrangement at all. That was almost certain.

"As soon as I unhitch the horse trailer, I'll come on up. Is everything okay, Lily?"

"Yes." She glanced over at Bryce, wishing he wasn't sitting right there. So close. Listening. "There are just some things I need to talk to you about."

"Do you need me to come back now? Just say the word, and I'm there. The boys can handle this run."

"No, no, everything's fine. Tomorrow will be soon enough." She hated how desperate and panicky her voice sounded, but she couldn't get her nerves to stop bucking like a young filly in a spring pasture.

"Are you sure?"

"Yes, Wade. It's not a big deal. It can wait until you get back."

"All right, but if you need me for anything, all you have to do is call. You know that, don't you?"

"I know." Her head drifted down into the softness her heart felt for Wade. He was a good friend. "Well, I need to let you go, be careful on your trip home, and we'll talk when you get back. Bye, Wade."

"Remember what I said. Call me if you need me. I'll see you tomorrow. Bye, Lily."

Lily was thankful Wade had carried a few horses to the auction over in Tennessee and wasn't at the ranch. Wade was like a big brother to her, and she knew he would be furious if he knew she was bringing a stranger onto the ranch when she and Joey were all alone, let alone allowing him to stay the night. Somehow, she would have to explain it all to him before Bryce returned from New York. The problem was, she didn't understand most of it herself.

She must be very fond of the old man, Bryce thought when he saw how her face lit up when she heard the man's voice on the phone.

"Sorry about that. I had to take that call."

"No problem. I guess I need to check my phone too. I haven't turned it on all morning." He pulled his own phone out of his pocket and turned it on. When the phone came to life, Bryce moaned when he saw the screen. He had 33 voice mails and 47 text messages. No doubt every single one was from one of his relatives.

He had too much on his mind and no patience or energy to deal with any of his family members, but he knew his mother wouldn't give up until she reached him. He reluctantly opened one of her texts.

Bryce, I know you're avoiding the family. You had better contact me ASAP!

He hit reply. *Mother, everything is okay. I will call you as soon as things are settled here. I give you my word.*

As if she could read his mind, without looking at him, Lily asked, "Have you told your family about this?"

"No, not yet. I don't want to deal with them right now. You met them yesterday. Should I say more?"

Lily raised and dropped one shoulder. "I guess not."

"After all, they're all twisted minded," he repeated Lily's statement from earlier.

She cut her eyes over at him and flashed him a smile. "That included you, too, you know."

To his surprise, his heart did a little dance. "So you can smile?"

"When I have a reason to," she answered, turning her face away from him and focusing on the road again.

"You should do it more often. It looks nice on you. I like it."

"Oh, you're a sweet talker, aren't you?" She rolled her eyes and huffed. "You know, I've heard your type say things like that before, but that stuff doesn't work on me. You should save it for the next girl who's anxiously waitin' in line because I'm not interested."

"I usually have several women standing in line at one time, if you must know," Bryce shot back, wounded by her cavalier attitude. "So, don't flatter yourself, sweetheart. I never said I was interested either. I was trying to be nice. But, don't worry, it won't happen again."

"Good, and I'm not your sweetheart. You can call me by my name or nothin' at all."

He went back to his phone just to have something to do. "Noted."

After several minutes of uncomfortable silence, Bryce finally abandoned the phone and asked the question that was playing tag with his mind. "So, is there anything I should know before we get to the ranch?"

"Such as?" she asked but never took her eyes off the road.

"How do I introduce myself to your son for one?"

"Ah, something like, Hi, Joey, my name's Bryce Fowler. I'm glad to meet you." A smirk toyed with the corner of her lips.

"Cute. You know what I mean, did you explain to him we're getting married? Am I suppose to be like his dad or —"

"Whoa, whoa." She lifted her hand in the air and cut her eyes over at him. "I don't want him to know we're getting married, not right now anyway." She shook her head with a snap. "I don't know why, but he's really excited to meet you. It could be perhaps because you're Martin's grandson, I don't know." She shrugged a shoulder. "But I don't want him to become attached to you or for him to think you're gonna to be around for a while and you're not when you realize a few weeks down the road you can't handle the ranchin' life and run off. I won't put him through that."

Bryce grunted, annoyed by her presumptive dismissal of him. "So, how are you going to explain to him why I'm at the ranch?"

"I've already told him you were Martin's grandson and you're coming to help us at the ranch for a while. He's only five-years-old. I don't think he'd understand this arrangement even if I did try to explain it to him. So for now, can we just take this one day at a time where Joey's concerned?"

Like Bryce had much of a choice. "I'll go along with whatever you think is best. Now, tell me more about Chapman's Quarter Horse Ranch."

A smile touched her mouth as pride flooded into her eyes. "We sell quarter horses. We typically run anywhere from eighty to one hundred head of the best-bred stock horses in the state of Alabama. Our horses are trained for all kinds of ranch work, steer wrestling, roping events, cutting, team penning, barrel racing, and general riding pleasure. As a matter-of-fact, a few of the horses we've trained and sold have placed first in competitions all around the state."

Bryce watched her rough edge fade away as she talked about the ranch, pride dancing across her face. "That's impressive. Who trains these horses?"

"We all do. Each of us has our own techniques, and they all just seem to fit. I guess you could say, we're like peas in a pod."

He smothered a laugh. He was finding her southern sayings delightful. But he knew if he laughed out loud she might think he was making fun of her. "I saw in the report, the ranch is over five-hundred acres. Is that right?"

"Yes, it's one of the largest ranches around." She looked over at him a bit longer and lifted a brow. "Do you know how to ride a horse?"

Bryce chuckled, but before he had a chance to answer, she blurted out, "I don't know why I ask such a stupid question like that. Of course you don't. I guess that's somethin' else we're going to have to teach you to do."

He nearly bit his tongue in half as he leaned back in his seat and smiled. "What makes you think that I don't know how to ride a horse?"

A soft giggle slipped from her lips, and her dark eyes filled with skepticism. "Oh, please, look at you. You look more like fast sport cars and expensive clothes than horses and cowboy boots."

He might not wear cowboy boots, but he definitely knew how to ride a horse. In fact, he'd been a police officer for the New York City Police Department's Mounted Unit for two years until his father pressured him into leaving the force and joining the family business. However, he wasn't going to share this information with her, not just yet. He wanted to let her think what she wanted, prejudice, misperceptions, and all.

Ten minutes later, Lily pulled the truck up in front of the house, pushed the gearshift into park, and shut off the engine. "Well, this is it. What do you think?"

He climbed out of the truck and took a long scan of the property. He had never seen pastureland so lush and green. The main house caught his attention as well. It was a huge two-story, white-sided farmhouse. The porch, with a spindled banister ran the full length of the front of the house. Two white rocking chairs sat to the left of the front door, and to the right of the door, a white porch swing hung suspended from the ceiling. Six green ferns hung in planters from the top rail. A few yards to the left of the house set a small replica of the main house. Bryce assumed it must have been the guesthouse, his home for the next few months.

A massive red barn was located across the yard with several other smaller buildings surrounding it. He gazed out across the rolling pastures and saw dozens of horses dotting the landscape.

Bryce let out a long, slow whistle. "Wow! This place is a lot bigger than I thought it would be."

Lily walked around the front of the truck, stopped at the bumper, and ran her gaze down his face. "C'mon, since you'll be staying in the main house tonight, let's get you settled in."

Lily unlocked the door and stepped inside, images of Martin's smiling face flooded into her mind. She closed her eyes as she took a deep breath, and she could still smell the fragrance of his Old Spice cologne mingled with his Captain Black pipe tobacco. Not wanting to open her eyes, she tried to hold onto Martin's memory as long as she could.

"Lily." Bryce whispered her name, sending a chill straight down to her toes.

When she opened her tear-filled eyes, Bryce stood inches from her, gazing at her with a look that came incredibly close to compassion. "You miss him, don't you?"

"It won't be the same around here without him." She blinked the tears away, pulled back her shoulders, and gave him a tight smile.

"I'm sorry for your loss." He touched her arm and gave her a sympathetic smile.

My loss? He was your grandfather! Anger bubbled inside her without warning. She bit her bottom lip to keep from saying something she would probably regret later. "I think you'll be just fine explorin' the place on your own. I need to change clothes. I have animals I need to tend to." She pointed to her right. "Go ahead and make yourself at home. The kitchen's that way, and if you need me for anythin', just stick your head out the door and holler. I'll check on you in a little while." She turned and slipped out the door, hoping he wouldn't protest or follow. Standing on the porch trying to steady her legs, she let out a slow breath. "Lord, what have I gotten myself into?"

CHAPTER FIVE

Bryce stood alone in the middle of the room after Lily's hasty retreat. When she closed the door behind her, he looked around the room. He was startled to see a deer head hanging above the mantel. The deer's eyes seem to follow him with every movement. A shiver streaked up his spine. "I feel like I've stepped into the twilight zone."

Even though his grandfather lived alone in the house, he saw Lily's touch everywhere, from the floral pillows on the sofa to the bouquet of silk flowers in the center of the coffee table. Plants, ferns, and candles were strategically placed all around the room.

This room spoke southwestern rustic. The sofa and matching chair were made of antique brown leather, and had leather buttons on the back and arms as well as decorating the front. Polished brass studs outlined the curves of the arms and base of the seats. The coffee table and end tables were a lighter shade of brown with wooden tops and wrought iron legs. A large western style area rug covered most of the hardwood floor. Beside the rock fireplace, he saw a box of toys. He assumed they belonged to Lily's son.

A well-worn pair of men's cowboy boots sat next to a wheelchair in the corner. Unexpected anguish pierced his heart. He pressed the palms of his hands into his eyes and shook his head vehemently.

He wasn't in the mood to go exploring his grandfather's home--a home he had never been a part of. Flopping down on the sofa, he laid his head back against the soft leather and closed his eyes. The ticking of his wristwatch sounded like drums, and his ears roared from the silence. He'd lived in New York all of his life, and he was used to the daily sounds of horns blowing, people shouting and bells clanging, to sum it up in one word . . . *NOISE*.

His eyes yanked open. "I've got to get out of here."

He wandered out onto the porch, stretched out on the top step, leaned against the banister, and stared out across his grandfather's land. Luscious green pastures stretched out for miles and ended at the base of a mountain. Dozens of horses grazed along the white fence that surrounded the pasture, and he spotted a herd of cattle in the distance. At any moment, he expected to see cowboys riding high in the saddle, with lassoing ropes looping high above their heads. He felt as if he'd stepped into a John Wayne movie.

A humming sound snatched Bryce's attention. He looked around and saw several brightly colored hummingbirds hovering around pink flowers blooming to the side of the house.

What had made his grandfather give up his life and successful business in New York fifteen years before to move here? What made this place so appealing?

Suddenly, he felt a slight sting on the side of his neck. He slapped it, and when he pulled his hand away, he saw a twitching bloody mosquito in his palm.

Disgust whipped through him. "What was I thinking? Why did I agree to live out in the middle of nowhere?"

Then he looked up and spotted her coming across the yard from the guesthouse. "Wow."

She'd changed out of her sundress and sandals, into a pair of slim fitting jeans, a pink sleeveless blouse, a white cowboy hat, and boots.

"Now that's what I call a real-to-life cowgirl," he said as he watched her stroll across the yard. Just as she neared the barn, a large hairy dog bounded out from behind the barn and lobbed up to her. She bent, scratched the brute on the head, and continued to speak to him as he followed her into the barn.

Bryce found himself staring at her far longer than he should have.

"Snap out of it, Bryce!" He rubbed his stubbled chin and grunted. "I think this mountain air is getting to my brain. One year and I'm out of here."

He shoved himself up from the step and turned to go back inside the house.

Suddenly, spine-tingling fierce barking whipped through the air and jerked his attention back toward the barn. Something was wrong!

♥ ♥ ♥

A low growl bubbled in Champ's throat, and the hair down his spine stood to attention. He looked like an angry porcupine ready to send its quills flying.

"Easy, boy," Lily whispered trying to calm the Leonberger next to her. The brown timber rattler was curled in perfect form ready to strike. Lily feared any sudden movement and she would certainly be his target. "Down, Champ, down."

The sound of the timber's rattler made the hair on the back of her neck stand on its ends as beads of sweat scattered across her forehead.

She wanted to kick herself for not being more vigilant as she stared at the rattler curled on top of a sack of feed. Her mind had been on other things, and not on things it should have been on. Now the snake was only inches from her thigh, and she knew if he struck her, the consequences could be deadly.

Champ whimpered but laid down beside Lily's foot. "Good, boy."

Suddenly the barn door swung open. "Lily, are you in here? What's wrong?"

Pulling on all of her training, Lily did not jump nor turn. Even a flinch could invite a reaction she knew she would not enjoy. For his part, Bryce froze in his steps when he saw her, and then his eyes traveled to the vibrating maraca sound. His eyes widened, and the color drained from his face.

"Stop." She spoke slowly, quietly, and through clenched teeth, trying not to move. "Don't come any closer. If you move too quickly, he'll strike, and I don't think I can move fast enough to get out of the way. I can't let him escape because it wouldn't be safe for any of us with this thing loose in the barn. We have to kill it." Her jaws ached from trying to speak without moving her lips.

"Kill it?" Bryce asked, and he swallowed. Fear etched his face as he looked from Lily to the snake and back to Lily. "What do you want me to do?"

"I need you to fetch my rifle."

"Your rifle?" He had to breathe that word down. "Where is it?"

Not moving was getting more and more difficult. Her muscles begged to be let out of their chains. "It's in the gun cabinet in my bedroom at the guesthouse. The key to the cabinet is hanging on a hook above the door."

"Okay, I'll be right back."

"Bryce."

"What?"

"Be careful with the rifle. It's loaded."

With Bryce gone, she returned her attention to the intruder. The rattler moved its head back and forth in a slow rhythm as if he was daring Lily to move. She wondered why this evil creature hadn't already struck, and even the thought made her heart thump so hard in her chest it sounded like thunder in her ears. *Breathe, Lily. Just breathe. God, please help Bryce. Help him hurry.* She had never considered herself a crier, but tears were beginning to pool in her eyes, either from the fear or not being able to move. She wasn't sure which.

Moments later, Bryce eased back into the barn, this time with the rifle in hand.

Lily slowly lifted her hand for the rifle, but when Bryce tried to move closer, the rattler jerked its head up and to one side.

All of Bryce's movement stopped too. "He's not going to let me get close enough to hand the gun off to you. I'll have to do it."

More fear kicked up in Lily's soul. "Do you even know how to shoot a gun?"

"I know a little."

"That's comforting." She beat the sarcasm down and instead focused on coaching him through the coming moments. "You can't miss. You have to get him on the first try."

She squeezed her eyes tight. *Lord, guide his aim. Please don't let him shoot me in the leg—or worse.*

Her breath bucked and jerked, giving her no oxygen as Bryce lifted the rifle and pulled back the hammer. The sound of the gunshot echoed against the walls, moving her without her help. She didn't feel any pain from a snakebite or a gunshot. Slowly she peeked out of one eye and saw the lifeless snake on the ground a few feet away with a gaping hole in the middle of it.

Relief plowed over her. "I can't believe you killed it."

That cocky arrogance from the lawyer's office returned as Bryce lowered the gun. "You don't know as much about me as you think you do. I have many talents."

Lily could only muster up a nod as the reality of the situation dumped into her soul. Her legs wobbled underneath her as her breath came in short rasps. Grabbing onto one of the stall rails to steady herself, she choked back tears.

"What no snappy come back?"

When she looked at Bryce, the smile dropped from his mouth and he took a step toward her. "Are you okay?"

"Yes, yes I am. Why wouldn't I be?" Her spirit jerked back in control with no effort at all. She refused to admit to him that her insides were whirling like a knife caught in a tornado. The last thing she wanted was to have him think she was weak or that she needed him for anything. "This isn't my first encounter with one of those things, and I can assure you, it probably won't be the last."

He nodded, gave her a smile, and looked over at the snake. "What are we going to do with it?"

"I need to get this thing out of here before Joey gets home. Would you grab that shovel for me?" She pointed to the shovel leaning against one of the stalls. Then before she could stop it, she shivered when she looked over at the thing lying lifeless on the ground. "Oh, I hate snakes. They make my skin crawl. Yuck!"

Bryce didn't comment. Instead, he took hold of the shovel and in one swift movement, scooped up the snake. "Show me where you want me to put it."

"We can bury it at the back of the barn. I just hope Champ doesn't dig it up."

"Champ?" He quirked a brow as he followed her out of the barn.

She pointed at Champ who was quick on her heels. "The dog."

"Oh, so Champ's its name? He's quite a hairy beast, isn't he?"

"Yes, Martin used to call him a carpet with a heartbeat." The pain of Martin's death pricked her heart again. Amazing how that happened so often.

"What kind of breed is he?"

"Champ's a Leonberger. He's a rescue dog." Champ responded to his name and flopped against Lily's leg. She scratched the top of his head. "When Joey and I first came to the ranch, Martin wanted to get a dog for Joey, and he found this boy at the pound." She bent and wrapped her arms around the dog's neck and kissed his head. "He was only three months old when Martin brought him home. Both of Champ's front legs had been broken from where his previous owners had tossed him from a movin' car. I think that's why Martin chose him. He wanted to show the pup there were people out here who would love him, and he'd never be mistreated again."

Lily looked up into Bryce's eyes. "That's the story behind this boy. Now, c'mon, I'll show you where we can bury that." She bobbed her head toward the snake and stood.

Bryce continued to follow her until they ended up at a small shed. She pointed to the ground. "Just shake the snake off right there and hand me the shovel." After he dropped the snake on the ground, she reached for the shovel, but Bryce pulled it back. "Why don't you let me do that?"

Jerking her jaw into lockdown position, Lily put her hands on her hips. "Why?"

He raised one brow and stepped to the solid ground. "Because, I'm a man and you're a —."

"Don't say it." Her eyes flashed with fury. She pushed her hat back on her head and poked her finger into his chest. What made him think she was weak? "I want you to know, I've been working on this ranch for the three years now. I know how to dig a hole, saddle a horse, hammer a nail, and shucks I even know how to drive a truck. I don't know how you do things in the big city, but here, we all carry our own share of the load. I'm not some fragile female who needs a man to do everything for her. I can do things for myself. So, let me dig my hole, and you can throw that thing in when I'm done." She grabbed hold of the shovel, but he didn't loosen his grip.

"Well, ma'am, the way we do things in the city is a gentleman always lends a hand to a *lady*," he said, mocking her tone. "The south isn't the only place that still has chivalrous men."

Not liking to lose one little bit, Lily bit down on her bottom lip and without a word released her grip on the shovel. Her pride hurt, but she knew arguing was ridiculous. "You're right. I was out of line, and I'm sorry. But," she held up her index finger. "I want you to remember one thing, I'm not helpless, and I'm capable of doing almost anythin' a man can do around here. Keep that in mind, and we should get along just fine."

His tone and face fell flat. "Noted."

She glanced down at his shoes, crossed her arms over her chest, and made a clicking sound with her tongue. "Just a word of advice, if you're gonna be workin' on this ranch, I'd suggest you invest in some boots. Those shoes won't last a week out here." She tipped her head to the side and glanced down at his expensive-looking pleated slacks as well. "And while you're at it, you might want to pick up some jeans, too."

She envisioned what he would look like all dressed up in jeans and boots. Her pulse quickened at the picture in her head. *Lord, this is going to be a long year.*

CHAPTER
SIX

After finishing the task of burying the snake, Bryce returned to the house to wash up. A laugh rumbled in the back of his throat when he glanced down at his one-hundred and fifty dollar pair of now-dust-covered Ecco Fusions and realized Lily was right, he definitely had some shopping to do.

What should he buy? He didn't have the first clue of what kind of clothing he needed. Of course, he knew he needed cowboy boots and jeans, but what kind did he need? What brand? He definitely wasn't going to ask Lily. She already had him pegged as a rich city boy who didn't know a thing about the "southern ways," and he wasn't about to prove her right.

He pushed his hand through his hair and grunted. He'd deal with it when he returned from New York in a few days.

He yawned, laid his head back on the sofa, and closed his eyes. Just relaxing felt so good that he let sleep tug him down into its embrace.

The sound of knocking on the door stirred him from sleep. He sat up, rubbed his eyes, and for a brief moment, couldn't remember where he was. Quickly looking around the room, he remembered.

The knocking continued, and he realized no one was going to answer it if he didn't.

Getting to his feet, he made his way to the door. He peered through the curtains and saw Lily standing on the porch holding a plastic covered bowl. Just seeing her caused his heart to take a perilous leap.

Calming his heart rate, he opened the door. "Hello again."

A young child with a huge grin stepped out from behind her. "Hi, I'm Joey."

"Sorry to bother you, Bryce. Joey thought you might be hungry, so we brought you some vegetable soup. Joey insisted." Lily handed the covered bowl to him and placed her hands on the child's shoulders.

The boy had the same dark eyes and hair as Lily did. He was definitely her son.

"This is my son, Joey. Joey, this is Mr. Fowler, Martin's grandson."

"Hello, Mr. Fowler."

Bryce held his hand out to Joey, and Joey slid his small hand into his. "It's nice to meet you, Joey. And, you can call me Bryce, all my friends do."

A smile stretched across the child's face, revealing a gap where a tooth once had been. "Did you hear him, Mom? He said I could call him Bryce, can I? He said I could."

"I guess it'll be all right." She patted Joey's shoulder and gave Bryce a quick nod. "I hope you enjoy your soup. The silverware is in the drawer next to the fridge, and I think there're some crackers in the pantry. If you need anythin' else, just give me a call. My number's by the phone."

Strangely, Bryce didn't want them to go. Being alone was starting to fray his nerves. "You don't have to rush off. Why don't the two of you come in? I could use the company."

"Can't we stay, Mom?" Joey tugged on Lily's arm. "Please."

When Lily looked up at Bryce, he shrugged one shoulder and grinned, hoping as much as her son that her answer would be yes.

"I guess we can, but only for a little while."

"Awesome!" Joey cheered and ran through the door and on ahead of them, off toward the kitchen. "C'mon, Bryce, you'll love my mom's soup."

"He's full of spunk, isn't he?" Bryce asked, tipping his head and smiling at her.

She rolled her eyes and shook her head. "You have no idea. Half the time he runs around here like a chicken with its head cut off."

Bryce creased his brow and chuckled. "I have no idea what that means."

Lily's lips curled into a grin as she walked past him into the house. "You will."

"Bryce, I can show you all of Grampy's horses. We have lots of them," Joey said when Bryce followed Lily into the kitchen only to find Joey spinning around and around on one of the barstools.

Bryce glanced over at Lily. "Grampy?"

"That's what he called Martin." Lily gave Joey's hair a tussle as she walked by him.

"He wasn't really my grampy, but he liked it when I called him that 'cause I don't have a real grampy."

"You don't?" Bryce asked.

Lily took the bowl of soup out of Bryce's hands. "Let me heat that up for you." She popped the lid off the bowl and placed it in the microwave.

"Where are your parents, Lily? Don't they live around here?"

Before Lily had a chance to reply, Joey blurted, "She don't have a mom and dad. I don't have a dad either, but we have each other, don't we, Mom?"

"Yes we do, Joey." She winked at her child.

"I don't understand," Bryce said. He didn't want to pry, but he did want to understand.

The hesitation was clear as Lily's gaze stayed on her son. "Joey, do you want to grab yourself a juice box?"

"Okay." He hopped down from the stool and darted to the refrigerator.

Lily leaned toward Bryce and lowered her voice. "You want the short and sweet version? I never knew my father, and my mother wasn't capable of caring for a child, so the state stepped in and took me away from her when I was seven. I was raised in foster homes until I turned sixteen, then I was on my own. I met Joey's dad when I was eighteen, had a husband and a child by twenty, and I was a widow by twenty-one. That's my life with a pretty little bow tied on top. Now," she pulled a memo pad and pen from the drawer next to the fridge and pushed them into his chest. "I need to make a grocery list of things we'll need. If you'll jot down some of your favorite foods, I'll pick 'em up for you when I go to the grocery store tomorrow."

She was a tough talker, and she put up a very brave front, but Bryce saw the pain in her eyes. "I'm not a picky eater, whatever you and Joey like will be fine with me."

"Are you sure you're up to some good old southern cookin'?" Lily asked.

The microwave beeped.

Bryce stepped over and pulled the bowl out. The aroma of the soup filled his nostrils making his stomach rumble. "If everything you cook smells as good as this does, I think I can adjust."

"It tastes good, too." Joey beamed. He came over drinking from the juice box. "Mom, can I have some cookies?"

Lily opened a cabinet, reached in and pulled out a pack of Oreos. "Bryce, would you like some crackers with your soup?"

"Yes, thank you."

She pulled out a sleeve of crackers and placed them on the bar. "Here ya go."

He snapped his fingers and asked, "Which drawer is the silverware in?"

"I'll get it." Lily pulled open a drawer, drew out a spoon, and held it out.

His hand covered hers when he took hold of the spoon. "Thank you." He wanted to look into her eyes so she would know the words meant more than just the spoon and soup.

However, she quickly pulled her hand back and rubbed it on her jeans as if to wipe his touch away. "No problem."

"Hey, Bryce, do you like sagetti?" Joey asked, climbing up onto one of the barstools and stuffing a cookie into his mouth.

"I haven't had it in a while, but yes I like it." Bryce grinned.

"Mom makes the best sagetti in the whole world. Do you like hamburgers, too?" Joey twirled in a circle on the barstool.

"Yes, I like hamburgers, too." Bryce slid onto the stool next to Joey, opened the sleeve of crackers, and began crumbling a few of them into his soup.

"Wade cooks hamburgers and chicken outside on the grill all the time. He cooks good, too. Do you know him?"

"No, I haven't met him yet, but I'm sure I will."

"I like Wade. He's funny." Joey put his hands over his mouth and giggled. "He rides Midnight sideways."

"Midnight?" Bryce tilted his head and lifted a questioning brow.

"Midnight is Wade's horse. Wade used to ride in the rodeo a few years ago, and he shows Joey some of his tricks from time to time. He really is good at it." Lily smiled and kissed Joey on top of the head. "Joey gets a kick out of it."

"He's going to teach me how to ride sideways when I get bigger."

How can an old man still pull off a stunt like that? Bryce wondered as he filled his spoon and took a bite. The savory soup made his taste buds perk up. "Wow, this is really good, Lily."

"See, I told you. My mom's the best cook in the whole world." Joey spread his arms open as if he could embrace everything.

"Well, maybe not the best but a close second." Lily lovingly smiled at Joey. "Now leave Bryce be, and let him eat his soup."

"Okay, okay."

However, the minute Lily turned her back to Joey, he whirled around on his stool and tugged on Bryce's sleeve. "I'm five years old, almost six. How old are you?"

The smile on Bryce's face traveled all the way through him to his heart. The kid was a fascinating combination of disarming and charming. "Well, Joey, I'm twenty-nine."

Joey's eyes widened. "Wow! You're older than my mom. She's twenty-four. Ain't that right, Mom?"

"Joey!" Lily slammed her hands on her hips and whirled around. Her cheeks flushed.

"Well you are." Joey giggled, tilted his head to one side, and looked back at Bryce. "Why don't you wear a cowboy hat? Wade always wears one."

Lily shook her head, tapped Joey on the arm, and looked over at Bryce. "I apologize for my son, Bryce. I don't know what's gotten in to him."

"Don't worry about it, he's not bothering me. Well, Joey, to answer your question, I don't have a cowboy hat. I guess I need to buy me one, huh?"

"You don't have a hat?" Joey's eyes widened again as if he never knew someone could not have a cowboy hat.

"No, I'm afraid I don't, but don't worry, I have some shopping to do when I get back. I'll pick one up then. How does that sound?"

"Wait! I know." Joey waved one finger in the air and hopped down from the stool. "I'll be back in a minute." With that, he darted out of the room.

"Joey, where are you going?" Lily called.

"I'll be right back," Joey yelled.

Bryce chuckled. "I wished I had that much energy."

"I never know what that boy's up to half the time. Let's just say, he keeps me on my toes."

Seconds later, Joey ran back into the kitchen with his hand behind his back. A smile stretched across his face.

"This is for you." He pulled his hand out from behind his back and offered a black cowboy hat up to Bryce. "This was Grampy's hat. He lives in heaven now, and he doesn't need it anymore. I got it for him for his birthday, and he said it was the best-looking cowboy hat in the world. Now, I want you to have it." Joey bounced up and down. "Try it on, try it on."

"Oh, Joey, thank you, but I can't take this from you." Bryce swallowed the knot in his throat, the soup barely making it past.

"Mom, tell him he can have it. He has to have a cowboy hat. He can't be a cowboy if he don't have a hat," Joey pleaded.

"Joey did all kind of chores around here to earn the money to buy that hat for Martin. If he wants you to have it, then it's yours. Besides, I think Martin would want you to have it, too."

"I'm not so sure about that." Bryce twisted the rim of the hat between his fingers, the soup completely forgotten.

"The hat's yours, Bryce. End of discussion. Now go ahead and try it on." Lily waved her hand motioning for him to put it on.

Bryce slid the hat around his hands once more before venturing to put it on his head. Not sure why it felt so important or so intimidating to him, he turned to her. "So, how do I look?"

Joey clapped. "Now you're a real cowboy!"

A real cowboy? He wasn't sure if that would ever be possible or if he even wanted to be one, and by the look on Lily's face, he could tell she wasn't too sure of the idea either.

After saying goodnight to Bryce two hours later, Lily held Joey's hand as they crossed the yard toward the guesthouse.

"Mom, do you think Bryce knows how to ride a horse?"

"No, I don't think he does. He's lived in a big city all of his life. He wasn't raised around horses like we were." It was so strange to her that two days before she had never heard the name Bryce Fowler and now every question somehow went back to him, to his life, to his future.

"Can I teach him?"

She bit back the laugh so she wouldn't hurt Joey's feelings. Bryce on a horse? She'd pay to see that one. "I don't know. It's a hard job to teach someone to ride, Joey. Don't you think Wade, Kyle, or Greg would be the best ones to teach him?"

Joey considered that, twisted his lips in concentration, and furrowed his brows. "You could teach him, and I could help you."

Lily knew her son all too well. When he got something in his head, it was like pulling an oak branch apart to get him to give it up. "We'll see."

"You always say that." He dragged his feet as they walked together. "Hey, I just thought of something."

"What?"

"He needs somebody to show him how to be a cowboy. I can do that. That will be my job." With that, he pulled his hand away and ran toward the guesthouse with Champ on his heels. Lily just shook her head. She was glad Joey liked Bryce. That was a good thing, right? At least she thought it was. Unless it didn't work between them. She shrugged back the thought.

That night, Lily tossed and turned in bed for hours. Every time she closed her eyes, she could still see the image of Bryce standing in the middle of the kitchen with Martin's black Stetson resting on his head.

When he smiled at her, the butterflies in her stomach felt more like angry, buzzing hummingbirds.

She sat up in bed, punched her pillow several times, and slammed it back behind her head.

"Lord, why does Bryce have to be so handsome? Why couldn't he have been ugly? Like one straggly tooth in his head, a long crooked nose, bushy eyebrows, or maybe a big fat wart on the end of his nose."

The image in her head made her giggle as she closed her eyes once more. Not that it helped her fall asleep, but it was worth a try.

CHAPTER
SEVEN

The next afternoon, Lily sat down at the kitchen table with Wade Haston and reluctantly told him about Martin's will and all the complications inherent in it.

"This has got to be the craziest thing I've ever heard." Wade slid his Stetson far back on his head, leaned back in his chair, and crossed his arms. His jawline tightened. "You told Mr. Hopper there's no way you're going to go along with this, didn't you?" Wade's brilliant green eyes darkened with his frown.

Lily had to smile. She thought back to the night before when Joey had called Bryce a real cowboy. That she wasn't too sure about, but the one thing she was sure of, Wade was a real cowboy in every sense of the word. When he had come to work on the ranch a couple of years back, she thought he resembled the Marlboro man. He was a downright handsome man. Right down to the slight dip in his chin. Not to mention his compelling green eyes, square face that had been bronzed by the sun, and his massive shoulders.

Lily bit her bottom lip and played with a loose string on the tablecloth. "Well, not exactly."

"Please tell me you're not seriously thinking about doing this." His eyes narrowed as he spoke through clenched teeth. Leaning in closer to her face, he waited for an answer. "Lily?"

She lifted one shoulder. "I didn't have any other choice."

"What?" Anger flared into his face. "You've already agreed to this, haven't you?" When she didn't answer, Wade pushed himself out of his chair, jerked his hat off, slapped it against his leg, and began to pace the floor. "Lily, be serious. You don't even know this guy."

Knowing he made far more sense than any of the rest of it, Lily got up, walked to Wade's side, and placed her hand on his arm. "Wade, you know that I have to think about what's best for Joey. His happiness is the only thing that matters to me, and I want to give him the best life has to offer. If all it takes is giving up my life for one year, well, then it's worth it to me."

With one slight turn, Wade tossed his hat on the table and took hold of both of Lily's arms. His six-foot-six frame towered over her five-foot-two stance. "I understand Joey's your first priority, but you need to think about what's best for you, too. You can't do this. You can't."

She never backed down, never even blinked as she faced him. Even though her insides felt like quivering Jell-o. "What's best for me is to secure Joey's future, and that's what I'm going to do."

The color drained from Wade's face. "You can't do this."

"I'm sorry, Wade, but this is my decision." She pulled free from his grip and folded her arms over her chest in defense.

"I can't believe this. Why didn't you call me? I would have talked you out of it. You can't move a complete stranger into your home."

"It's not what you think, Wade. Besides, he won't be living in the house with Joey and me. He's going to be living in the guesthouse." Lily felt the ground shift beneath her carefully constructed rationalizations. "And, it's not going to be a traditional marriage; it's just a marriage of convenience. Trust me when I say I'm not his type, and he's certainly not mine."

He ran his hand down the stubble on his face and then grabbed her again. When Lily gasped at his forcefulness, Wade released her. "How can you be sure he'll follow the plan? You're a beautiful woman, Lily, and any man would be crazy not to want you."

"I don't believe he'll try anythin'. Besides there's somethin' about him I trust. Remember he is Martin's grandson after all. Martin wouldn't put me in harm's way. You know that."

Wade sighed heavily and shoved his hands in his pockets. "You trust him?" He blew out a long breath. "You trust a complete stranger?"

"I'm not asking you to trust him. I'm asking you to trust me, and trust that I'm making the right decision."

Wade shook his head and sighed heavily. "And there's nothing I can say that will make you change your mind, is there?"

"No, I'm afraid not."

"Okay then. So, tell me, how are you going to explain him being here to the boys?"

She shrugged that question away. "He's Martin's grandson, and he's here to help us out for awhile. Then after a few weeks, we'll start dating, and, well, I think you know how it will line up after that. But remember he's only going to be here for a year, and then he'll be gone."

"I still don't like it. I don't like it at all." Wade exhaled slowly, his jaw working back and forth as if he was chewing on the situation. "So, when is he going to be back?"

"He flew back to New York this morning to pack up his things. He said it shouldn't take but a couple of days to get everythin' in order. I imagine he'll be here by Friday or Saturday, Monday at the latest. That's why I wanted to explain this to you now, before he gets back. I didn't want you to get the wrong idea, Wade. Like Bryce said, it's a financial investment, that's all."

"Bryce, huh? I thought it was Mr. Fowler." He lifted a dark brow and clenched his jaw. One brown lock of hair fell across his forehead. His sharp eyes burned into her face.

Why did she feel the need to defend herself? Just because Wade had always been like a big brother to her didn't give him the right to make her feel like she had to answer to him. She knew Wade was only concerned for her and Joey, but that didn't keep her from being irritated with him.

Exhaling in aggravation, she placed her fists on her hips and squared her shoulders. "Wade, I'm going to do this. End of discussion."

His shoulders tensed as he thrust his chin forward. "Does the city boy know anything about ranchin'?"

"Living in New York all of his life, I wouldn't imagine he'll know much about it, but I'm sure you'll have him learnin' the ropes in no time."

"Oh, you can count on that. As long as I'm foreman, I won't tolerate a slacker."

A twinge of guilt tugged at Lily's heart. She knew Wade all too well. She could read it in his face; he wasn't going to make it easy on Bryce. Then again, why did she care? Bryce was a grown man, he could hold his own…but still.

"Wade, I want your word you won't be too tough on Bryce when he gets here. Remember he's just following Martin's wishes, too. If he hadn't agreed to this, I would be out today looking for a place to live."

"You know I wouldn't let that happen." Wade looked at her, weighing his words. "There are other options, you know."

Options? What other options do I have? Living in my truck? That's appealing.

"And one more thing, I know you're not going to like it, but I want you and the boys to take off Friday. Y'all can enjoy a three day weekend."

"What? Are you crazy, girl?" He lifted his hands and waved off her request. "No. I don't think so. I'm not doing that."

"Wade, the next few days are going to be stressful enough as it is, and I think it would be best to give Bryce a few days to get settled in here. If I need you for anything, I'll give you a call. Trust me, I know what I'm doing."

"Lily—"

"Please, Wade. Do this for me."

His jaw went slack, and he shook his head in defeat. "Only if you promise me, you'll call me if he does anything out of the way."

"I promise, and Wade there's one other thing I need to tell you."

He lifted a wrinkled brow. "What?"

She might as well get this over with. She sucked in a deep breath and gave him the sweetest smile she could pull to her lips. "He doesn't know how to ride."

"Great. That's just great." Wade flopped down in the chair again, snatched up his hat, and slammed it on his head.

Bryce knew he'd been acting like a coward for the past couple of days by slipping in and out of his apartment to pack up his belongings, taking great care not to turn on any lights, and keeping his phone shut off. He'd hoped he could get in and out without running into any of his family members. He didn't want to be bombarded by all of their questions or to be ridiculed for his actions by agreeing to marry Lily, a woman they thought was their father's gold-digging girlfriend.

Only twisted minds would think that. He grinned when Lily's statement replayed in his head.

Just as he tossed his last bag on the bed, he heard a familiar female's voice behind him. "Where have you been?"

"Hello, Mother." He turned around, knowing he was about to be berated with both barrels. She stood in the doorway dressed to the nines in her designer clothes like she always was, with her arms folded over her chest, and tapping her foot.

He knew his family would eventually find out all the details of his grandfather's wishes, so rather than tap dance around it, he took a deep breath and told his mother everything.

"Bryce, I can't believe you fell for the tricks of that girl! Don't you see she's behind all of this? She wanted to sink her claws into the old man's money and marrying you will be a definite way of getting it. I can't believe you were so gullible." His mother laughed bitterly and plopped down on the edge of the bed. "Are you seriously moving down there to become what? A pig farmer?"

"It's not a pig farm, Mother. It's a ranch. And, trust me, I know what I'm doing," Bryce argued as he emptied one of his dresser drawers into a suitcase.

"Oh, please, Bryce. Open your eyes. What kind of woman would marry a man she doesn't even know? A woman after an old man's fortune, that's who. I wouldn't be surprised if Father's attorney wasn't in on this scheme every step of the way. I wonder how much money he gained from it." She pulled her cell out of her purse. "I have to call Sid."

Bryce reached across the bed and grabbed her phone. "Mother, I'd appreciate it if you'd wait until after I'm gone to stir up trouble."

"What a hateful thing to say to me! I am your mother, remember?" she snapped, and then puffed out her bottom lip.

Holding his patience with her was not easy. "Look, I'm not trying to be disrespectful, but I just want to get out of here without having to deal with Father, Sid, and Meg." He held out her phone just beyond her reach. "Do you promise to wait until after I leave before calling them and telling them about Grandfather's request?"

She didn't look particularly happy about that. "I guess so, but if you've set your heart on going through with this ridiculous plan, I want you to do whatever it takes to make sure you take everything away from that girl. She's not a Chapman. She shouldn't be entitled to anything."

"Whatever you say." He handed her the phone and then slammed his suitcase shut. "I need to go, or I'll miss my flight. I'll call you soon." He dropped a kiss on the top of her head. As he started past her, she grabbed his arm.

"I can't believe you are seriously going to do this."

He gently pulled his arm away. "Well, believe it because I am." With that, he grabbed up his other suitcases, hastened into the hallway, and punched the elevator button.

"What are you going to do about your position at your father's office?" He heard her yell just as the elevator opened. "What do you want me to tell your father?"

"Tell him I quit. I've had a better offer."

Stepping onto the elevator, Bryce silently prayed the doors would close before she followed him inside.

"Bryce Monroe Fowler, you wait just one minute!" she yelled just as the doors closed.

Hours later, when his plane touched down on the strip in the Huntsville International Airport, Bryce's stomach did a little dance. Lily had plagued his dreams for the past couple of nights, and he was looking forward to seeing her again.

After he gathered his luggage from the baggage claim, he headed for the lobby to wait on Mr. Hopper.

"Bryce, do you care if we sit with you?" Tina, the cute little blonde-haired woman who'd sat across the aisle from him on his flight, asked as she sat down on his left. Billie, her brunette friend, sat on his right.

"Well, I am waiting for someone."

"It's okay, we'll wait with you." Tina giggled.

Normally he would have loved the attention, but today was different. Why?

"Bryce?"

The voice he heard made his heart thump against his ribs. He lifted his eyes and saw Lily standing in front of him with her hands on her hips. She was dressed in jeans and a red-plaid sleeveless blouse. He thought he would never find denim and plaid attractive on anyone, but he was wrong.

This woman wasn't at all his type. So why did his heart skip a beat or two every time he saw her? He liked how the corner of her mouth twitched when she tried not to smile and how her southern accent was as soft as silk to his ears.

His attraction to her was stronger than he anticipated and that wasn't good. Not good at all.

"Excuse me, ladies. My ride's here." He scrambled to his feet and ran his hand through his hair, feathering it back. "I wasn't expecting you, Lily."

She looked past him at the girls, pinched up her nose, and rolled her eyes.

"They were just keeping me company. I thought Mr. Hopper was picking me up."

"He was, but about an hour ago he called and asked if I could come get you. He had a meeting he couldn't reschedule. Are you ready? Or do you have other plans?" She hiked a brow at the two groupies who were literally hanging all over him. Why hadn't he told them to get lost on the plane?

Both girls had their arms wrapped around his like twisting vines around an oak tree. "Who's this, Bryce?"

"We found him first," the other one said with an irritating giggle.

He politely pulled his arms free and smiled. "Tina, Billie, I'd like for you to meet Lily, my fiancée."

Lily's eyes widened and her mouth fell open. Apparently she wasn't the only one surprised by the announcement.

The girls gasped simultaneously. "You didn't tell us you were engaged." They untangled their arms from around him as if he'd suddenly developed leprosy. The blonde girl flipped her hair, glanced at Lily with a look of derision, and then both girls pranced away.

Lily looked almost as horror-stricken as they had. "Just what do you think you're doin'? Why did you tell them that?"

Bryce shrugged and picked up his carry-on. "I thought it was the fastest way to get rid of them, and it was, don't you agree?"

She twisted her mouth into an angry frown. "I don't appreciate you introducing me as your fiancée just to shake off unwanted females. It had better not happen again. Let's just go." She turned away from him.

"What makes you think this will happened again?"

She whirled back around like an angry ballerina. "Oh, please, I know a Casanova when I see one."

She sure was pretty when she was angry.

"Casanova, huh? Is that what you think?"

"I don't think it. I know it." She thrust her fists into her sides, narrowed her eyes, and bobbled her pretty little head.

"Oh, really? So tell me, how did you come to that conclusion?"

"Shall I make a list? Let's see." She held up one finger. "First there was Mr. Hopper's secretary and now, not one, but two girls from the airplane? This is normal for you, isn't it? Having girls following you around like lost puppies?"

"What can I say?" He shrugged. "Are we a bit jealous?"

"Jealous? Don't be ridiculous? I'm telling you, you'd better not use me as your pawn in your little games again. I don't appreciate it." She sent him a warning glare.

"I don't understand why you're getting so upset. After all, technically, in three months we are getting married, remember?"

She sharply sucked in her breath, and her face turned several shades of red.

Bryce let out a thunderous laugh. "Come on, Lily. I'm only teasing you." He swung a couple of bags and his leather laptop case over his shoulder. He grabbed the handle of his rolling luggage bag, which had two smaller bags stacked on top of it. "I think we need to get moving. People are beginning to stare."

A breathless gasp escaped her lips as she looked around the airport. Tucking a loose strand of hair behind her ear, she leaned in and whispered, "Well, it isn't funny."

When she spun around on her heels to leave, he grabbed a hold of her arm, and pulled her back around to face him. "Okay, okay. I shouldn't make light of the situation, and I'm sorry. "

"Fine, but don't let it happen again."

When she turned, he followed her as they weaved through the crowd making their way to the sliding glass doors. Immediately when they stepped outside into the heat, perspiration beads began to gather on Bryce's forehead and neck, and rolled down between his shoulder blades. He glanced over at Lily, who didn't seem to be affected by the heat in the least. "This heat is sweltering."

"It's only the middle of May just wait until July and August. What's the temperature like in New York this time of year?"

"It was fifty degrees when I boarded the plane this morning. It didn't seem this hot when I was here two days ago." His shirt was drenched and clinging to his skin by the time they reached her truck. If he had been a snowman, he would certainly be a puddle by now.

"We'd had some storms move through a few days ago, and it brought some cooler temperatures in behind it. The temperatures are back to normal now."

He tossed all of his bags into the bed of the truck and climbed into the cab. Lily started the engine, flipped the air conditioner on max as she pulled out of the parking space, and gave him a sideways grin. "This should help."

"Aw, thank you," he said as he adjusted the vents to blow in his face.

It might be hot, but so was she in her own way, and he found himself actually looking forward to getting to know the feisty little thing better. Heaven help him.

CHAPTER EIGHT

"If you can't handle the heat now, you're in for a big surprise."

"Oh, I assure you, I'm tougher than I look."

She cut her eyes over at his callous-free hands and snorted. "I don't see you lasting one week out there, but I guess we'll all find out just how tough you really are."

I hope he has something tucked away in one of those bags he can wear when we put him to work. The thought zipped through her head as she glanced over at his expensive-looking, pleated, black pants. If she had to guess, she probably could have purchased four or five pair of jeans from the local clothing store with the money he paid for those pants.

Pushing that aside, she turned her attention to more important issues. "Bryce, I'd like to discuss a few things with you before we get to the ranch."

"Such as?" he asked, still fiddling with the vents.

"First of all, I'll get the minor stuff out of the way." She swallowed the lump in her throat and pulled a deep breath. "I know most men don't like to cook, so you're more than welcome to eat your meals with Joey and me. On a normal day, Wade and the boys usually eat with us too, so one more mouth to feed won't be a problem."

"I appreciate the invitation."

"Now, I've had some time to think about our arrangement. I think people will be suspicious if we begin dating right off the bat, so I thought we should wait for at least a couple of weeks before we are seen out in town together as a couple, don't you agree?" She gripped the steering wheel and tried to ignore how damp her hands were, swatting away the urge to wipe them on her jeans. There was no way she was going to let him know how nervous she felt around him.

"That does sound logical."

"So, we agree then? We should wait for a bit."

When he readily agreed, the uneasiness in her stomach began to settle.

"I'm fine with it, if you are." When he dipped his chin in agreement and smiled, her pulse skittered alarmingly.

Why did his smile have such an effect on her? He was just another man, for mercy sakes.

"Good, so until then, if you want to date any of the women around town, I'd appreciate it if you don't bring any of them home with you to stay overnight. Remember, I do have an impressionable five-year-old child. I don't want him subjected to anything like that, and there'll be absolutely no drinking on the ranch." She knew she sounded bossy, but Martin never allowed drinking on the ranch, and she was going to continue to honor his memory. "Whatever you do on your own time is your business, but I don't want it brought back to the ranch. Martin never allowed it, and neither will I."

"Lily, I want to set your mind at ease right now. I don't drink, and I never have. That's certainly one rule I don't have a problem complying to."

"I'm relieved to hear that." The uneasiness settled even more. Her breathing felt more relaxed and the knot between her shoulders loosened. *Thank you, Lord.*

"But, I do want to make a minor adjustment to one thing you said."

"What's that?" She figured he wasn't going to like the "*no bringing women home*" rule. He was a handsome man, and she had no doubt once all the single women in Trinity caught sight of him, they were going to be knocking down her door wanting to meet him. One thing Lily was sure about, Bryce wasn't going to be lonely while he was here.

"Lily, not all men are incompetent in the kitchen. I make a mean chicken cacciatore, and if I do say so myself, my parmesan crusted steak, baked Ziti, and my stuffed Chicken Siena…" He kissed the tips of his fingers, looking like a TV chef. "They're absolutely delicious."

"You can cook?" The shock in her voice startled even her. An unwelcomed blush crept into her cheeks. "I mean, it just surprised me, I'm not used to having a man cook for me, unless it's from the grill."

"I may not know how to operate a grill like Mr. Haston, but I do know my way around the kitchen. So, I don't mind cooking a meal for us from time to time."

Us? Feelings of anxiety rushed through her, causing every single nerve in her body to twitch. She swallowed the knot in her throat and suppressed the panic trying to surface. "That would be fine. Be my guest."

"You won't be disappointed. Cooking is only one of my many talents."

"I guess we'll see, won't we?"

Lily couldn't believe her ears. This man could cook. She couldn't imagine Bryce even knowing how to boil water, and here he was naming off dishes she'd never heard of before. First impressions were overrated.

"Oh, and one more thing, if we're expected to take the next three months to become better acquainted, I don't think I'll have time to be involved with anyone else but you."

Lily's breath hitched and a flutter played in her stomach.

"Who knows," Bryce shrugged a shoulder. "You might even learn to like me before it's over with. I, myself, could find it rather easy to like you." He turned the knob on the radio and began to whistle along with a Blake Shelton tune.

Later, as Lily loaded the breakfast dishes into the dishwasher, her mind continued to replay Bryce's statement. *"I myself could find it rather easy to like you."*

What did he mean by that? Did he plan to break the rules? Well, she knew if he said or did anything out of line, all she had to do was call Wade. That's what she would do, what she should do, right?

She shoved another plate into the dishwasher, and tried to get her mind off Bryce. A smile tickled the corner of her lips when his smile flashed across her mind. Sighing, she sucked in her bottom lip and wondered how it would feel if he kissed her.

After drying her hands on a kitchen towel, she dropped into one of the kitchen chairs, and brushed a loose strand of hair from her face. "What's wrong with me? He's only gonna be here for a year, then he's gone. I can't let my emotions get the better of me because if I do, I'll be the one who's left with a broken heart."

Why did Bryce Fowler have such an impact on her?

It had to be the stress of Martin's death and dealing with all the changes over the last few days that had her feelings muddled and her mind in shambles.

"Is he here? Is he here?" Joey yelled as he stormed through the kitchen, throwing his backpack on the table.

"Joey! Is that any way to come into this house? You know better than that. Where are your manners? You scared the life out of me."

"I'm sorry, Mom. I didn't mean to."

Lily gave him a smile and pulled him close. "We'll let it slide today, but let's not let it happen again, okay?"

"Your heart really is beating fast." He laid his head against her chest and listened. "And it's loud."

"I told you, you scared me to death. Now, tell me, Mr. Meyers, what has caused you to come barrelin' into the house this way? Is a stampede behind you?"

"Is he here?" Joey sprang back and forth from foot to foot.

"He? Does this 'he' person have a name?" Lily placed her hand under her jaw and tapped her index finger on her chin.

"Ah, Mom, you know who I mean. Is Bryce here? You said he was 'pose to be here today."

A giggle escaped her lips. She didn't want to damper Joey's excitement any longer. "Yes, he's here. He's at the guesthouse unpacking his things."

"Yippee." Joey turned to run out the door, but Lily grabbed his collar, barely managing to snag his exit.

"Hold on a minute, young man. Bryce needs time to settle in, and you're not going to disturb him. You can come on into the kitchen with me, and I'll fix you a snack."

"But, I wanted to see him," he moaned, but he followed Lily into the kitchen dragging his feet just the same.

"He'll probably be over here in a little while. If he's not, I'll let you go visit him in a bit, okay?"

"Okay." He sounded sadder than a whippoorwill on a lonely Saturday night. After dragging himself up on the barstool, he propped both elbows on the bar and placed his face in his hands.

Lily picked up the platter of sliced apples, cheddar cheese sticks, and a scoop of peanut butter she'd prepared earlier and set it on the bar in front of Joey. "How was school today?"

Joey's eyes lit up with excitement. "Oh, I almost forgot. We're going on a field trip on the last day of school; I have the letter from my teacher in my backpack."

"Do you know where the field trip is to?"

"Wait." He hopped down from the barstool and ran out of the kitchen.

Seconds later, he darted back into the kitchen waving a piece of paper in the air. "We're going to the Briminghand Zoo."

Lily giggled. "The Birmingham Zoo, Joey."

"My teacher said they had lots of monkeys, and elephants, and tigers, and bears, and alligators, and tall giraffes." His voice climbed a notch with each animal he named.

"Wow, and we'll get to see all of them. But, we have to watch out for the monkeys, they may want to tickle you." She bent down and ran her fingers up and down Joey's belly.

"Get away, monkey!" he squealed in delight. "Get away!"

Lily began to chatter like a monkey, and then she scooped him up in her arms, and whirled him around the kitchen. "Oh, no!" She began to screech like an eagle. "Watch out for the giant eagle! It might fly away with you."

After several seconds of spinning around, she sat him down on the top of the counter. "Whew. You're getting so big I won't be able to do this much longer," she said gulping air.

"One day I'll be big, big, big." Joey stretched his hands high above his head.

"I know, but don't grow up too fast. I sure will miss my little boy."

He put his hands on both sides of her face. "You don't have to miss me. I'm always going to live with you, even when I'm big."

"I sure do hope so. But, when you're a grown man, I don't think your wife would like that very much."

"Wife? Yuck, girls aren't any fun." He wrinkled his nose and shook his head in disbelief. "They don't like frogs, they scream and scream when I catch one at school and try to show it to them."

Lily gasped in horror at the image of Joey chasing little girls around the playground with frogs. "Joey, you don't chase them with it, do you?"

"Just a little, I only wanted them to look at it, and they don't want to even do that." He shook his head in disbelief again. "That's why I'm never gonna get married. Never, ever, ever."

Lily stifled a laugh. "Oh, I think when you're a big boy, you're gonna have lots of girlfriends, and then one day you'll love one of them so much you'll want to marry her."

Joey slightly tilted his head to the side, and a questioning look swept across his face. "Why don't you have any boyfriends? So, one day you will want to marry one of them, and then you'll have a husband and I can have a daddy."

Lily's mouth fell open, but she was rendered speechless. How could she answer this question? She frantically searched through the fuzziness in her brain, trying to find a suitable answer she could offer to her son.

"Joey, I—"

Joey's eyes darted over Lily's shoulder, and then he hopped down from the counter. "Hey, Bryce."

Butterflies fluttered in her stomach when she turned and saw Bryce leaning against the doorframe, smiling.

How long had he been standing there? Had he overheard their conversation?

Bryce thumbed over his shoulder. "I knocked, but no one answered, so I let myself in. I hope that's okay?"

"No one ever knocks. Do they, Mom?" Joey turned toward Lily for a brief moment with wide eyes waiting for her to answer.

She licked her dry lips and a nervous laugh slipped from her throat as she tried to hide her flushed cheeks. "What Joey means is, it's hard to hear anyone at the front door from back here. So, all the boys know if the front door is open, they can come on in. I guess that applies to you too now."

Bryce only nodded, not taking his eyes off her face.

"Guess what, Bryce?" Joey asked, bouncing in place. He looked like a jack-in-the-box waiting for the last turn of the crank so he could pop out.

"What's that, little man?" Bryce pushed himself away from the doorway as he looked down at Joey.

Releasing a trapped breath, Lily was thankful of Joey's interruption. Why did Bryce have to look at her that way?

"I'm goin' to the zoo." Joey's excitement bubbled out of him.

"The zoo, huh? That explains it then. I thought I heard some wild animals in here." Bryce displayed a wide grin and drummed one foot on the floor.

"That wasn't wild animals. It was just Mom being silly." Joey waved his hand in her direction. "She does stuff like that all the time."

"Oh, she does?" Bryce's question was meant for Joey, but he lifted a teasing and questioning brow in Lily's direction.

"Yeap and sometimes she—"

"Okay, okay." She stepped up, took hold of Joey's shoulders, and gave him a gentle shake. Lily had no idea what he was about to say, but she knew whatever it was; she certainly didn't want it to be shared with Bryce. "You need to finish your snack."

Half turning to Bryce, she went back to the counter. "Would you like a sandwich or somethin'? Joey and I go into town every Friday night to eat supper, but I can whip somethin' up for you before we leave."

Bryce pointed at the platter of apples. "Do you mind?"

"No, go ahead. Help yourself."

Bryce slid onto one of the barstools, picked up a couple of apple slices, and popped one in his mouth. His eyes widened. "Wow, these are delicious."

"We buy them fresh from a family-owned orchard just outside of town," Lily said over her shoulder as she pulled a gallon of milk from the fridge.

Joey crawled up onto the other barstool beside Bryce, swept up an apple slice, and chomped down on it. "I love it when Mom buys the apples because she makes apple pies, jelly, and apple butter with them. They're all so yummy," Joey mumbled with a mouth full of apple as he rubbed his belly.

"Joey, don't talk with your mouth full." Lily poured Joey a glass of milk and set it down in front of him. She held out the gallon toward Bryce. "Would you like a glass?"

"Yes, thank you, if it's not too much trouble."

"Not any trouble at all." She pulled another glass from the cabinet, filled it, and held it out to him.

"Thank you." His hand covered hers as he took hold of the glass.

His touch made her heart rate climb. When she looked into his face, she thought he had a smile that could melt butter.

Lily jumped when the house phone rang and pulled her hand away. "I need to get that." Turning as if the room was on fire, she hurried out of the room to answer it.

CHAPTER NINE

As Bryce watched Lily leave the room, he suddenly realized he was holding his breath. He breathed out slowly, reached up, and rubbed the back of his neck. Just the way she looked up at him caused a quiver to shoot through his body.

"Bryce? Bryce?" Joey pulled on his sleeve. "Did you hear me?"

Shaking out of the dreams and visions floating in his head and heart, Bryce recalibrated his focus on the child. "What? I'm sorry. What were you saying?"

"I said, do you like to go bowlin'?"

"I can't say I've ever been." Bryce downed his glass of milk, picked up Joey's empty glass, and slid off the barstool.

"You don't ride horses and you don't go bowlin'? What do you do?"

A bark of laughter bubbled from Bryce's throat as he walked across the kitchen and placed the glasses in the sink. "Well, little man, I don't know what to tell you."

"Would you like to go bowlin' with me and my mom tonight?"

The idea was appealing, but he wasn't sure if Lily would approve of it. "I think it might be best if you okayed that with your mom first."

"She won't care. Kyle and Wade go with us sometimes too. Greg don't go 'cause he don't like to bowl."

"I still think you'd better ask her." Bryce hoped Lily wouldn't mind him going along. He liked the idea of spending more time with her.

Joey jumped to the floor, grabbed Bryce's hand, and pulled him into the living room. "Come on, let's go ask her."

"Ask me what?" Lily asked as she placed the phone back in its cradle.

Joey crossed the room and put his arms around Lily's waist. "You don't care, do you, Mom?"

Her arms came around the child as if made to go there. "I don't care about what?"

"You don't care if Bryce goes bowlin' with us tonight, do you? I told him you wouldn't care, but he said I had to ask you first. Tell him you don't care. You don't care, do you?" Joey rushed his words as he tugged on her.

She opened her mouth and then closed it just as fast. A cute shade of pink started at the base of her throat and crept up into her cheeks.

"Well? Can he?" Joey asked.

"Joey, I'm sure Bryce doesn't want to go with us. He probably still has some unpacking to do." Looking up at Bryce, her eyes pleaded with him to agree.

"Nope, I'm all unpacked. If you don't mind me tagging along, I'd love to go. We have to start somewhere." Bryce gave her a wink and watched a blush sweep into her cheeks again.

She sighed in defeat. "If you want to come along, then you're welcome to. We will be leaving here at five."

Bryce nodded. "Great. And dinner will be on me."

"Yay! Thanks, Mom. I'm going to go and get ready. Can I wear my blue shorts?" Joey asked.

"Yes, and don't forget your socks this time," Lily yelled after Joey as he darted from the room. She grunted, placed her hands on her hips, and turned to face Bryce. "I thought we discussed this. Two weeks, remember?" She narrowed her eyes, and then tilted her head to the side waiting for him to respond.

Bryce shrugged. "We can't disappoint your son. Besides, it won't be a date. It'll be just you and Joey taking your houseguest out to see the town. What's the harm in that?"

Lily tucked a wayward strand of hair behind her left ear and bit down on her bottom lip. "You know you don't have to go if you really don't want to. I can make an excuse for you with Joey. I know he can be pretty persistent."

"No, it sounds like fun. Besides, I wasn't looking forward to being here alone all evening."

"Okay then, but you know we may have to put up the bumper rails for you."

"I take it that's something for beginners?"

"You could say that." Lily covered her mouth with her hand and stifled her laugh. "I'm gonna get a kick out of watchin' you bowl."

"Why's that?" He quirked a brow.

"Because you just don't look like the bowlin' type. This is going to be an interestin' night."

"You've made quite a few assumptions about me." With one stride, he closed the gap between them and loomed over her. "So, tell me, Lily, what type am I?"

Lily's eyes widened, and he saw a tremor rake over her body. "Let's just say, I know your type."

"I don't think you know me as well as you think you do." He slanted his head and whispered close to her ear. "I may just surprise you."

"Mom, I can't find my blue socks. Do you know where they are?" Joey's voice echoed into the room.

Lily put her hand on Bryce's chest, pushed him away, and headed for the door. She stopped, and without turning around, said over her shoulder, "Not much surprises me anymore."

Later that night when they entered the bowling alley, the strong smell of popcorn and fried food assaulted Bryce's senses. The sound of bright colored bowling balls rolling down the lanes and crashing into the wooden pins echoed throughout the place. People laughing, children screaming, babies crying, and the red and blue jukebox in the corner playing an old country tune all seemed to intertwine into one thunderous roar.

Lily leaned in and raised her voice above the noise. "C'mon. Let's get our shoes."

"Shoes?"

She stopped in her tracks, twisted her head slightly, and blew out an exasperated breath. "Bowlin' shoes." She pointed at his deck shoes. "If you bowl in those, you would wind up on your fanny out there."

A few minutes later, carrying his red, white, and blue shoes, Bryce took a seat in the hard plastic chair.

After he tied up his bowling shoes, he lifted one foot in the air and moaned. "These are the ugliest things I have ever seen."

Lily looked up from lacing her shoes and bopped a shoulder. "Don't be silly, I think they match your eyes." Her voice held a hint of humor as a smile ruffled her pretty pink lips.

Blood pounded in Bryce's brain. She sure did make a captivating picture when she smiled. He hoped to see more of it.

"Mom, can I go first?" Joey appeared in front of Lily carrying an orange bowling ball with both hands. He held it against his stomach like it weighed a ton.

"You sure can. I'll get our game ready." She stood, leaned over, and touched Bryce's arm. "You need to go pick out a ball if you plan on bowlin' tonight."

The mere touch of her hand sent a warming shiver through him. "I guess you're right. It would be hard to bowl without one, wouldn't it?"

"Come on, Bryce, I'll help you." Joey grabbed his hand and pulled him toward the racks on the wall that held several bowling balls of all colors.

"What color do you want?" Joey asked as they reached the racks. He ran over and slapped a blue one that had a yellow stripe around it. "I like this one."

"If you like it, then I guess this one will be mine for the night." He picked up the bowling ball and held it in the crook of one arm before taking hold of Joey's shoulder with the other. "Let's bowl."

Lily had already entered their names in the computer by the time they returned to their lane. She looked up at the bowling ball he was holding and smiled. "Joey picked that one out, didn't he?"

"How did you know?"

"Because he loves the way the stripe spins when it rolls down the lane. He would bowl with it himself if it wasn't too heavy for him." She shifted in her seat and waved toward Joey. "Okay, it's your turn, little man."

A chuckle rumbled in the back of Bryce's throat as he watched Joey squat down, hold the bowling ball between his knees, and with all his might, roll the ball down the lane. The ball rolled one small roll at a time making its way down the lane. When it finally reached its destination, the pins began to slowly fall one-by-one, leaving only one standing.

"Woo whoo!" Lily bounced out of her chair and gave Joey a high five. "That was awesome."

"Did you see me, Bryce? Look all of them fell but one." Joey eyes sparkled with excitement.

"Good job. I may need some pointers from you."

Joey's second roll missed the lone pin completely, and he came back dragging his feet.

"That's okay," Lily said, holding up her hand for him to give her a high five. "Nine is a great start." She fiddled with the scoreboard for a second and then turned her attention to Bryce. "Okay, Bryce, it's your turn." Lily slipped a strand of hair behind her ear. She sure did look lovely without her cowgirl hat hiding her face and eyes.

Bryce picked up his bowling ball and stared down at it. He didn't want to look like a complete idiot, but he wasn't even sure how to hold the ball. He knew the holes in it were important, but why?

"Is there a problem?" Lily asked with an arched brow.

"Just strategizing." He just stuck his index finger and middle finger in the top holes and his thumb in the bottom hole. Then walked onto the lane and gave it a throw. The moment the ball left his hand, he knew instantly that wasn't the way to do it.

Blood pounded in his ears and his face grew hot with embarrassment as he watched the ball sail straight up in the air. Bryce stood frozen in terror as it came crashing down to the floor with a thundering boom that echoed throughout the bowling alley, and then it bounced over into the next lane.

"That was so funny!" Joey yelled out and started laughing. Several people around them began to laugh too. When Bryce turned around, Lily was standing directly behind him with her arms crossed over her chest. She sucked in her lips trying to keep from smiling and lifted a brow. "So, do you think you might need to rethink your strategy?" As soon as the last word left her lips, laughter bubbled out of her, which caused a tickle in the pit of his stomach.

He tilted his head to one side and rubbed his chin. "I think you may be right."

The next morning, after listening to the third ring, Lily started to hang up when Bryce's sleepy voice said, "Hello?"

"Oh. Were you asleep? I didn't mean to wake you. I just thought you'd be up by now." A tingle of embarrassment swept up the back of her neck and across her face. Why had she called him at 6:05 on a Saturday?

Shoving the pan of biscuits in the oven, she cleared her dry throat. "I'll let you go so you can go back to sleep."

"No, that's okay. I needed to get up anyway. What can I do for you?" he said through a yawn.

"I was about to start breakfast, and I was just wonderin' if you were gonna eat with us. So I'd know how much to make."

"I believe I will. Thank you. I'll be up there in about fifteen minutes or so. See you then."

"Okay. Bye." She pushed the *Off* button on the phone and dropped it on the counter. "What is wrong with me? Why did I invite him to breakfast? And to make it worse I woke him up to do it." She blew a loose strand of hair out of her face and shook her head.

"Mom, Kyle's here." Joey came scampering into the kitchen with Kyle the youngest ranch-hand, right behind him. When she looked down at Joey in his swimming trunks, she slapped herself in the forehead, remembering Kyle's mom had called earlier in the week and asked if Joey could go swimming with their family today. Kyle had two younger brothers that were close to Joey's age, so they always included Joey when they went on outings.

"Joey, I completely forgot." She gave Kyle an apologetic smile. "Give me a minute to get some things together for him."

"Okay, I'm not in any hurry." Kyle slipped off his hat and twisted the brim of it in his hands. He'd worked on the ranch for over two years yet he was still shy around her. He towered over her by at least a foot and a half. She wouldn't say he was skinny, but if he stood sideways, you may not be able to find him. There wasn't an ounce of fat on his entire body. His handsome face was kindled with a sort of passionate beauty. When he looked at her with his gentle brown eyes and tender sweet smile, her heart melted.

She hurried down the hallway with Joey on her heels. His excitement was obvious as he was speed talking the entire time she tossed an extra change of clothes and a towel into a bag.

A few minutes later, she stood on the front porch and waved to Kyle and Joey as they drove away. Leaning against one of the porch posts, she watched the truck until it disappeared. Turning to go back into the house, her eyes snagged on the guesthouse. Her heart thumped as apprehension crept up into her throat.

She stared at the guesthouse until her eyes burned. Why had she invited Bryce to breakfast? Now, it was just going to be the two of them, eating breakfast together, in the house, alone. Gnawing on her bottom lip, Lily wondered if she could un-invite him. No, she couldn't do that. How rude would that be?

Shaking off the uneasy feeling in the pit of her stomach, she scolded herself. "C'mon, Lily, it's just breakfast." With that, she jerked open the screen door and forged ahead into the house.

A few minutes later, Lily was taking the pan of biscuits out of the oven when Bryce walked into the kitchen. "Good morning, Lily."

Lily's insides vibrated at the sound of his voice behind her. The spicy scent of his aftershave and soap filled the kitchen.

Without turning, she said over her shoulder. "If you want coffee, the cups are in that cabinet. How do you like your eggs?"

"Scrambled is fine." After getting a cup from the cabinet, he poured himself a cup of coffee and leaned against the counter. "Can I help? Like I said before, I do know my way around the kitchen."

"No, thank you. I got it. Besides, everythin' is done except for the eggs." After cracking and whipping the eggs in a bowl, she poured them into the hot skillet.

Lily turned her head slightly, gave him a once over look, and then with a grunt, shook her head. He was wearing a white polo shirt, navy khakis, and deck shoes—hardly riding and roping attire.

"What?" He looked down at his clothes and shrugged one shoulder. "What's wrong with what I have on?"

A bubbly laugh eased from her lips as she wagged her head. "I'm glad we made plans last night to go clothes shopping for you today. If any of the boys saw you now, they would laugh you right off this ranch." She slid the eggs into a bowl and pointed the spatula at the table. "Sit."

He pushed himself away from the counter and dropped into one of the chairs. "I assure you, in my circle of friends, this is normal attire."

"You're not in the same circle of friends anymore."

"So, we are friends?" Bryce took hold of her hand that held the spatula, and with a squeeze, he lowered his voice. "I sure hope so."

Lily's lungs tightened when all the oxygen seemed to have vanished from the room. The very air around her felt electrified. Pulling her hand away, she awkwardly cleared her throat. "After you're finished, we'll head on into town."

"I'm sure you have better things to do than to chauffeur me around."

"I don't mind helping you out until you become familiar with the area. Besides, it would be easier to show you than to give you directions, too many back roads. Oh, that reminds me." She walked over to the key hook next to the back door and took down a set of keys. "Here are the keys to the truck Martin left to you. I think you'll like it. Every man needs a truck, even a city boy."

"Thanks." He pocketed the keys and then looked around the kitchen. "Where's Joey? Will he be going with us today?"

"No. Kyle came by this morning to pick up Joey to go swimmin' with him and his family. Kyle has two younger brothers who are around Joey's age, so Joey's gone for the day."

"So it's just the two of us?" Bryce arched a brow.

"Yes, I guess so." A tingle galloped through Lily's stomach as she rubbed her sweaty hands on her apron.

CHAPTER
TEN

On the ride into town, Lily's mind went back to the night before. Bryce certainly wasn't a bowler. If someone scored big with gutter balls, Bryce would have been the champion. Out of the ten frames, at least half of them went in the gutter. Each time, Bryce only laughed.

A giggle made its way to the surface when she cut her eyes over at him.

"What's so funny?" Bryce cocked his head to one side and bumped up a brow.

"Oh nothing, Mr. Gutter man. You know, I think Joey is available to give lessons."

"Funny, very funny."

They laughed together.

Following Lily's direction, Bryce parked the truck in an empty space in front of the *Western Days* clothing store. Lily climbed out of the truck, and he followed her toward the entrance.

In three quick strides, he stepped ahead of her, pushed opened the door, and waited for her to go inside. A musical note sounded as they entered the store.

"Can I help you?" a woman about Lily's age asked as she met them at the door. She flashed Bryce a pearly white smile and picked up a brow. "And your husband?"

"He's not my husband." Lily's cheeks warmed at how quickly she corrected the woman. "Mr. Fowler needs some jeans, shirts, and boots."

The woman's smile widened, and she breezed past Lily so her full gaze was on him. Then she snaked both of her arms around one of his. "Well, Mr. Fowler, I'm sure we can find something. Mmm, someone's been working out. Follow me and we'll get started on you."

Bryce smiled down at the sales girl. "Lead the way. I'm all yours, Ma'am."

The woman's giggle crawled over Lily's skin.

"Please, call me Angie."

Bryce glanced back at Lily. "Are you coming?"

"Oh no, you two go ahead. I think you're in good hands," Lily said through tight lips.

Angie pulled him along toward the menswear department, giggling.

Is it like this everywhere he goes? Lily moaned, letting her eyes go closed for a second.

She breathed a heavy sigh and plopped down on a padded bench with a thump. Angie's giggling and Bryce's throaty laugh could be heard throughout the store. Jealousy tried to etch its way into her heart, but Lily refused to let it take hold.

Twenty minutes later, Angie walked up to Lily and cleared her throat. "Excuse me. Bryce wants to know what you think."

Bryce, huh? Well, that was quick. Why was she surprised?

When Lily lifted her eyes in Bryce's direction, her breath caught in her throat, and her heart rate spiked.

"Isn't he handsome?" Angie leaned in close and whispered.

Wow! Lily couldn't speak as she watched Bryce saunter toward her. He was dressed in perfectly fit Wrangler jeans, a black t-shirt, and a pair of black cowboy boots.

"Well, what do you think? Do I pass inspection?" Bryce gave her a crooked grin. Then he did a manly full circle turn. "Am I cowboy enough?"

She shoved her shaky, damp hands, down into the front pockets of her jeans. "It's better than what you had. At least now you can go to work."

"Is that all you have to say?" Angie wrinkled her nose at Lily, turned, and took hold of Bryce's arm. "Well, I think you look gorgeous."

"We don't need him to look gorgeous. We need him dressed for work." Lily grabbed her bag, tossed it over her shoulder, and moved past him. "Be sure to grab a couple extra jeans and a few more shirts. Then if you're finished shopping, I'll wait for you in the truck." She'd wait for him in the truck all right. She couldn't stand to watch that woman clinging to him like a dryer sheet, and she didn't like that feeling one little bit.

♥ ♥ ♥

"Lily," Bryce called after her, but she hastened toward the front door without looking back.

"Don't worry about her. I'll take care of you." Angie ran her hand down his arm and linked her fingers in his. "Who is she to you anyway? I noticed when you first came in she called you Mr. Fowler. Is she your employee?" She flicked her other hand in Lily's direction as they made their way toward the small stack of clothes he had already chosen and then headed toward the checkout counter.

He smiled when he remembered Lily's words of warning not to use her as a way of escaping women. "I guess you could say she's a friend."

"I was hoping you'd say something like that." Angie picked up a pen from off the counter, took hold of his hand, and scribbled numbers in his palm. "Here's my cell phone number. Give me a call if you need anything. I get off at six on the weekends, and since today is Saturday, that means I'll be free after six tonight."

"I'll keep that in mind."

"You'd better." Angie ran her fingertips over the numbers on his hand, grinned up at him, and then glided around behind the counter.

He usually loved this kind of attention; he'd always had a way with women. He knew exactly how and when to turn on the charm, and with little effort he could win the heart of any woman he wanted. From time to time, he'd been referred to as, a *lady's man*. A title he liked and tried to live up to.

Angie smiled and every time she rang up one of his items, she batted her long eyelashes at him. She was a beautiful young woman, with shoulder length red hair, sparkling green eyes, and a figure that haunted every man's dreams. This girl definitely fell right into the category of the women he'd dated back in New York.

So why wasn't he enjoying this attention from Angie? Instead, his mind traveled back to the cute little cowgirl with the sweetest southern drawl waiting for him in the truck. A quiver started in the pit of his stomach and moved up his body until it turned into a smile. Just thinking about her caused an adrenaline rush to rocket through his body, making him light-headed.

Sunday morning, when Bryce stepped up on the porch of the main house, he saw a note taped to the door.

Bryce,

Joey and I have gone to church. We should be back home around one o'clock. Breakfast is on the stove and I have the coffee pot ready for you. All you have to do is flip it on.

Lily

When he wandered into the kitchen, the smell of fried bacon and freshly baked biscuits hit his nostrils making his stomach rumble. He glanced around the kitchen and thought this looked like a kitchen you'd see pictured in a country home magazine. A vase of handpicked wild flowers sat in the middle of the table giving the entire room a warm and cozy feel to it.

He'd only been here two days, but strangely, he found himself missing Lily and Joey's company. He wasn't used to being around children, but he liked Joey. He was a smart and funny kid.

After eating breakfast, he leisurely walked out onto the front porch and plopped down on the top step. Champ stretched out on the porch alongside of him, and Bryce patted the dog's head. "It's lonely around here without them, isn't it, boy?"

Champ whimpered.

Bryce was still sitting there when he saw Lily's truck coming down the drive. Champ jumped up and darted toward the truck, barking happily.

When the truck stopped in the drive, Lily shut off the engine, and Joey leaped out of the truck waving at Bryce. "Hey, Bryce."

Bryce waved back, but when Lily stepped out of the truck, his hand froze in the air. He was awestruck as he watched her sashay across the yard toward him. She looked like she had just stepped out of a glamour magazine. Her thick dark hair hung in long graceful curls over her slender shoulders and bounced with every step she took. The sleeveless, knee-length, pale pink dress she wore made her honey-bronze skin glow. Her hips tapered down into long, straight tan legs. She had delicate features that would make any man sit up and take notice.

"Whatcha doing?" Joey asked as he raced past Lily and ran up on the porch.

Reluctantly, Bryce pulled his attention away from Lily and bobbed his head at the hyperactive Champ who was now licking Joey as if he were covered in syrup.

"Not much. I was just keeping your dog company until you came back home."

"He always misses me when I'm gone. Watch what he can do. Come on, Champ." Joey took off running across the yard with the dog at his heels. He stopped and picked up a stick.

"Stop right there, young man, you know you have to change out of your Sunday clothes before you can go play," Lily yelled, shaking her finger.

Joey groaned loudly. "Ah, Mom, I wanted to show Bryce how Champ can fetch a stick."

Lily placed both hands on her hips and exhaled noisily. "After you change."

"Okay, okay." He ran back upon the porch, stopping only for a moment to tell Bryce he would be right back.

"Did you enjoy church this morning?" Bryce asked when Lily reached the steps.

Her smile reached her eyes. "Yes I did. It was a good service, but I'm starvin'." Touching her hand to her stomach she continued, "I put a ham in the oven this mornin' before I left. It should be ready by now. Are you hungry?"

"I sure am." Bryce bolted to his feet and held the door open for Lily. "After you."

"Thank you." When she smiled up at him, his senses leapt to life.

After the three of them had lunch, Lily and Joey gave Bryce the grand tour of the ranch. Lily showed him some of the things he'd be doing come Monday while Joey introduced him to some of the horses, cows, and chickens.

After a while, Joey became bored with it all, and he and Champ ran off to play.

"So, what do you think about all of this?" Lily tucked her hands in her pockets and rocked back on her heels. "Do you think you'll be able to live out here in the sticks for a year?"

He smacked a mosquito on his neck and exhaled sharply. He didn't like being eaten alive by bugs, but he had a point to prove to Lily and to himself. "I think I can manage."

"Moving from the big city to this, I don't know." Her head swung lazily from side-to-side as she gave him a lopsided grin.

"Are you trying to discourage me?" He quirked his eyebrows questioningly.

Lily bumped up a shoulder. "Would it work?"

"Sorry, but you're stuck with me for a year."

"A girl can dream, can't she?"

Inching closer to her, he whispered close to her ear. "You sure do make a guy feel wanted."

She lifted her chin upward, and her lips curled into a soft smile. "I try."

His eyes moved over her face and settled on her lips. A quiver surged through his veins as his heartbeat skyrocketed. He had never wanted to kiss a woman as much as he wanted to kiss her right now. To pull her into his arms and kiss her until the world around them disappeared. From the glimmer he saw in her eyes, he knew she wanted his kiss too. When he moved closer, Lily slowly closed her eyes and lifted her chin.

"Mom!" Joey's voice pierced the air causing them both to jump.

"Joey." Lily's eyes flung open, and her expression darkened. She shoved him away and stumbled backward.

Whirling around, she dropped to her knees just as Joey ran up behind her. "What's wrong, Joey? Are you okay?"

"Look, Mom. We have babies." Joey held up his cupped hands, and Bryce saw a ball of yellow fuzz.

Relief flooded over Lily's face as she pulled Joey into her arms. "You almost made me have a heart attack."

Joey wiggled out of her arms. "Mom, you're going to squash the little baby."

Lily let go of Joey and slid her hands under his. "So we have babies?"

Joey bobbed his head excitedly. "There are eight of them. Ain't this one cute?"

"Yes, it is. But, do you hear that sound? Listen." Lily lifted her head in the air.

Bryce listened too and heard a clucking, screeching sound.

"Is that the mommy chicken?" Joey asked.

"Yes, she's calling her chick, and I think she's sad because she doesn't know where it is."

"I should put it back." Sadness filled his eyes, and his shoulders drooped.

"Why don't you let me do it for you? I don't want her to peck you, but you can go with me."

"Okay."

Lily smiled lovingly down at Joey. "You're such a good helper." She held the chick close to her chest with one hand and took hold of Joey's hand with the other.

Watching Lily with her son stirred up something deep down in Bryce's soul. Silently he followed them toward the chicken coop.

After putting the chick back with its mother, Lily stepped out of the coop and dusted her hands off on her jeans. "Well now that that's taken care of, are you ready for your first ridin' lesson?"

Bryce leaned his head back and gazed into her eyes. "What? Now?"

"I'd say the sooner the better. You're not afraid, are you?" A faint light twinkled in the depths of her dark eyes brightening her entire face.

"Of course not. I'm ready whenever you are."

She pointed at his brand new western boots. "It'll be a good time to break those in." Turning, she called over her shoulder, "Come on, Joey, we're going to teach Bryce a thing or two about ridin'."

"Yay!" Joey sprinted into sight.

Bryce tagged along behind Lily and Joey all the way to the barn.

"I'll saddle up our horse Quarter Roy for you. He's one of the oldest horses we have here on the ranch, and he's the one I trust the most to put a greenhorn on. Once you learn how to ride him, we'll get you on another horse."

"So, you think I'm a greenhorn, huh?"

"Oh, yeah." She snickered and entered the barn with Joey right behind her.

A few seconds later, one at a time she led three horses out of their stalls.

"Mom, will you saddle Big Red first?" Joey asked as he rubbed the nose of one of the horses.

"Don't I always?" She patted Joey on the shoulder and then turned to Bryce. "He likes to sit in the saddle while I saddle up my horse, Lady Blue." She skillfully saddled Joey's horse and then gave Joey a leg up into the saddle.

She then tossed a thick black blanket over the back of the horse she called Quarter Roy. "Bryce, follow me." With a wave of her hand, she motioned for him.

He stepped into a room that had several saddles mounted on the wall. "This is the tack room." Looking over several of the saddles, she pulled down one of them and handled it as if it were weightless. "For the time you're here, this one will be your saddle. Once I get Quarter Roy saddled, you can mount him, and then I'll adjust the stirrups."

He reached for the saddle. "Do you want me to carry that for you?"

With an adventurous toss of her head, she shoved the saddle into his chest. "I guess there's no better time than the present for you to learn how to saddle up a horse."

Bryce pretended to follow her instructions as she told him how to get the horse saddled, which was as complicated as he remembered.

She rubbed the horse between the eyes. "Quarter Roy, this is Bryce, he's gonna be ridin' you today. You mind your manners now."

Giving the horse one last stroke on the head, she turned to Bryce. "Always saddle and mount from the left side of the horse. Now, put your left foot here, grab the horn, hoist yourself up, and at the same time throw your right leg over the horse."

Bryce tossed her a smile of satisfaction and accomplishment when he mounted the horse on the first try.

Joey clapped his hands. "You did it. Good job, Bryce."

A tinge of guilt pulled at his heart, but it quickly slipped away when Lily shrugged and said, "Not too bad, but you'll get better with time, hopefully."

Irritation crawled up his neck. What was it about him that made her think he was useless when it came to anything regarding this ranch? He was about to show her he wasn't some brainless city boy.

"If you'll pull your foot out of the stirrup, I'll adjust it for you." Lily's shoulder brushed against his leg as she worked to adjust the stirrup. A tingling sensation traveled up his leg and thumped into his belly.

After she adjusted both of the stirrups, she mounted her own horse and pulled on the reins. "Let's ride."

They trotted across the yard and stopped at the gate leading into the pasture.

"Do you want me to open the gate? I can—" Bryce began to dismount when Lily motioned for him not to move.

"Just stay in the saddle." She hopped off her horse, unlatched the gate, and swung it open. "Go on through."

"I could have done that, you know," Bryce grunted with a sigh.

"I thought it would be faster for me to do it. Just because you mastered getting on that horse on your first try doesn't make you an expert rider."

"No it doesn't. But I think this just might." He sank his heels into the sides of his horse and tore off into the pasture. After a couple minutes of proving his point, he slowed the horse and galloped back to where a dumbfounded Lily stood with her hands pressed into her hips and her mouth agape.

Joey cheered, pumping his hands in the air. He gave Bryce a high-five when he stopped his horse beside him. "Wow. That was awesome."

"You lied to me." Her voice sliced through the air, causing Joey to flinch as his gaze snapped to his mother.

Bryce shifted forward in the saddle, and his lips broke into a leisurely smile. "No, Ma'am, I didn't."

"Yes, you did. When I asked you if you knew how to ride, you told me no."

"That's not exactly how it happened, Lily. Let me refresh your memory. You asked me if I could ride, but before you gave me a chance to answer, you just assumed I didn't know how. So, I just played along."

"I…" She crossed her arms and shook her head. "Okay, I suppose you're right, but you could have at least had the decency to tell me before I made a complete idiot out of myself back at the barn." She climbed up on her horse and jerked on the reins. "Come on, Joey, let's go."

"Is my lesson over?" Bryce asked innocently.

Instead of seeing anger in her eyes, he thought he saw a flicker of sadness. "I can't believe you did this. I guess I deserved it, but I don't appreciate being made a fool out of, especially in front of my son."

CHAPTER
ELEVEN

The next morning, a rapping on the door stirred Bryce out of his sleep. He stretched and slowly opened his sleepy eyes. Sunlight streamed through the window, filling the room with its warmth. He glanced over at the alarm clock on the nightstand. "Six o'clock. Who gets up at six o'clock?"

The knocking continued, becoming more persistent with each passing second.

"I'm coming. I'm coming." He scrambled out of bed and staggered to the door. He opened it to find Joey standing on the porch, grinning.

"Mornin', Bryce. Mom asked me to come and wake you up. She said if you want to eat your breakfast hot, you need to hurry."

"Good morning to you too, Joey. Thank you for coming to wake me. It won't take me more than a few minutes to get dressed." He yawned and rubbed the sleep from his eyes.

"Okay. Don't forget to wear your hat today."

"I'll remember." He smiled down at Joey and nodded. Even though Bryce hadn't been here very long, he was already growing attached to this little guy.

"Can I wait on you?"

"Sure. Come on in." He opened the door wide and stepped aside as Joey came in and bounced down on the sofa.

Bryce went back into the bedroom, quickly dressed, collected Joey once more, and headed out across the yard with the boy by his side. "Good morning," he said when he stepped into the kitchen. After his comment to her the day before, he wondered if things were going to be awkward between them.

"You really look like a cowboy now, Bryce. Don't he, Mom?"

"You look like you're ready to go to work," Lily said as she gave Bryce a quick, head-to-toe scan. He saw her mouth twitch with what he thought was a hidden smile.

Bryce shrugged. "So you approve?"

She gave him a thumbs-up, turned back to the stove, and pulled a fresh pan of biscuits from the oven. He saw her shoulders droop slightly.

Was she still upset? Bryce had to make things right between them. He eased up behind her and laid his hand on her shoulder. "About yesterday, I—"

When Lily turned, she shifted to the side making his hand fall away from her shoulder. "There's no need. I know I overreacted. Everythin's fine."

"Then we're okay?"

"Yes, we're okay. Now sit so I can finish breakfast."

Bryce still had an unsettling feeling in his chest. Even though she said everything was fine, he knew different. He'd hurt her feelings. He didn't know how, but he was determined he was going to make it up to her.

After breakfast, Bryce pushed his plate away and rubbed his stomach. "I do believe that's the biggest and the best breakfast I've ever had."

"I told you my mom's the bestest cook in the world." Joey grinned with a mouthful of eggs.

"Joey, you know better than to talk with food in your mouth," Lily scolded.

Suddenly a loud rumbling sound filled the kitchen.

"What's that noise?" Bryce asked.

Joey giggled as he wagged his head. "That's not noise. It's Wade's in the big tractor."

Lily crinkled her brows. "Bryce, go ahead and finish your coffee. I need to speak with Wade alone, and I only need a couple of minutes." She then turned to Joey. "Joey, finish your breakfast, and then you can bring Bryce out to meet Wade. Do you want to do that?"

Joey wiggled in his chair and bobbed his head up and down as he chewed on his eggs.

"Good boy." Lily kissed the top of Joey's head as she walked by him, and then slipped out of the room.

After Joey wolfed down the rest of his eggs and finished off his milk, he slipped away from the table. "Are you ready to meet Wade? You'll like him," he said as he pulled up the bottom of his t-shirt and wiped his mouth.

"Ready whenever you are, little man." Bryce looked down at the wet spot on Joey's t-shirt and smiled to himself. He remembered doing the same thing when he was a little boy. His mother was always so preoccupied she never even noticed. Nevertheless, he wouldn't be surprised at all if Lily noticed the little wet spot on Joey's shirt.

Joey jumped out of his chair, ran over, and grabbed his backpack off the counter. "C'mon."

Bryce pushed his chair back and stood to his feet. "I'm right behind you." He tagged along behind Joey toward the front door.

When Bryce stepped out onto the front porch with Joey, he looked out across the yard and saw Lily standing next to a tall cowboy who was leaning against one of the work trucks. She laughed, and the man reached out and put his arm around her waist. He pulled her close and whispered in her ear.

She tossed her head back and laughed.

An unfamiliar feeling shot through Bryce's chest. "Who's that?"

"That's Wade," Joey answered.

"That's Wade? I thought…" He'd imagined Wade to be an elderly man like his grandfather, but this man was definitely not an old man. He was probably in his early thirties, and he was built like a young John Wayne. Bryce groaned. "I guess it's time I meet the illustrious Wade Haston."

When Lily spotted them, she nudged Wade away from her. He looked up at them from under the rim of his hat, and his smile faded into a dim, dark frown. Every old western shoot-out movie Bryce had ever seen played out in his head. He knew from the expression on Wade's face this wasn't going to be a friendly meeting.

Bryce crossed the yard with Joey at his side and came to a stop in front of Lily and Wade.

Lily hesitated only a second before turning her attention to her son. Then her eyes traveled down to the bottom of his shirt, and a moan escaped her lips. "Joey, did you wipe your mouth on your shirt again?"

Bryce's insides warmed with a smile. *I knew she would notice.*

"Yes, Ma'am. I'm sorry I forgot." Joey bumped up a shoulder and tugged at one of the straps of his backpack trying to avoid his mother's stare.

The sound of the bus' engine filled the air.

"Joey, here comes the bus." She adjusted his backpack and kissed him on top of the head. "Have a good day at school."

"Shoot. I wanted to talk to Wade." Joey kicked the ground and looked up at Wade.

"We'll see each other after school, buddy," Wade said with a glance at the child although his gaze never really left Bryce.

"Okay, bye, Wade. Bye, Mom. Bye, Bryce." He waved and ran off toward the bus.

Crossing her arms as she watched her son, Lily waited until the bus pulled away. Then, with a sigh, Lily looked from one man to the other. "Bryce, this is Wade Haston, our ranch foreman. Wade, this is Bryce Fowler, Martin's grandson."

Neither one of them extended a hand. Instead, Wade pushed his hat back on his head and gave Bryce an icy stare. "So, this is the city boy who thinks he can make it out here in the dirt?"

"I don't see it as a challenge," Bryce said, winding his arms over his chest, clicking his tongue in his cheek.

Wade narrowed his eyes until they were just slits. "Why don't you go back to where you came from? You don't belong here."

"You don't worry about me. I'm here, and I plan to stay."

Lily stepped in between them. "That's enough. I don't want either one of your *who's the biggest bull in the pen* attitudes around here. If you have somethin' to prove, then you can do it somewhere else."

Wade ran his hand down Lily's arm. "He doesn't belong here, Lily, and you know it. Look at him, with his shiny new boots and jeans. He won't last one day out here with the real men."

Lily sighed heavily and gave him a black scowl. "Wade, please. This isn't helping anythin'."

"You'd better get used to seeing my face, Haston. I'm not leaving anytime soon." Bryce thrust out his chin and eyed Wade with a stare of cold triumph.

"Bryce, you're not making it any better either." Lily's lips puckered with annoyance.

Wade gritted his teeth. "You can leave on your own, or I can make you leave."

"I wouldn't be too sure about that. I believe in three months I'm going to become your boss. If anyone's leaving, it just might be you."

Wade yanked off his hat and took a step toward Bryce. Lily placed her hand on Wade's chest and gave him a push. "That's enough out of both of you! Wade, Bryce is going to be here for the next year whether you like it or not." Then she turned to face Bryce, her back on Wade lest he actually charge. "And, as for you, Wade has been here for a long time, and that's not about to change. So, both of you had better put your egos away, learn to deal with it, and play nice. I mean it!"

With a turn on her heel, she stared both of them down and then waved her arms in the air, turned, and stormed off toward the house.

Wade chose not to add anything. Instead, he kicked the ground, slapped his hat against his leg, and climbed into the work truck. The motor roared to life. Then he pulled up beside Bryce and leaned out of the window. "Lily wants to wait until tomorrow morning before I can put you to work. She thinks you need one more day to get the feel of the place. But come mornin', let's just see how long you hang around after a couple of days working out here in the real world."

"Don't you worry yourself, Wade. I'll be hanging around for a long time. I'm not going to let some dirty cowhand run me off."

"Don't mess with me, boy. You won't win. I guarantee it," Wade snarled.

Suddenly and without any warning, Wade popped the clutch and did a quick tailspin, kicking up a monstrous cloud of dust and gravel that pelted Bryce. Wade's boisterous laugh knotted with a "*yee-haw*" that echoed in Bryce's ears.

He tried to fan the dust out of his face, but it was too late. As the dust cloud swirled around him, it filled his eyes, mouth, and nose. When the dust reached his lungs, it started a chain reaction of choking coughs as he struggled, trying to catch his breath. His eyes burned, his nose burned, and his throat felt as if he'd swallowed a piece of hot coal.

A few seconds later Bryce felt someone take hold of his arm. "Bryce, are you okay?"

"I—" Bryce's throat constricted from the dust when he tried to speak.

"Come on, we need to get you to the house."

She led him across the yard, up the steps, and into the house.

"The sofa's right behind you. Sit down, and I'll get you some water and the eyewash. I'll be right back."

Within seconds, she returned and placed a glass of water in his hand. "Here's some water. It'll wash down some of the dust in your throat."

Bryce swallowed the offering like a man dying of thirst. "Thank you."

"Now lay your head back. I'm going to try to flush some of the dirt out of your eyes. It may burn a bit, but I promise it doesn't burn as bad as that dirt does."

She held his eyelids open and poured the eyewash into it.

"Ugh!" Bryce moaned.

"Sorry."

After she finished flushing out both of his eyes, she placed a cloth in his hand. "Here's a wet cloth to wash your face."

"Thank you, Lily." He pushed himself up into a sitting position, propped his elbows on his knees, and held the cloth against his eyes.

"You want to try and open your eyes now? I need to see if I should wash them out one more time." She spoke gently to him as if she were speaking to Joey.

He slowly opened his eyes. His vision was blurred, and his eyes still burned, but at least he was able to keep them open.

"How do they feel?" Lily chewed on her bottom lip as she looked intently into his face.

"They still sting, but they do feel better. It's nothing I can't live with. Thank you again, Nurse Lily."

"Now do you see the necessity of a cowboy hat? It doesn't just help to block the sun. If you'd have been wearing the Stetson Joey gave you, the rim would have shielded your face."

"I forgot about it and left it on the breakfast table. I guess I learned that lesson the hard way."

"I'd say you did. I'll have a talk with Wade because it's one thing if the two of you don't like each other and you butt heads from time to time, but this?" She reached over and picked up the first-aid kit she'd brought with her and pulled out a couple of antiseptic wipes.

The frustration in Lily's voice let Bryce know that she wasn't too happy about what Wade had done. Bryce hid his smile at that thought—some because she was mad at Wade, some because she had landed on his side in the fight. He was glad for that. Maybe more glad than he should have been.

Picking up the washcloth she had brought in, Lily turned to him. "You have a couple of nicks on your face, probably caused by some loose gravel." Her hands were as soft as daybreak as she examined first one scratch and then the other with the soft tips of her fingers. "Here, lean back again, and I'll clean them up for you."

Tenderness for her gentleness touched him. Before she could touch his face with the cloth, he took hold of her hand. "You don't have to do this. I can do it myself."

However, when her gaze brushed his, her dark, sad eyes matched the apology on her face perfectly. "I don't mind, besides I feel somewhat responsible. I shouldn't have left the two of you out there alone." Then like a leaf on the autumn wind, the tenderness flitted away and her tough side reasserted itself. "Now, hush and lay your head back."

Still, Bryce couldn't let it go. He had to make her understand. "This isn't your fault."

The growl of frustration started low in her throat but quickly jumped to the forefront as her hands worked to mend him despite his protests. "Would you please let me tend to you and stop your arguin' with me?" Anger and determination flashed across her gaze. "Now, lay your head back already."

What else could he say? "Whatever you say, boss lady."

Bryce obeyed and laid his head back on the sofa. Lily leaned over him, and dabbed his injuries with the wipes. The sweet smell of apples mingled with the scent of her floral perfume filled his nostrils, and the touch of her fingers was as soft as rose petals to his skin. He closed his eyes and savored the moment. Suddenly, his heart played rat-a-tat-tat against his ribcage. He yanked in a jagged breath.

"Sorry. This stuff does sting a little, but I'm all finished now."

He opened his mouth to speak, but nothing came out. The antiseptic wipes weren't the problem…her touch was. Just what he was going to do about it, he had no idea, but he was looking forward to finding out.

CHAPTER
TWELVE

That evening, Bryce tapped on the screen door, opened it, and walked in. "Can I come in?"

Lily laid aside the cookbook she was flipping through. "Sure, c'mon in." Bryce's cologne filled her senses. When she breathed the scent in, a chill tickled down her spine.

Bryce strolled over to the sofa, took a seat, glanced down at Joey, who was lying in the floor coloring. "Hey there, Buddy. What are you doing?"

Joey looked up from his coloring book and gasped. "What happened to your eyes and face?"

"Ah, it's nothing, Joey. I just had a battle with an angry dust cloud this morning." Bryce winked at Joey.

"I got dirt in my eyes 'fore too. It really hurts, don't it?" Joey looked up, wrinkled his nose, and examined Bryce's face. "It will feel better tomorrow."

"Thanks, Joey." He pointed at the coloring book that lay opened in the floor. "What do we have here? I didn't know you were an artist."

"You wanna look at them?" Joey asked as he rolled over, and with coloring book in hand, he sat up.

"I sure do."

Joey handed the coloring book to Bryce, who began to flip through the pages. "These are really good, Joey."

Lily whispered a silent prayer of thanks that Bryce had diverted Joey's attention away from the injuries to his face. She didn't want Joey to know what Wade had done. He thought Wade was a hero, and this definitely wasn't what a hero would do.

Leaning forward, she swept Joey's bangs away from his forehead. "Yes, he's my little artist."

"Well from what I see, I'm impressed." Bryce continued flipping through the book. "You know I need something on my walls to brighten up the place, and I think one of your pictures will do the trick. Joey, would you color something for me?"

Joey's face glowed as he puffed his chest out. "Do you like this one?" He pointed at one of a cowboy on a bucking bronco.

"That one's pretty cool," Bryce said, nodding.

"Can I give it to him, Mom?" Pleading filled Joey's eyes.

"Of course you may, Joey. They're yours."

Joey tore the page from the book. "If you tell me how to spell your name, I can write, to Bryce from Joey. I can already spell my name you know."

"That would be great. There's nothing like having an autograph from an artist on his work."

It amazed Lily how good Bryce was with Joey, especially when he had admitted to her just a few days before that he wasn't use to being around children.

Joey giggled. "Mommy says my daddy was an artist, too. She has some of his drawings in her bottom dresser drawer, and she lets me look at them sometimes. They are really pretty."

"You dad was an artist too, huh?" Sympathy stirred in Bryce's eyes as he looked square into Lily's face.

Lily squirmed under Bryce's pity stare. Looking away, she leaned over and touched Joey's shoulder. "Joey, why don't you go wash up? I'm about to put supper on the table."

"Ah, Mom! I already washed my hands." He held his hands in the air for her to inspect.

Lily took hold of his hands and shook her head when she saw streaks of dirt, which ran from the tips of his fingers to his wrists. "When was the last time you washed your hands, Joey, this morning? Look how filthy they are. Now go."

"Okay, okay." Joey turned to leave the room, then he stopped and looked up at Bryce. "You better make sure your hands are clean." He shook his head and frowned. "Mom hates dirty hands."

"I'll keep that in mind," Bryce said with a wink and patted Joey on the shoulder. "Now, go get cleaned up."

"You'd have thought I'd just sent him to face a firing squad. Boys."

"I remember being that age, too." A mischievous smile tickled Bryce's mouth.

After she knew Joey was out of earshot, she looked into Bryce's face.

"I'd like to thank you for not tellin' Joey about what happened today with Wade. Joey adores Wade, and it would break his heart if he knew Wade is the one who did this to you. You know, if I hadn't seen it with my own eyes, I wouldn't have believed it. This just isn't like him. I don't even know what to say."

Bryce moved in close to her. "You don't have to say anything."

"Do they still hurt? They look painful. I guess I should have taken you to the doctor." She wrinkled her nose, sighed softly, and gave him a sympathetic smile.

"I didn't need to see a doctor. It's not as bad as it looks, Lily. Stop worrying."

"I really want to apologize for Wade's behavior today. I just don't know what's gotten into him. He's not normally like this."

"You don't have to keep apologizing. Wade and I will work this out among ourselves like men, don't worry."

"I'm not so sure about that. I knew when I first told him about…well…us. He was extremely upset about the whole situation, but I would've never dreamed he would do something like this. This is just mean."

"They're clean now," Joey yelled as he raced back into the living room and pushed his hands inches from Lily's face in case she didn't hear him or believe him. "See."

She laughed as she pushed his hands down. "I see, Joey, I see. Okay, do you want to help me get supper on the table? Bryce, I hope you like meatloaf."

"I can't say I've ever had it, but I'll try anything once. Besides, it certainly does smell delicious. I'd better go wash my hands. Don't want Joey to think you're showing favoritism."

Lily watched Bryce leave the room. She was going to have a talk with Wade just as soon as possible. This was uncalled for, and she was going to let him know it.

At that moment, Wade and Kyle came through the door.

"Ah, Lily's famous meatloaf. I could smell it when I stepped up on the porch. It's only the two of us. Greg already left for the day." Wade stopped in his tracks when he saw Lily glaring at him.

"Joey, would you please go ahead and start setting the table?" She turned and looked at Kyle. "Kyle, would you mind giving Joey a hand? I'd like a moment alone with Wade, please."

"Yes, Ma'am." Kyle pulled his hat off, gave Lily a quick nod, and followed Joey into the kitchen.

Lily waited until Joey and Kyle were out of the room, then she slammed her hands on her hips and tried to control the anger, which was threatening to erupt. "Wade Haston, how dare you deliberately try and harm another person on this ranch!"

A shadow of innocence crossed his face as he reached for one of her arms. "What are you talking about?"

She put a hand on his chest and pushed him away. "Hold on there a minute, buster. And, don't play dumb with me, Wade. I saw what you did to Bryce with my very own eyes. Why would you do such a thing?"

He bit his tongue and shrugged. "You saw that, did you?"

"Yes, I did, and it was hateful, cruel, and malicious." She glared at him with burning, reproachful eyes. "You could have caused serious injuries to his eyes. You know better than to do something like that. What on earth is wrong with you?"

"Ah, come on, Lily. I was just joking around with the boy." His response held a hint of irritation.

"Joking?" Anger bubbled up inside of her so strong she could taste it in the back of her throat. She took a slow deep breath trying to control her temper. "Oh, I see, causing someone else pain is 'joking around' to you?"

"I didn't hurt him, Lily. How can a little dust hurt anyone?"

"Have you seen him? Have you seen his eyes?" She struggled to keep her voice low, not wanting Joey to hear her agitation.

"No, he's been hid out in the guesthouse all day, but it can't be that bad."

"Trust me, it is. Did it even occur to you, what would have happened if Joey had seen you do that? You know how much Joey looks up to you."

"Joey was long gone, but I guess I wasn't thinking. I'm sorry." The corner of his mouth twisted in exasperation as he heaved a sigh.

"No, you weren't thinkin'." She licked her lowered lip, trying to suppress her anger. "I want you to promise me you'll never do anything like that again. Promise me."

"Okay, if it will make you happy, I give you my word that I'll give the boy some slack, but I still don't trust him, and I'm keeping an eye on him." He took hold of her arms and looked into her face. "So, are we okay?"

"No, we're not okay." She didn't push him away this time. Instead, she crossed her arms while he still held onto them. "I'm still angry with you, Wade."

He gave her a playful shake and successfully disarmed her with his infectious smile. "What can this old cowboy do to make it right?"

"Apologizing to Bryce would be a good start."

Wade looked up at the ceiling and blew out a sharp breath. "Okay, I'll do it for you."

"That's all I ask."

"So then, am I forgiven?"

"I'll still have to think about that." She unfolded her arms, slapped his chest with both hands, and gave him a lopsided smile.

Wade chuckled, pulled her close, and kissed her forehead.

"Well, I'm all washed up and ready for…"

When Lily heard Bryce's voice behind her, her heart slammed to a stop as she flinched away from Wade. She turned just in time to see a brief flicker of anger sweep across his face. "Bryce," she took a step toward him. "Wade here has something to say to you."

She glanced over her shoulder at Wade, raised a brow, and dipped her head in Bryce's direction. "Well?"

Wade shrugged, grunted, and shifted his gaze to Bryce. "Lily seems to think I owe you an apology, Fowler. I just figured you'd move out of the way and not just stand there."

Bryce laughed without a smile. "Hey, don't worry about it. I assure you I won't be caught off guard again."

Wade took a step forward, his jaw working back and forth as if he was chewing on something he didn't like. His fists clenched at his sides. "You think so, huh?"

Bryce set his jaw, and the vein on the side of his neck throbbed as he moved a step closer to Wade, too. "I know so."

The hair on the back of Lily's neck prickled as the temperature in the room rose by ten degrees, and it wasn't due to the weather.

She stepped between them and lifted her hands up in front of both men. "Okay, boys, that's enough. You two are going to have to find some common ground here." She lowered her voice and glanced toward the kitchen. "Look, for some reason or another, the two of you have made it perfectly clear that you don't like each other, so I'm not going to ask you to become best friends or anything like that, but can't you at least be civil to one another? If you can't do it for my sake, can you at least do it for Joey?" She dropped her hands to her sides and released a weary sigh. "The next twelve months is going to be stressful enough without the two of you acting like three year olds, don't you think?"

"You're right, Lily. Why don't you run along into the kitchen and finish up with supper while Fowler and I have a little talk?" Wade asked, clearly holding himself in control so she would believe he wasn't about to punch Bryce in the nose.

"Wade, I don't know if that's a good idea or not."

"I'm sure Wade and I can come up with a mutual understanding." Bryce took a step back and shoved his hands into his pockets.

"We'll play nice, I promise." Wade took her arms, turned her toward the kitchen, and gave her a gentle push. "Now, get. We'll be along in a few minutes."

"Okay, I'll go, but if I hear the slightest sound of an argument, you'll both go without supper, and I mean it." Lily glanced once more at each man then reluctantly left the room.

Bryce didn't like the feeling that twisted in the pit of his stomach when he saw Wade holding Lily in his arms. He tried to rationalize with himself. So what if Wade was holding her? So what if they had a thing going on? So what if they even had feelings for each other? None of this was any of his business. However, the rationalizations weren't helping much. If he didn't care, then why did his blood pressure soar? Finally, standing there glaring at the man, Bryce concluded that he just didn't like Wade Haston.

Both men stood in silence and watched her exit the room. Wade turned toward Bryce and spoke in a low tone. "Okay, Fowler, I'm going to lay it all out on the table for you to understand. I care a lot about Lily, and I do mean a lot.

What I'm trying to say is she's mine, and I'm not gonna let some slick-talking city boy waltz in with his fancy clothes and money and mess it up for me. Just because you and Lily have this ridiculous arrangement going on doesn't mean a thing to me. You don't belong here, and the sooner you leave, the better off we all are. And nothing would please me more than to put a boot in your pants and be the one to throw you off this ranch."

Wade took a step back and bobbed his head toward the kitchen. "But, for Lily's sake, I'll back off for now. But you'd better listen to me and listen good. If you do anything to hurt Lily and that little boy of hers, you will answer to me. Do you feel where I'm coming from?"

Wade's threat wasn't going to intimidate Bryce. "Oh, I feel where you're coming from all right, but now I want you to know where I'm coming from. Trinity, Alabama, is definitely the last place on earth where I want to be. But this is my grandfather's ranch, and not you or anyone else is going to be able to throw me off this place. When the year's up, I'm gone but not one day before then. I'm giving you fair warning right now, Haston. I don't appreciate being threatened, and I don't need a woman to protect me either. I can handle myself just fine."

The darks of Wade's eyes lowered three levels. "You better hope you can. Because before it's over, we may just have to find out how tough you really are. I can make things easy on you around here, or I can make your life a living nightmare. It's up to you which road you want to travel. Because even though Lily is upset with me right now for what happened this mornin', she will always and I mean always, back any decisions I make when it concerns this ranch. In other words, when it comes down to it, she'll always be on my side of the fence. You're nothing to her, Fowler, nothing."

"Boys, supper's getting cold." Lily appeared in the doorway, face pale and questioning. "Is everything okay out here?"

"Everything's just peachy out here. Ain't that right, Bryce?" Wade slapped Bryce on the back and let out a throaty laugh.

"Everything's just fine, Lily." Bryce faked a smile and fought not to cough.

"Well," Lily's brows knitted as she looked from Wade and then to Bryce. "C'mon before supper gets any colder than it already is."

"Right behind you, girl," Wade said.

Bryce waited until Lily disappeared into the kitchen. "Wade, I have to correct you on one thing."

On the heel of his dirty boot, Wade spun. "And, what's that?"

"You were wrong. I think I am something to Lily that you're not."

"Oh, you think so, huh? And just what would that be?" Wade growled.

Bryce moved in beside Wade, returned the slap on the back, and said with a smile, "I'm going to be her husband."

CHAPTER
THIRTEEN

Every muscle in Bryce's body throbbed. Would his legs carry him to the tailgate of the truck to where the bright red cooler was? He shook off his gloves, thrust his hand into the ice, and grabbed a bottle of water from the cooler. He downed the chilled liquid in one long gulp, collapsed onto the tailgate, and drew in a deep breath. He jerked his hat off and wiped the sweat from his forehead.

He had never worked this hard a day in his life, not even his regular morning jogs in the park followed by a trip to the gym for his hour-long workout compared to this.

Sweat, dirt, hay, and manure all cling to his skin and clothing. This certainly wasn't the lifestyle he was accustomed to.

He massaged the back of his neck and looked out across the land. "I'm beginning to wonder if any of this is worth it."

Then Lily's words danced around in his head. *I can't see you lasting one week out there.*

He found her to be irritating, stubborn, and even bossy at times, and yet he couldn't explain the attraction he felt for her. What was it about this woman that made him smile every time he thought about her? Maybe it was just the thought of what he would gain by their arrangement. At least that made some sense. The truth was, back in New York, he would have never looked twice at her. Anger and pride bubbled in his core. He would not quit this ridiculous game especially because everyone was out to prove he would fold under the pressure.

"I'm going to do this even if it kills me." He shoved his hat back on his head and stood. "And, it just might."

Sharp whistles seized his attention. He grabbed another bottle of water from the cooler and followed the sounds around to the left of the barn. Lily stood in the middle of a round pen with a rope in her hand while a horse circled the pen in a steady lope. Lily shouted a command, the horse stopped, and galloped in the opposite direction, then back again.

Greg stood against the fence, his arms slopped over the top rail, and one foot propped up on the bottom as he chewed on a piece of straw.

"Wow, that's impressive," Bryce said as he joined Greg.

"Yeah, Lily's the best trainer around. That thing she's doing right there is for Western Pleasure. It's the most popular horse show class in the country. She's only been working with that stud colt for a short time now, and he's already obeying her commands. Don't tell her I said this, but around here we call her the horse whisperer."

"The horse whisperer, huh? She does have skills, I give her that."

"I think it's her second nature. People who have been doing this a lot longer than she has have brought their own horses to her to train."

They watched her for a few more moments in silence. The horse obeyed every command she called out to him with ease.

She called out a command, the horse stopped and gaited to her. She gave him a pat, spoke softly in his ear. He backed up and then took a bow.

"Yee-haw. Way to go, Lily!" Greg yanked off his hat and waved it in the air.

Lily whirled around, and a smile radiated across her face. "Did you see that? Did you see that?"

An electrical jolt shot through Bryce's body as if he'd grab hold of a live wire. He had been here for almost a week, and this was the first time he'd seen Lily truly smile. It wasn't a stressed smile, it wasn't a nervous smile, and it wasn't a tense smile. It was a smile of pure excitement and joy. It was a beautiful smile.

She snapped the lead onto the halter and led the horse toward the gate.

Greg cupped his hands to his mouth and yelled, "I'll get the gate for you."

Lily nodded, and her chocolate brown hair bounced around her shoulders.

Greg walked over, unlatched the gate, and swung it open. When Lily came out with the horse, Greg held his hand in the air, and Lily gave it a slap.

"I'll take him for you." Greg took the lead rope from Lily and led the horse toward the corral.

Bryce was glad he had grabbed an extra bottle of water when Lily pulled off her hat and swiped her forehead with the back of her gloved hand.

Twisting off the bottle cap, he strolled over and held it out to Lily. "This should hit the spot."

Lily pulled off her gloves, tucked them in her back pocket, and took the water. "Thanks, I appreciate it. Where's Kyle? You're workin' with him today, aren't you?"

"Wade needed his help, so Kyle told me to take a break. I was about to go back to work when I heard you." He bobbed his head toward the round pen. "You were amazing with that horse."

"No, he was amazin'. We won't have a bit of trouble sellin' him, and I'm sure the bid will be high." She took another long drink and began to walk toward the house.

"How long have you been training horses?" Bryce followed her, and they sat down at the picnic table beneath the large oak tree in front of the house.

"After I was taken from my mother, I was shuffled from foster home to foster home. When I was twelve, I was placed with a family that raised horses. The two years I was there, I learned a lot just from watching my foster dad work with the horses. The desire to learn more never left me. Then when I moved in here to care for Martin, Mr. Horton was the trainer, and I trained under him for a year. When he had another job offer in Tennessee, I took over the training job."

"You've only been training for three years?" Admiration mingled with surprise sounded in his voice.

She took another sip of water. "Give or take a month or two."

"Is that why they call you the horse whisperer?"

A soft giggle slipped from her lips causing a slight tremor to rush through him. As always, his ears hungrily soaked up the sound.

She bumped him with her shoulder. "Greg told you that, didn't he? He's the culprit who started it."

"It's a well-deserved name for you. If I didn't know any better, I would think you've been doing this your entire life."

"Nope, but I can say, I'll be trainin' horses for the rest of my life. I love working with them. Each one of the horses I train has its own unique personality, just as people do. Once I figure it out, it makes the training process a breeze."

The sun danced in her eyes as she spoke. "I've never had two horses exactly the same. I use several different techniques with each animal, and it seems to work. The only problem is, I become attach to every one of the horses I train, and when they're sold, it kinda breaks my heart to see them leave."

When he didn't respond, she twisted around and looked at him. Her cheeks pinked. "Sorry. I don't know why I rattled on and on like that."

"This is the first time since I've been here that you've share a little piece of yourself with me. I like it."

Her brows shot up, and her lips parted with a slight gasp. "I think it's time for me to get back to work. I'm wastin' daylight."

"Yes, I need to get back to work too. Kyle may be young, but he can be a drill sergeant at times."

Lily's laugh caused a rippling effect in his stomach. "You think he's bad, wait 'til you have to work with me."

♥ ♥ ♥

A few days later, Lily was piling uncooked hot dog wieners onto a platter when Joey scampered into the kitchen through the backdoor. "Mom, how much longer are you going to be? Wade has the fire pit ready."

"I'm almost ready," Lily said over her shoulder with her back to Joey. The back door opened again, and instantly she knew it was Bryce. His aftershave filled the kitchen, and Lily's skin tingled when she breathed it in.

"I love it when we roast hotdogs over the fire." Joey's excitement filtered through his voice.

"I know you do." Lily turned, grinned down at Joey, and winked. "I do too."

"And we tagged along with Joey to see if you needed any help," Bryce said and thumbed back at Kyle who was standing close behind him.

Lily wasn't expecting to see Kyle too.

"As luck would have it, I have a job for each of you." She stepped up to Kyle and handed him the platter of wieners. "Here you go, Kyle. You can take these on outside to Wade for me."

"What about me? What can I carry?" Joey asked.

Grabbing the chips and buns off the counter, she handed them to Joey. "You can take these outside."

"Come on, Kyle. I bet I can beat you back to Wade," Joey said and barreled out the back door.

"I guess the race is on." Kyle laughed and hurried out the door after Joey.

Lily snickered and nodded her head toward the refrigerator. "Bryce, if you'll follow me, I have a job for you too."

She pulled a bowl of potato salad and a bowl of slaw out of the fridge and handed them to Bryce. "Let me grab the clothes hangers and you can carry those too. I'll grab the pot of chili myself, and we'll be all set."

Bryce's brows crunched. "Clothes hangers?"

"Yeah, we could use roastin' forks, but it's so much more fun for Joey to use the hangers."

In a clench, Bryce watched her skeptically. "What am I missing? I don't get it. How on earth do you use a clothes hanger to cook with?"

She walked over to the pantry and took the straightened hangers off a hook on the back of the door. "See, we twist the hangers open, straighten them, and presto, the perfect roasting fork. Then all you do is slide the hot dog weenie on the end of it and hold it over the fire until it's cooked to your likin'."

His smile unclenched his face. "Oh, now it makes sense."

Lily laughed. "I can't wait to see you do this. I promise you, you'll never want to go back to boiled hot dogs again."

"What now? You havin' to school the city boy on how to roast a hot dog?" Wade grunted from the door and laughed dryly. "Shall we put it on the bun for you, too?"

Bryce clenched his jaw.

Lily put her hand on Bryce's arm and gave him a smile. "Don't pay any attention to him. Nobody knows everythin'." She stepped past Bryce and narrowed her eyes at Wade. "Be nice. We were about to head out. Was there somethin' you needed?"

He pointed at the hangers. "I came for those. Joey's getting impatient, and he's ready to get started." He looked over her shoulder at Bryce and then back to her. "Are you coming now?"

"Yes, let me grab the chili. You can go ahead, we'll be right behind you."

"I think I'll wait." Wade spoke to Lily but stared in Bryce's direction.

Two hours later, after everyone left for home, Lily tucked Joey into bed and finished putting the leftover food away. As she rinsed the last plate, she glanced out the window and noticed the fire pit still had a few flickering flames.

If Martin were still here, they would both be out there, still sitting around the fire. Lily shook her head to get the tears to stand at bay. "Martin, it just isn't the same without you here, but I'll carry on our tradition for you." She dried her hands and slipped out the backdoor.

When she sat down in one of the chairs, Champ came over and laid his head in her lap. "I know, you miss him too, don't you?"

Champ whimpered as if he understood what Lily had said. She stroked his head and began to hum, *Amazing Grace*. It was one of Martin's favorite songs.

"Do you mind if I join you?"

Lily jumped, sat up straight, and looked around at Bryce. "You scared me."

He picked up one of the folding chairs and moved it closer to the fire. "I didn't mean to startle you. I should have made some noise when I came out."

"It's fine. I thought you had already gone to bed."

"I couldn't sleep. I got up for a glass of water and noticed the fire was still burning. I came out to check on it, and then I saw you sitting out here. Why are you out here at this time of night?"

Bittersweet memories flooded over her like a swollen riverbank that had just crested. Memories of Martin in his wheelchair with his smoking pipe in his hand, playfully spouting out rhyming lyrics off the top of his head. Their laughter being carried away into the night like a falling leaf swept up in a whirlwind. Even though the fire radiated heat, she rubbed her arms as if she had a chill. "On nights like this, Martin and I used to sit out here for hours. Sometimes we never even spoke. We just enjoyed the love songs of the night, underneath the stars."

"Love songs?" He tilted his head and raised a questioning brow.

"You really are a city boy, aren't you? Listen. Do you hear the frogs and crickets? They're singing their love songs into the night, hoping to catch the attention of that one special female who will be drawn in by his song."

"No offense, but it sounds like noise to me."

"You need to enjoy the simpler things in life, Bryce." Lily put her head back, breathing in the moment. "It's not all about expensive cars or clothes, or fancy houses. It's about the little things in life that give you joy and contentment and things that don't cost you a dime."

"My grandfather enjoyed this?"

"Yes, he did. He would sing along with the frogs sometimes, adding his own lyrics to the music." The laugh died in her throat as grief tugged at her heart.

Bryce didn't respond, but his gaze stayed on her for a lingering minute.

They sat in silence for a while until Bryce shifted and leaned forward in his chair. "I once thought my grandfather was the greatest man on earth, and when he left…" Bryce picked up a twig, broke it into pieces, and threw it in the fire. "My world fell apart. I felt abandoned. I felt betrayed. But most of all, I felt unloved by the one person I loved the most. When he ran off, he didn't even slow down long enough to tell me goodbye. Can you imagine what that did to a fourteen-year-old boy? I always wondered what I did to make him leave."

"I don't know why Martin left his family, we may never know, but—"

"I'm a grown man now, Lily. I don't need answers anymore." He ran his hands down his jeans. "Joey had a blast tonight, didn't he?"

"Changing the subject." She gave him a thumbs-up. "Smooth."

Fighting the smile, he picked up a stick and tossed it at her.

"Hey." She picked it up and flicked it back at him. "And, yes, Joey did have a blast. There's somethin' about cookin' over an open fire. He just loves it."

"I actually enjoyed myself, too."

She tucked a wayward strand of hair behind her ear. "I'm glad. You just might start likin' this place after all. So, tell me, how is ranchin' life so far?"

Moving his leg very slowly, Bryce rubbed the top of it. "It's pretty intense, but I think I'm learning my way around."

"I have to admit, I'm surprised. I didn't think you'd last a day, much less a week. As much as it pains me to say it, you're doing a good job."

His smirk did funny things to her heart. "I knew I would squeeze a compliment out of you sooner or later."

"You actually deserve this one." Lily lifted her face and smiled. No smirk of her own accompanied it. She really was very impressed with his effort.

"But I can't take all the credit. Kyle may be young, but that boy's stronger than he looks, and Greg's a powerhouse."

"They know as much about this ranch as Wade and I do. Those two boys are like two peas in a pod."

"They certainly know what they're doing. How old are they, anyway?" Bryce picked up another stick from the ground and tossed it into the fire. Sparks danced above the fire like fireflies.

"Kyle's eighteen, and Greg just turned twenty-three a couple of months ago. Both of them came right out of high school to work here. They're good boys." Pride filled Lily's heart. Kyle and Greg both were only a few years younger than her, but when she thought about them, she felt like a lioness with her cubs.

"I have to agree with you again. I'm impressed at how hard they work. They don't let up either. They're relentless."

"That's my boys."

They shared a laugh.

"Joey is being taught by the best. It wouldn't surprise me at all if he's not breaking horses by the time he's ten."

"Oh, he already wants to learn now."

For a second, Bryce let the conversation be over taken by the frogs. "Was his father a rancher, too?"

Lily exhaled softly, pulled her feet up in the chair, hugged her legs, and propped her chin on her knees. "Chad? No, he worked for a construction company."

Bryce nodded. "If it's not too personal, would you tell me about him? Like how did the two of you meet?"

"There's not much to tell, really. We met and began dating in high school. We were young and did some foolish things, which I'm ashamed of now, but two months before graduation I found out I was pregnant. Against his parent's wishes, we were married right away. Four months later, Chad was killed by a drunk driver."

"He never got to meet his son?"

"No." Painful memories of Chad's death surfaced in her heart again, bringing tears to her eyes.

Gentle sympathy brushed his face. "I'm so sorry, Lily. I didn't know. What about his parents? Don't they help you?"

"No, his parents said it was my fault Chad died. They said I tricked him into marrying me by getting pregnant because if it wasn't for me, he would have been safe at college instead of working for a construction company to support a family. They told me never to contact them because they didn't want anything to do with my unborn child or me. So, I respected their wishes."

"You've raised Joey all on your own then, with no help from anyone?"

"I did. Then God sent Martin into our lives. He took us in and made us a part of his family. I will always be grateful for that. The Martin I know and the Martin you knew are two completely different people." Lily yawned and quickly covered her mouth. "Oh, excuse me. Must be getting late."

Bryce yawned and stretched his arms over his head. "I guess that means its bedtime. I think I'll head back to the guesthouse. I'll see you in the morning. Good night." He pushed himself up from the chair.

"Good night, Bryce."

However, instead of leaving, he stood with his back to her, staring into the fire. Lily watched him rake his hand through his hair. "Lily?"

Worry drained into her spirit. "Is something wrong?"

"When I saw my grandfather's video in Mr. Hopper's office, there was no doubt in my mind he had been in terrible health for quite a while. Even though my feelings toward him are still raw," he turned and stared into her eyes. "I want you to know, I'm glad he had someone like you who cared about him in his final days, so he didn't die all alone."

His sad smile touched her heart in the deepest of places. "Me too." She wanted to take his hand in hers and comfort him, but she thought better of it.

Lily watched Bryce stroll off across the yard and disappear into the guesthouse. She had enjoyed this time alone with him, matter-of-fact she'd enjoyed it a little too much, and she knew that was a very, very bad idea. In a year, he would be packing up and going back to his life in New York.

There was only one thing she could do if she didn't want to be left nursing a broken heart again; she had to keep their relationship on a business level and nothing more. But, how easy was that going to be?

CHAPTER
FOURTEEN

"Mom! Mom!" Joey shouted as he ran into the laundry room.

A violent quake ripped through Lily's body, and her blood pressure spiked. She dropped the basket full of freshly dried clothes onto the floor. When she whirled around, her elbow struck the bottle of liquid washing detergent, dumping its contents right on top of the spilled clothes and all over the floor. "What is it, Joey? What's happened? What's wrong?"

"Can I go to town with Bryce? He asked me if I wanted to. We're gonna get ice cream."

Relief mixed with unspent panic flooded her as she dropped back against the washing machine. "Joey, you scared the life out of me. You've got to stop yellin' like that. My heart's beating faster than a June bug on a string."

"Sorry." He wrinkled his nose. "Can I go with him? Please Mom?"

Lily looked down at the clothes on the floor, now covered in the blue detergent, and she groaned. "Look at this mess."

"Mom, can I go?" Joey impatiently wiggled back and forth.

"I don't know, Joey." She started to pick up the clothes and put them back into the washer.

"Please, I promise I'll be good. I promise." He clasped his hands together as if in prayer. "Please."

"Okay," she shook her finger at him. "But you'd better mind your manners and listen to Bryce."

"I will." He bolted out of the room like lightning and was as loud as thunder as he ran through the house.

"Joey, don't run in the house!"

"Yes, Ma'am," Joey yelled back, and then the sound of the slamming the front screen door echoed through the house.

With a grunt, she placed her hands on her hips as she stared at the blue detergent still on the floor. "Well, my day just got a little longer."

Knowing it was too much liquid to mop up, she looked around the laundry room and spotted a dustpan. She grabbed it off its hook, dropped to her knees, and began to rake the liquid into it.

Just as she dumped the second dustpan full of detergent into the mop bucket, Bryce stepped into the laundry room.

"Do you want to ride into town with—" Bryce pushed his hat back on his head and stopped in one stride. "Oh. What happened? Do you want some help?"

Heat flushed her cheeks when she thought what a sight she must be. Here she was on her hands and knees in the middle of the floor with detergent dripping off her fingers. And to make matters worse, some of her hair had fallen out of her hair clip and was hanging in her face.

"Naw, all I have to do now is mop the rest of it up." When she started to get up, Bryce took hold of her arm, and helped her to her feet.

He didn't let go of her arm right away, but he held onto her and inched closer.

His closeness caused her heart to flutter and her muscles to lose tension. When she moved her head to look away, a loose strand of hair fell down across her face.

"Let me get it, you don't want that blue stuff in your hair." Bryce hooked his finger around the strand and positioned it behind her ear. "There, is that better?"

Looking into his eyes, she couldn't really remember what the word better even meant. "Did you need somethin'?"

"Joey and I are going to get ice cream, and I wanted to invite you to come along."

With a shake, she disengaged herself from his grasp. It was either that or be pulled into those blue orbs and lost forever. "I think I'll pass. I have house chores to do."

"Ah, come on. It's ice cream." He shifted even closer. "I won't take no for an answer."

"I can't. I need to get this mess cleaned up." When she tried to move past him, she stepped in the slippery liquid, lost her balance, and slid right into his arms.

Her heart nearly didn't make the trip with her.

"I've got you." He tightened his arms around her, pulled her into him, and murmured against her ear. "I like having you this close. A guy could get used to this."

She sucked in a deep breath and blew it out slowly, trying to calm her racing heartbeat. His cologne tickled her nose. "You know, I think I could go for that ice cream now. But, I need to change first." She righted herself with difficulty and glanced at the blue stains on the front of his shirt from where she'd grabbed him. "From the looks of it, you need to go change shirts, too. Sorry."

Bryce didn't even bother to glance down at his shirt. "If Joey wasn't waiting for me, I wouldn't let you get away this easy."

A ripple zipped through her stomach like a rock skipping across a pond. "Like you said, he's waitin'. You'd better hurry. He isn't a very patient child."

When he shifted to the side, she carefully eased around him, and slipped down the hallway. *Remember he's only here for a year, and then he's gone.*

Later that night, after Lily returned from the kitchen with two glasses of milk and a plate of cookies, Joey crawled up next to her and asked, "Mom, do you like Bryce?"

She stiffened, momentarily speechless. "I… well… I think he's a nice guy. Why do you ask? Do you like him?"

"I like him a lot. He's funny, and he makes me laugh. I had so much fun with him today. It was funny when he climbed in the tunnel with me at McDonald's." He slapped both hands over his mouth and snickered. "The people at McDonald's didn't like it too much, did they?"

"No, they didn't." Lily laughed when she remembered how one of the workers asked Bryce to not climb in the tunnel because he was too tall for it.

Joey snuggled in next to her. "I hope he stays here forever."

Her chest tightened. "I don't know about forever, but he'll be here for awhile."

"He works hard too, don't he?" Joey's big brown eyes stared up at her, melting her heart.

Lily pushed his hair to the side and kissed his forehead. "Yes, he does."

To her surprise, Bryce was a natural at working on the ranch. He took to it as a fish takes to water. If a person didn't know any better, they would've thought he'd been born and raised in this kind of lifestyle.

After the dust incident, Lily thought it might not be a good idea for Wade and Bryce to work together just yet. She'd decided it was in the best interest for everyone if Greg and Kyle were the ones who taught Bryce the ropes.

A tap on the door snagged Lily's attention.

Joey got up, ran to the door, and yanked it open. "Hey, Bryce, me and Mom were just talkin' about you."

Jauntily he slanted his head to one side and arched a brow indicating he wanted to hear more. "Really? What were the two of you saying about me?"

"I asked her if she liked you."

The beginning of a smile tipped at the corner of his mouth. "And what did she say?"

"Joey, come pick up your crayons before they get stepped on," Lily interrupted the line of conversation. Her face and neck warmed when Bryce looked over at her, working on keeping the smirk from his face. "Did you need something, Bryce?"

He held up two plates and a bowl. "I was bringing back some of your dishes I've taken home with me."

"At 7:30 at night?" Lily slanted her head and crossed her arms.

"Okay, okay, you found me out. It's Saturday night, and I'm bored out of my mind. Can I hang out with the two of you for awhile?"

Lily tapped her index finger on her chin and made a clicking sound with her teeth. "I don't know." She turned to Joey and arched her eyebrows playfully. "What do you think, Joey? Should we let him stay?"

"Yes, yes, yes." Joey grabbed Bryce's hand and pulled him into the living room. "Hey, Mom, can all of us play Go Fish? Bryce, do you know how to play Go Fish?"

"I don't think so, but I'm willing to learn as long as I can have some of those delicious looking cookies." Bryce licked his lips and rubbed his stomach.

"Joey, get the cards, and I'll get Bryce a glass of milk."

"You don't have to do that." Bryce flopped down on the sofa and snatched up a cookie.

"Are you kiddin'? You can't eat cookies without milk."

An hour later, and after several games of Go Fish, Joey yawned. Lily noticed his eyes drooping.

"I think it's bedtime for you, little man," Lily said as she leaned over and tugged on Joey's shirt.

"Ah, Mom, I'm winning, and Bryce is here," Joey whimpered and pushed out his bottom lip.

Bryce yawned too, and Lily couldn't tell if it was real or fake. "I'm getting sleepy myself. If your mother doesn't care, maybe we can finish our game tomorrow."

Joey's expression went from sad to happy in a matter of seconds. "Is that okay, Mom?"

"I suppose." When Lily shifted to stand, Joey slid over and threw his arms around Bryce's neck. "Good night, Bryce. So we'll play Go Fish again tomorrow?"

Bryce wrapped his arms around Joey. "You can count on it."

Tears burned in Lily's eyes. Suddenly and without warning, the cold, hard truth hit her like a wrecking ball. Joey was already forming a bond with Bryce. For Joey's sake, this fact scared her to death.

"Great." Joey slapped his hands together. "Good night, Bryce. I'll see you tomorrow."

Lily reached out and took Joey's hand, and then she gave Bryce a momentary glance. "I'll be back in a few minutes. I need to tuck Joey in."

"Take your time." Bryce picked up an Oreo cookie, popped it in his mouth, and settled back on the sofa.

She walked with Joey into the bathroom and waited while he brushed his teeth. After saying his prayers, he climbed into bed. "I'm ready."

Lily snuggled in beside him and began to hum a lullaby, something she had done ever since he was an infant.

However, instead of listening, Joey turned big, curious eyes on her. "Mom, can I tell you somethin'?"

"Sure, baby, you know you can tell me anythin'."

"I wish I had a daddy like everybody else."

Lily's heart crumbled into a million pieces and fell down around her feet. She pulled him closer into her arms. "Oh, Joey." She fought to suppressed the tears bubbling up. "I'm so sorry, but you know your daddy would be here if he could. You know that, don't you?"

"Yeah. I know he would, but he can't because he's in heaven." Joey looked up into her eyes and snuggled closer to her. "Now, can I ask you somethin'?"

"Sure, baby. Ask." Her stomach tightened as she braced herself for his question.

"Do you think Bryce would be a good daddy?"

A heavy feeling thumped in her stomach as her throat constricted. She swallowed hard and struggled to form the words to answer Joey's question. "Well, I... I don't know, Joey. What do you think?"

"I think he would be a great daddy. He plays with me all the time, he's strong with big muscles, and he knows how to ride a horse. I think he would be a good daddy for a little boy, 'specially if the little boy don't have a daddy. Can I pray and ask Jesus if Bryce can stay forever?"

Lily was thankful when she saw Joey yawn and rub his eyes. She kissed his forehead. "I think it's time for you to go to sleep now."

"Will you tell Bryce good night for me again?"

"I sure will. Good night, my little prince." Lily kissed him once more and eased out of the bed. Leaning against the wall outside of Joey's door, Lily squeezed her eyes shut and tried to regain some kind of control of her raging emotions before returning to the living room where Bryce was waiting.

"So, what was your answer?" Bryce asked when Lily finally came back in to the room and plopped down in the chair.

"To what?" She crimped her brows as she looked up at Bryce and saw a glint of humor cross his face. She raced through her mind trying to think of what he was talking about.

"When Joey asked you if you liked me, what did you say?" He leaned forward with a grin on his lips and waited for her to answer.

Her cheeks flamed as if she had a fever. Turning away quickly to hide her blushed face, she shrugged. "Not much, I only said I thought you were a nice guy."

"So you think I'm a nice guy, huh?"

"You have your moments, but don't let it go to your head. Even a blind hog finds an acorn every now and then." There was no way she was going to tell him what she really thought of him. That was something she was still struggling to figure out for herself.

♥ ♥ ♥

A few days later, Bryce walked by the barn and saw Lily inside brushing down one of the horses.

Seeing her there, her long dark hair flowing down her back, her slender waist, her tight-fitting jeans, gave new meaning to the term adrenaline rush.

Bryce grabbed another bottle of water out of the cooler off the tailgate of the truck and walked into the barn. He would find any excuse he could to be near her. "Looks like you could use one of these."

She looked back over her shoulder and smiled. "You read my mind."

He twisted the cap off one of the waters and held it out to her. "I haven't seen much of you over the last few days. Have you been hiding?"

She accepted the water from him, took a long drink, and shook her head. "No, I've just been busy, had a lot to do."

"Same here." Nodding, he bobbed his head at the horse. "Have you been training?"

"No, I got caught up on my chores and then went for a ride before starting lunch. Are y'all finished mendin' the fence already?"

"Not quite. We ran out of water. Greg sent me to reload the cooler."

"Yeah, it's hotter than a two dollar pistol today."

Bryce leaned against one of the posts, took another drink of water, and then twisted the cap back on the bottle. "I got an idea. Why don't we get all dressed up and go out to eat tonight?"

Her smile vanished as she tilted her head down so the brim of her hat concealed her face. "Out to eat? I don't know."

Pushing himself away from the post, he moved in closer to her. "We did say we would begin dating in two weeks, remember? It's been way over that now. Don't you think it's time we start? Does Joey like lobster? If he doesn't, we can pick him up something from McDonalds."

A soft gasp escaped her lips. "You wanna take Joey, too?"

"Of course, after all we're all going to be a family soon."

"Don't joke about something like that." Her chilled tone made it evident that she was not amused.

He edged even closer, trailed his fingers down her arm, seized her hand, and pulled her in. "Do you see me laughing?"

She pulled her hand free and backed away. "Greg is probably wonderin' where you are. You need to get back out there."

"Don't you like me being so close?" Closing the gap again, he stood so close to her he could smell her strawberry shampoo. He breathed the fragrance deep into his lungs as goose bumps tickled his skin.

"No. Wade is on his way back. I don't want him to get the wrong idea."

The muscles in Bryce's shoulders went rigid as he said through clenched teeth, "Who cares what Wade thinks?"

"I do. Wade's very important to me."

Her words were like a knife to the heart, and jealousy reared its ugly head. He kicked his head back an inch and stared down at her. "Ah, I'm beginning to see now."

Lily scrunched her brows. "See what?"

"This thing between you and Wade, I thought it was just him, but apparently you feel the same way. You know the reason he doesn't want me near you is he thinks I'm moving in on his territory."

"Territory?" Lily's head jerk up as she shook her head in disbelief. "Don't be ridiculous. You're dumber than a box of rocks if that's what you think. Wade and I are just friends."

"Friends? Right. Is that why every time I come within breathing distance of you Wade gets all upset? He's jealous. I see the way he looks at you, Lily. And I can't say I don't blame him, you are something to look at."

"Look," she said, her face flushed with anger, "I don't have to explain myself to you. What goes on between Wade and me isn't any of your business, and I'd appreciate it if you'd keep your nose on your own face where it belongs."

Throwing his hands in the air, he shrugged. "Hey, I was only stating the obvious, but if you're in denial, I guess I can play along." He took a step back, crossed his arms, and grinned at her. "There's nothing going on between you and Wade, right. Got it. No problem."

From the expression he saw on her face, it was clear she was growing more and more agitated with every second that ticked by. Her nostrils twitched every time she inhaled as her eyes narrowed into tiny slits, and her bottom lip quivered slightly.

His fingers ached to reach out and touch the side of her delicate face. Delightful visions danced around in his head of him pulling her into his arms and kissing her until they both had to come up for air. But it was quite clear now that that wouldn't be happening at least in the foreseeable future.

However, for whatever reason he couldn't explain to his heart, no woman had ever had this kind of effect on him before, but he liked it…he liked it a lot. And as he stood there, Bryce Fowler decided he wasn't going to let Wade just have her. The only problem was, how was he going to convince her to take a real chance with him?

CHAPTER FIFTEEN

Lily wanted to smack that smug smirk right off of his face. Feeling like a pressure cooker about to explode, she balled her fist into her hips. "What's it to you anyway? Sounds like you're the one who's jealous."

The moment the words tumbled out of her mouth, she wished she could have sucked them back in especially when Bryce didn't reply but only smiled.

Why in the world would he be jealous of me? He could have any woman he wanted. Why would he want me?

Catching Lily off guard, Bryce slipped one arm around her waist, pulled her into him, and ran his fingers down the side of her face. "Maybe I am. You are so beautiful when you're angry. Do you know how much I want to kiss you right now?"

She pulled in a jerky breath as her mouth fell open.

For a moment, neither one moved. Neither one spoke a word. Neither one looked away.

He held her so close she could feel his breath on her face. A shiver traveled down her spine. She wondered if he could hear her hammering heart.

She ran her hands up his arms, locked them around his neck, and lifted her face up to him.

"Lily." He slid his hand behind her neck and ever so slowly began to lower his head.

She closed her eyes, waiting, wanting, ready.

Just as Bryce pulled her to him, Champ leaped up on Lily, causing her to stumble sideways. Dumbfounded about what had almost happened, she barely caught herself on a bale of hay, and standing there, she fought to regain her composure. "Bryce, we have to stop this."

"Stop? Why?"

When he reached for her again, she dodged his hands. "I don't want to be just another fish on your hook."

When she tried to push past him, he caught hold of her hand and pulled her back into his arms. "It's not like that, Lily. Please don't go."

"I have to," she whispered.

"Lily," he whispered back, pulling her to him so his words brushed against her ear.

Just the way he said her name made her pulse speed up so fast she became dizzy. Her head was screaming for her to pull away, but her heart wouldn't let her move.

"Why do you have to go?" His breath was heavy, and she thought she felt his body shake.

"Because I don't trust myself when I'm around you and I don't want my heart broken again." With all the willpower she could muster, she pulled away from him and rushed from the barn. Just as she stepped out of the barn, she ran headlong into Wade almost knocking him off his feet.

"Whoa, girl. Slow down." At first, Wade laughed, but when he looked down into her face, he immediately realized something was wrong. "What's wrong?"

"Nothing," Lily said, her voice shaky as she pulled herself out of his arms, and she glanced back at the barn door.

Just then, Bryce ran out of the barn behind her. "Lily. Wait."

Wade's eyes filled with rage. He pushed Lily to the side, grabbed hold of Bryce's shirt and shoved him against the outside barn wall. "What did you do to her?"

"Wade, stop it! Stop it! Let go of him." Lily jumped forward and tried to pull him off Bryce. "Wade! I said stop!"

"Get off of me." Bryce shoved Wade back.

"I knew you couldn't be trusted. If you ever touch her again, I'll—" Wade took a swing at Bryce, and his fist connected with Bryce's chin.

"Hey!" Greg yelled as he and Kyle bolted up past Lily, each of them grabbing for a combatant.

Bryce returned the punch just before Kyle and Greg pulled them apart.

"Let go of me, Greg." Wade yanked his body forward, but Greg didn't let him go, much to Lily's relief.

"Not until you calm down," Greg said.

"Wade, stop it. It's not what you think." Lily's voice raised a notch or two.

"How is it then, Lily? You come running out of the barn and almost knock me over. Your face is all red, and you're out of breath. It looked to me like you were running from somebody, namely him." Wade's nostrils flared.

"No. I wasn't running. Not like you mean," Lily said. "We had a little disagreement, and I lost my cool. That's all. That's all it was, I promise."

"He didn't try anything?" Wade asked.

"If I made a move, Wade, I assure you she wouldn't be running away from me." Bryce spat out a mouth full of blood, lifted his chin, and grinned. "She would still be in the barn with me."

Wade jerked free from Greg and jumped toward Bryce, but Lily stepped in between them and put her hands on Wade's chest. "Stop it. Stop it right now. Come on, Wade, let's go for a walk." She wrapped her arms around Wade's arm and pulled him toward the house. He wasn't happy about it, but he reluctantly went with her.

The first fifty yards she was practically dragging him, but once they reached the house, Wade turned to her and clutched both of her arms. "I want to know what happened, and I want the truth."

She tried to pull free, but he tightened his grip. "You have to believe me when I tell you, nothing happened."

"I don't believe that! Tell me what happened." His eyes were black and dazzling with fury.

His chiding tone caused anger to creep up into her throat, but she swallowed it away because she just didn't have the strength to go into battle with Wade right now. "Nothin' happened," she said through clenched teeth.

"Then why did you come running out of the barn like that?"

"It was nothing. Now leave it at that. Please."

He slid his hands down her arms and locked his fingers in hers. "If he ever does anything, and I mean anything, I need to know."

Lily sighed in pure exhaustion as she fought to erase the images of Bryce's face out of her head. His touch still lingered on her skin. "And I'll tell you if I need your help. It was just a misunderstanding, and that's all. Please, Wade, I can't have you and Bryce fighting every time you're around each other. I'm tired of playing referee."

"All I want to do is protect you, Lily."

"And, I appreciate it, I really do, but I'm a big girl, Wade. I can take care of myself. You can't come in swingin' every time you think I'm in trouble, and then ask questions later."

He wrapped his arms around her and kissed her on top of the head. "I know I overreacted, but now that Martin's gone, I feel like I have to be the one to watch out for you."

"I made it on my own long before I came here." She pulled back and looked him in the eyes. "You're gonna have to stop bullying Bryce. First, you pelted him with dirt and gravel, and now this. If it continues, I know it will escalate into somethin' worse, and you know it too."

He heaved in a breath and blew it out hard and loud. "I know, but I can't stand the idea of him touching you. From what I saw at the barn, that's exactly what he was trying to do."

"I can handle myself, Wade." She turned her head and glanced toward the barn. *I can handle myself just fine, but it's my heart I'm worried about.*

"Lily—"

Ring. Ring. Ring.

"Hold on a second." She stepped inside the house and picked up the receiver. "Hello?"

"May I please speak to Bryce?" The female voice oozed over the phone.

An icy feeling spread through Lily's stomach as she bit down on her bottom lip until it throbbed in pain. "Yes, may I ask whose callin'?"

"Tell him it's Hannah. He'll know what it's about. When we spoke yesterday, I promised him I would call him back today. I tried his cell phone, but he didn't answer. Then I remembered he called me from this number a few days ago."

Lily's lungs constricted making it hard to breathe. "One moment, please, and I'll get him for you."

"Oh, wait, I have a…, hold on a minute. Never mind, I have another call. I'll just call him back later. Tell Bryce I love him."

Click.

Suddenly, Lily's mind flooded with the images of how she'd seen women buzzing around him like flies around honey not to mention how much he seemed to enjoy it. In fact, she knew how they felt. She'd foolishly found herself drawn in by his good looks and sly smile, too.

He's a good player. That's for sure. What made me think I'd ever be any different from all the others? Nothing. How brainless can I be?

Her stomach cringed at the thought of being so gullible. Why had she let down her guard with him? She knew better.

Wade had followed her in and was now staring into her face as he ran his hand down her arm. "What's wrong? Who was that?"

Fighting to hide the hurt in her voice, she lifted her head and straightened her back. "It was for Bryce."

"You look upset. Who was that?"

"It was someone named Hannah."

"Hannah? See I told you he couldn't be trusted. How do you think it's going to look if he's seen in town with another woman?"

"Wade, I've told you. This isn't any of your business. Now, I need to get back to work, and so do you."

"Lily, I—"

"No, we're not talking about this anymore. This ranch isn't going to run itself." She tried to play all of it off as no big deal, but she was sure Wade didn't buy into that for a moment.

He leaned in and kissed her cheek. "I need Kyle's help. I'm taking him along with me."

"That's fine."

He lingered one more second before he went out the door. Lily stepped outside right after him. He leaped off the porch, and he crossed the yard to where Bryce still stood talking to Greg and Kyle. Lily gripped the porch rail, and hoped Wade would keep his word about not pounding Bryce into oblivion. She didn't have the energy or the willpower to stop him this time. And from the sharp pain in her chest she wondered if she'd even try.

Wade motioned for Kyle, and just like that they climbed into his truck and drove off.

Leaning against one of the porch posts, she watched Bryce talking to Greg. Pictures flashed in her mind of him holding her in his arms in the barn and in the laundry room. Her arms still tingled from his touch, and her lips still hungered for his kiss. What was wrong with her? She knew what he was, what his game was, and still she was letting herself get lost in that fantasy? What could she possibly be thinking?

She took a deep, jagged breath, squared her shoulders, and brushed off the feeling of disappointment. She wasn't going to be another woman for him to string along.

However, in Bryce's defense, he had made it perfectly clear to her from the very beginning exactly what he wanted from their arrangement, hadn't he? After all, he did say no strings attached, no commitments, and no obligations. He'd made it perfectly clear that this was just an investment, nothing more, and she'd agreed to those terms.

Moreover, they were becoming friends, and she didn't want to jeopardize their relationship. There was too much at stake for her to be caught up the illusion of something that wasn't ever going to happen.

"It's back to the original plan, a financial investment only." She turned and slipped inside the house. Now she just had to convince her heart of that fact.

♥ ♥ ♥

"You might want to get some ice on that before going back to work." Greg waved his hand toward Bryce's jaw.

Bryce moved his stiff jaw back and forth. "I suppose so." He flipped open the cooler, scooped up a chunk of ice, and pressed it to his face.

"I just don't get it."

"What's that?" Bryce asked as he slammed the tailgate shut.

"This ruckus between you and Wade." Greg pulled out a bandana from his back pocket and slipped off his hat. Sweat and grime had his short brown hair plastered to his forehead. This boy was tall, lean, beardless, and had an innocent face like a child. "What's going on between you two?"

"It's personal."

"It must be 'cause for the life of me, I can't figure it out." Greg walked around to the driver's side of the truck, opened the door, and looked over at Bryce. "You ready to finish unloadin' the trailer before we lose daylight?"

"Let's roll."

As they headed back to the field, Bryce stole a glance at the house, hoping to catch sight of Lily, but she still hadn't emerged from the house.

More than ever before, he wanted to see her. He wanted to be near her. He wanted to hold her in his arms, but most of all, he wanted to kiss her. Oh, how he wanted to kiss her.

What was it about this woman that had his insides twisted in knots? From the first time he'd laid eyes on her in

Mr. Hopper's office, he knew there was something different about her. She wasn't like the other women he'd dated. For the first time in his life, he'd finally met a woman who had captured his heart. Her words about how she didn't want to be just another fish on his hook splashed through his mind. Is that what she was to him? He sure didn't think so.

Lily lingered on his mind for the rest of the day and so did her words.

At suppertime as Bryce crossed the yard, Greg came up behind him. "I hope Lily has some fried chicken ready. I'm starving." Greg slapped him on the back and leaped up on the porch.

"I'm right behind you." Anticipation danced in the hollow of his stomach, and it had very little to do with the food.

"I didn't think Friday would ever get here," Greg said, slipping off his hat. Their boots sounded like thunder on the hardwood floor as they all marched into the kitchen.

"What's got you all fired up, Greg? You got another date with Mindy Dyson again?" Kyle asked as he pulled out a chair.

"You'd better believe it. Why don't you and Carrie come along with us tonight? We're going down to Hank's place on the river for a bonfire." Greg punched Kyle in the arm as he took his seat.

Kyle nodded. "Sure. I'll give her a call after dinner."

"What about you, Bryce?" Greg elbowed Bryce when he sat down. "Why don't you come along with us tonight?"

Bryce glanced up at Lily as she set a platter of chicken in the center of the table. "I don't think so, boys. I think I already have plans."

She turned without so much as glancing at him.

"Ah, come on, Bryce. You'll have a great time. You need to get out and see more of Trinity." Greg glanced at Lily then back at Bryce.

"Come on, Bryce. Go with us. You don't have to stay long. I'd like for you to meet Carrie," Kyle added as he removed his hat and smoothed down his hair.

"Sounds like a great idea to me. Who knows you just might find you a lady-friend who will keep you company while you're here," Wade said when he entered the kitchen from the other way. "I'm sure that charm of yours will work on some unsuspecting female."

Bryce clenched his jaw. "You're hilarious, Wade."

"Wade." Lily turned back from the sink and scowled at him.

"What? I'm just having a little fun with him." Wade walked up behind Lily, grabbed her around the waist, pulled her close, and kissed her on the side of the head. "Don't go getting mad. I'll mind my manners. Promise."

For a brief moment, she met Bryce's stare from across the room, and then she quickly looked away.

She gave Wade a nudge toward a chair. "Sit."

Flames burned hot in Bryce's throat. How dare he touch the woman who was to be his wife like that.

"What do you say, Bryce?" Greg asked, and then he yanked his attention toward Lily. "Talk to him, Lily. You're the boss. Tell him he has to go."

"Why don't you go with the boys, Bryce? Who knows, you just might enjoy yourself." However, Lily didn't say it with too much conviction.

What? Did she want him to go? What about their date? Confusion buzzed through Bryce's mind until he finally concluded if that was what she wanted, then that's what he'd do. "Sure, if that's what you want, why not? I guess I can go for a couple of hours. Looks like I don't have plans after all." He didn't take his eyes off Lily until she turned away.

"Hey, Lily, since Joey's not going to be home tonight, why don't you come along, too? You never go anywhere unless it's with Joey. You just might have some fun," Greg said.

"I don't think so." Lily shook her head as she came back to the table to make sure everything was ready.

"It's a family thing, Lily. You know Hank's a preacher man, so there won't be any drinking or stuff like that," Kyle added.

"Not this time. Y'all go on and have a good time. I'll be just fine." Lily took her seat beside Greg but never looked over at Bryce.

Disappointment gnawed at his gut, but if that's what she wanted, so be it. He would go, and he would enjoy himself.

CHAPTER
SIXTEEN

Saturday morning, as Lily made her way to the kitchen, she was startled when someone knocked on the door. When she opened the door, there stood Bryce.

"Good morning," Bryce said with a smile that caused her heart to melt into a puddle around her feet.

"Mornin'. You're up early. Come on in. I was about to start breakfast."

"Aren't you going to ask me how my night went?" Bryce asked as he followed her into the kitchen.

"I'd rather not know." She grabbed the coffee pot and began to fill it with water.

He leaned against the counter next to her and stared at the side of her face. "Are you sure?"

"What you do on your own time is none of my business." Turning away from him, she poured the water into the coffee maker. After Lily flipped it on, she turned to face him. "Which reminds me, Hannah called you yesterday."

"Hannah?" His face dropped into a scowl. "I don't know why she didn't call my cell phone. Oh, well. I'll call her back Monday." He pulled two cups from the cabinet. "Hey, I've got an idea. Would you like to ride into town with me today? I need to pick up a few things."

He hadn't even flinched when she'd mention Hannah. It didn't bother him that she knew he was seeing another woman? Then again, why should it? In this completely illogical nightmare she had somehow stumbled into, it made absolute, soul-crushing sense. She had told him she was fine with him dating other women, hadn't she? So why did her chest feel as if it had a hole punctured in it.

Lily shrugged. "I'm sure you don't need me to go with you. I can give you the directions to wherever you need to go."

"I don't *need* you to go with me, but I'd *like* for you to join me."

His closeness made her dizzy. She licked her lips, tucked her hair behind her ear, and tried to hide her shaky hands from Bryce. "Okay, I'll ride into town with you. I guess I could go ahead and pick up some things while I'm there, too. What time do you want to leave?"

"We can leave right after breakfast if that's all right with you."

Lily reached out and lightly touched his arm. "Tell you what. I have a suggestion if you're interested."

"What's that?"

"There's a mom and pop's diner in town called Sara's Place. They serve a pretty good southern breakfast. Would you rather eat there this mornin'?"

"Sounds good to me, and while we're there, we can discuss our plans for tonight, too. Like I said in the barn yesterday, I think it's about time we start going out together, don't you? I need to run and make a phone call first, but then I'll be ready to go in about fifteen minutes." He pushed himself away from the sink and took several strides toward the door but then came to a halt in the doorway. With his back to her, he said over his shoulder, "I want you to ask me why I didn't enjoy myself last night."

She felt suddenly anxious to escape from his disturbing presence. "What?"

"I want you to ask me why I didn't enjoy myself last night," he repeated.

Sighing in frustration, she leaned against the counter and crossed her arms. "Okay, Bryce, tell me, why didn't you enjoy yourself last night?"

"Because I couldn't get you out of my head." And with that, he strolled out of the kitchen.

A flush of adrenaline coursed through her body causing her to clutch the edge of the kitchen counter to steady her rickety legs.

She stared at the empty doorway. Had he really meant what he just said? If he didn't, that had to be the most effective pick-up line printed in the Casanova handbook.

With one breath, Lily blew a wayward strand of hair out of her face. "What have I gotten myself into? If I fall for every line like that, I'm going to be left alone and with a broken heart again. No. I refuse to go through that twice in one lifetime. I refuse."

Twenty minutes later, Bryce strolled through the front door and tossed her a smile when he saw her fluffing the sofa cushions. "Are you ready to go?"

Lily's nose perked up when the fresh scent of his woodsy cologne filled the living room. A tingle zipped through her body all the way down to her toes.

"Yep, whenever you are." As she sashayed toward the door, she grabbed up her bag that was hanging on a hook beside the door, and flung it over her shoulder.

Bryce took hold of her elbow and walked her to the truck. "Your chariot awaits," he said when he stepped ahead of her and opened the door.

Twenty minutes later, Bryce pulled his truck into a parking space near the entrance, put it in park, and shut off the engine. "Do you eat here often?"

"Not really. Joey and I eat here every couple of months or so. I'm usually too busy at the ranch."

"Lily, there's more to life, than the ranch you know." He crinkled his brows, and the smile disappeared from his face.

"Not in my world." When she reached for the door handle, he reached across the seat and took hold of her arm.

"Wait." He bounced out of the truck and hurried around to her side. He opened the door and held out his hand.

Without hesitation, she placed her hand in his and slid out of the truck. Then they walked into the diner together.

As soon as Bryce pushed the door open, the smell of freshly brewed coffee mingling with gravy, bacon, buttery biscuits, and syrup, tingled her senses. An old twangy-sounding song flowed from the vintage jukebox in the corner. Not much had changed since she'd been in the last time. Down the left side of the diner were black vinyl-covered booths, which matched the black and white tiles on the floor. Tables with four chairs at each one were crowded throughout the majority of the restaurant each had a black and white checkered tablecloths on them. All the stools at the diner-length counter were filled.

Bryce leaned in close. "Wow, I feel like I've just stepped through a time machine. What a good job on recreating the sixty's era."

"I don't think it was intentional."

Lily grinned when Bryce murmured under his breath, "You're joking, right?"

"Afraid not." She grinned. "Do you see an empty table? Anywhere?"

They scanned the diner for an empty table. Then Bryce nodded to one in the back. He fastened his hand on her elbow and guided her through the crowd. When they reached their destination, he pulled out her chair.

She sat down and smiled up at him. "Thank you."

His smile reached his eyes causing her heart to gallop like a wild stallion on an open range.

"Let's see, what looks good." He pulled the menu from a holder and opened it. "What do you recommend?"

"The Cowboy Breakfast is good. It's two eggs cooked to your likin', two sausage links, three pieces of bacon, gravy on the side, biscuits, and a bowl of grits."

He leaned over the table and whispered, "What in the world is grits?"

She giggled. "It's a southern thing. If you don't like 'em, you don't have to eat 'em."

He wagged his head in amazement. "Do you eat this size of a breakfast?"

A humorous gasp slipped from her throat. "Gracious, no. I order the smaller version."

"Don't tell me, it's called the Cowgirl breakfast?"

She covered her mouth and laughed. "Yes. Actually it is."

"Don't hide it." He reached across the table and laid his hand on hers. Her eyes traveled to his and stayed. "I like to hear you laugh."

Her chest tightened and then quivered at his touch and at the look in his eyes. *That boy's smile could melt butter and those eyes... Lord help me. In a year he's gone, in a year he's gone, in a year...*

"Well, hello there, Sweetie." Sara, the owner of the diner, came up to their table, wrapped her arm around Lily's shoulder, and squeezed.

"Hi, Sara, how are you doin'?"

"Same old, same old. It seems odd you comin' in without old Martin. We sure do miss him around here."

"I know. It's the same way at the ranch, too."

"For the last five years, that man had the same breakfast every other Sunday mornin'. I sure do miss seein' his smilin' face in here." Sara smiled lovingly at Lily, and then looked over at Bryce. Placing a hand on her well-rounded hip, she asked, "Now, who do we have here?"

"Sara, this is Bryce Fowler, Martin's grandson. Bryce this is Sara Stover. She's the owner of this place."

"It's nice to meet you, Mrs. Stover." He stood, dipped his head, and shook her hand.

"Mrs. Stover? Honey child, you'd better call me Sara, and it's nice to meet ya, too. So, you're Martin's grandson?" She took a step back and gave him a long once over. "Ya know, I can see the resemblance. I'm sure we met at Martin's funeral, but the sad truth is my mind just ain't what it used to be."

"Sara, I need you in the kitchen," someone yelled from behind the counter.

She let out a loud grunt and then laughed. "They can't run this place without me." Sara grabbed one of the waitresses by the arm as she passed by their table. "Brandi Sue, I want ya to take good care of these two." She patted Lily's shoulder. "I'll talk to ya later, honey."

After Sara waddled away from the table, Brandi Sue smiled down at them. "Are y'all ready to order?"

"Yes, I think so," Lily said.

After they polished off their breakfast, Lily pointed her fork at Bryce's empty bowl. "So, what did you think about the grits?"

"Didn't like them, didn't like them at all." His lopsided grin made her chest quiver. It began to worry her how easily he could make her feel this way with just the simple act of a smile.

"Well just look at you, Mr. Bryce Fowler, in all your cowboy gear and everything. Nice." The bubbly salesgirl from the *Western Days* clothing store pranced right up to their table and trailed her fingers down his shoulder. "Fancy meetin' you here."

Lily searched her brain trying to remember the girl's name, but it kept jamming into *would you go away already?*

"Oh. Hello, Angie. How are you?" Bryce leaned back in his chair and smiled.

Of course, he would remember her name.

Angie slid one of the chairs close to Bryce, plopped herself down, and crossed her long legs. "You bad boy, why haven't you called me? I gave you my number." She picked up his hand and circled the palm of his hand with her finger. "Remember I wrote it down right here."

"Sorry, I've been busy. You know, getting settled in and all." He politely smiled and pulled his hand away. "You remember, Lily. Don't you?"

Angie turned her head slightly, her lips stiff. "Oh, yes. Hello." She didn't even bother to make eye contact with Lily before turning back to Bryce. "Now, as for you, Mr. Fowler, I'm not leaving until you give me your word you'll call me."

"Well, I—" Bryce mumbled.

Angie leaned in close to his ear and whispered something Lily couldn't hear.

Surprise splashed through Lily when she saw Bryce's face turn a deep shade of red.

"Ah, did I embarrass you?" Angie giggled, moved onto Bryce's lap, and ran her hand down the side of his face. "Cute, cute, cute."

Anger seared through Lily like acid. She bit down on her tongue, fighting to keep the words in her heart from spewing out.

Just who did this girl think she was? Blatantly throwing herself at Bryce with Lily sitting right there.

Lily's common sense took a leap out the window when she reached across the table and took hold of Angie's arm. "You know, I would really appreciate it if you'd get out of my fiancé's lap."

Angie released a sharp squeal and leaped to her feet. "What? You're... what? Is this true? Are you engaged to her?" She pointed a well-polished nail at Lily as her words echoed through the diner, loudly.

It all happened so fast that Lily had no clue what his answer would even be.

However, Bryce looked up at Lily, picked up her hand, and gave her a tender smile. "Yes, it certainly is."

"Well, I never..." Without another word, Angie wheeled around on her heel and stormed away, making the bells on the front door ring with her angry exit.

The sound of silverware dropping onto plates filled the diner as a hush crept its way through the space. How could a place with so many people be so quiet?

Heads turned.

Eyes widened.

Mouths hung agape.

Then, slowly, whispers filled the silence.

Lily closed her eyes. *Oh, no. What have I done?*

"Well, why didn't you tell me y'all were getting married?" Sara broke the silence as she waddled up to the table, drying her hands on her apron.

"Well, I…it…all happened, so fast, I…we…," Lily babbled, her eyes bouncing from Sara to Bryce as heat spread through her body, making her feel nauseous.

"Girl, I didn't even know you were dating." Vicki, Lily's hairstylist, chimed in as she hurried up to the table.

Lily's jaw dropped. "I…Um…"

Bryce lifted her hand to his lips and kissed her fingers. "I guess you could say it was love at first sight."

Vicki grinned. "Awesome."

"Have you already set a date?" Sara boomed and grabbed Bryce's arm, pumping his hand as if she might get water out of it.

Bryce looked from Sara to Lily, then back to Sara. "Yes. August 21st."

"August? Good heavens, dear, that doesn't give us much time, but I think we can manage it. Hey, folks, it looks like we're gonna have a weddin'." Sara's boisterous voice echoed throughout the diner.

And just like that, people in the diner began filing up to congratulate them, hugging Lily and shaking Bryce's hand with a few slaps on the back.

Lily's heart was in an all-out panic. *How could this get any worse?*

"Mom?"

She looked up to see Joey pushing through the crowd. From the expression on her son's face, Lily knew he'd overheard everything.

A tingling feeling started in her stomach and spread down her arms, up into her chest, and in to her head, making it swim like the creek down by the holler. "Joey."

The panicked look on Bryce's face probably perfectly matched the one on her own. "I didn't know he was here. I'm sorry, Lily," Bryce whispered.

"Bryce, we need to get out of here. I can't do this here. I have to explain this to him in private."

"You got it." He pulled a handful of bills out of his pocket and dropped them onto the table.

"Thanks, everyone, but it's time for us to be on our way." When Joey reached them, in one swift motion, Bryce gathered him up in his arms, wrapped his free arm around Lily's shoulder, and guided them through the crowd and out the door.

On their way out, Lily took only a second to inform Kate, the mother of the little boy Joey had spent the night with, that she was going to go ahead and take Joey on home with her. When they were finally outside, Lily heaved a nervous sigh.

"Mom, is it true? Are y'all really getting married?" Joey asked as soon as they stepped out onto the sidewalk away from the noise.

His eyes widened as he waited for an answer.

What could she say? She couldn't tell him no because whether it was an arranged marriage or not, she was still marrying Bryce.

How was he going to react to this news? Would he be upset? Would he cry? Lily braced herself for the worst. She swallowed hard, took a deep breath, and whispered, "Yes."

However, when she reached for Joey, he smiled and threw his arms around Bryce's neck. "Yes! That means I'm gonna have a daddy just like all of my friends. This is the bestest news ever!"

Hugging the child to him, Bryce looked over at her. "So, Joey, does this mean I have your consent to marry your mom?" Bryce asked, and then he gave Lily a wink.

Joey wrinkled his brows. "Co-sent? What's that?"

Bryce chuckled. "Consent. That means, is it okay with you if I marry your mom?"

"Oh. Then yes, yes, yes, I give you my consent to marry my mom."

Lily breathed a sigh of relief. Thankful Joey wasn't distressed about any of this. She hugged him and kissed his cheek.

He wrapped one of his arms around Lily's neck, too. "See, I told you, Mom, Bryce is going to be a great dad."

"Yes, you did."

Joey then turned and looked straight into Bryce's eyes. "Will it be okay if I call you daddy?"

CHAPTER
SEVENTEEN

The lump in Bryce's throat felt more like a boulder, and the tightness in his chest wouldn't allow him to speak. For the first time in his life, he felt loved. His heart swelled. Is this what it felt like to be a father?

He swallowed hard. "Yes, I would be honored for you to call me your dad."

Joey's eyes brightened even more. "You can call me son if you want to."

Bryce drew in a slow, steady breath. "I'd be proud to, Joey." He enclosed Joey in both of his arms and hugged him tight.

Glancing over at Lily, he saw the tears glistening on her cheeks, but she quickly swiped them away. "How about we get out of here?"

With Joey still tucked in his arms, Bryce followed her across the street toward the truck.

"Can we go home now?" Joey asked.

"You want to go home? Don't you want to go shoppin'?" Lily's chin quivered when she attempted to pull a smile onto her face.

"Are you kidding me?" Joey wiggled, and Bryce put him down. "I have to call Alex and tell him I'm going to have a daddy," he shouted as he ran toward the truck.

"Lily, I'm sorry about all of this." Bryce slipped his hand under her elbow, drew her closer and whispered, "I know things got out of hand back there, but we'll work through it."

"You don't have anythin' to apologize for." Shaking her head, Lily blew out a hard breath as she rolled her eyes to heaven. "All of this is my fault. I should've never said anything to that girl, but she was so…" She clenched her jaw and grunted. A second and she dragged politeness back to her. "But none of that matters now because in this little town gossip travels fast. By the end of the day, everyone I know will know about this. I'm sure of it."

"Well, everyone was bound to find out eventually anyway."

"I guess you're right, but now Sara's talkin' about a weddin'. I didn't want that."

"What did you want, Lily?"

"I thought we would just hop on down to the justice of the peace and get it done there."

"I think you're going to have to change your plans now." He bobbed his head back in the direction of the diner and grinned. "That lady won't let that happen."

"Are y'all comin?" Joey yelled from the truck. "I'm ready to go. I have to call my friends."

Suddenly color drained from Lily's face. For a moment, Bryce thought she was going to be sick. "Lily, what's wrong?"

"Did you see Joey's face when he thought you were going to be his dad? Do you even know how to be a father? You said it yourself, you didn't know how to be one." She whirled around to face him and flung the next word at him like a dagger. "You'd better not hurt my son!"

Her words sliced him to the core, and heat flushed through his body as he gripped Lily's arms. "Do you really think I'd intentionally hurt Joey? Do you think so little of me that you think I'm not even capable or could have the ability to be a father?"

"What makes things so different now?" She hissed through clenched teeth. "Less than a month ago, you had no intention of ever being a father."

"You're right, I didn't know how to be a father, but I do know how to love your son." He released his hold on her and dropped his arms to his sides. "You want to know what makes the difference now? The difference is, I met Joey. And just so you know, your life isn't the only life that's been affected by all of this, Lily. Do you think I enjoy having blisters and calluses on my hands? I gave up my home and life in New York for you and Joey. What did you give up, Lily, huh? What? I've made sacrifices to make this work. Yes, for myself but for you and Joey was well. Not that any of that has ever mattered to you." He shouldered past her, jerked open the truck door, and slid in behind the steering wheel.

Without a word, Lily followed him, climbed in the truck, and sat rigid against the door.

However, once inside, Bryce wanted to kick himself for snapping at her. His anger and pride had gotten the better of him. He'd wanted to hurt her the way she had hurt him, but now he regretted his words.

How could he take back the things he'd said? Would she believe him even if he told her he didn't mean a word of it? Without putting a single thing in his heart into words, he started the truck and headed back to the ranch.

The second the truck stopped in front of the house, Joey unbuckled his seatbelt and hopped over Lily. "Mom, I'm going to call my friends." He opened the truck door and took off running.

Lily still didn't move even when Bryce shut off the engine. She sat with her hands folded in her lap. Her head lowered.

"Lily, I'm sorry for—"

"Look, Bryce, I think we both said some things we didn't mean. Let's just forget about it." She twisted her hands together and then rubbed them down her jeans. "There's something I think I need to tell you. Your family members aren't the only ones who have accused me of being a gold digger. When I first moved in to care for Martin, for a long while people around here thought the same thing about me. They said I was a poor single mother who was on the prowl for someone with money and someone who would take care of her child. It took a long time for the people to accept me, and now, if people found out about our arrangement…" Her voice cracked, and she cleared her throat. "I don't want to go through all of that again, and I don't want the kids at school to tease Joey. Kids can be so cruel."

Bryce suppressed the rage boiling on the inside. He wanted to pull her into his arms to protect her, comfort her, and he wanted to erase the pain he saw in her eyes. However, he knew this wasn't the time.

"And so can adults. Whatever you need me to do, all you have to do is ask."

"I think the best thing is just to take it one day at a time. Like you said, we were going to get to this point in a few weeks anyway, it just happened earlier than we had planned. Let's just play the part of a happily engaged couple and move on."

"So tell me, what will '*playing the part*' entail?" He tilted his head to the left and lifted his brow.

It took her a whole 30 seconds to answer through the scowl on her face. "For appearances only, when we're around other people, we'll just act like a couple in love who's about to get married."

"No, Lily." Bryce turned all the way to her. "I need to know what lines not to cross."

She folded her arms with a sigh and rolled her eyes. "Oh, I'm certain you already know some of the lines not to cross because you've already tried to cross some of them. However, if I have to spell it out for you, what I mean is, things such as, holding hands when we walk down the street or maybe your arm around my shoulder. You're a big boy. I think you can figure it out on your own." She slid out of the truck.

"What if I pulled you into my arms and kissed you breathless. That would certainly be convincing, wouldn't it?"

Before closing the door, she angled her head to the side and said, "Who says your kisses would leave me breathless?"

Adrenaline mingled with excitement zipped through his body. "Oh, I take that as a challenge."

With a shrug of her shoulder, Lily's lips curled upward into a mischievous smile. She slammed the truck door shut and quick-stepped it into the house.

"I feel like things are about to change dramatically." His lips twitched into a smile when he saw her silhouette appear in the window. "Well, Mrs. soon-to-be Lily Fowler, I'm eagerly looking forward to this adventure."

The next morning, just as Lily switched on the coffee pot, she heard a pounding on the front door.

She darted through the living room and jerked open the door. "Wade, what on earth are you doing here this early on a Sunday mornin'? What's wrong?"

"It's all over town, Lily. Everybody knows about you and Fowler. I guess he must've thought if he told everybody about the two of you, then he would have a chance with you."

"Wade, what are you talkin' about?" She wavered, trying to comprehend what she was hearing.

"I'm not blind, Lily, I see the way he looks at you."

"He doesn't look at me any differently than you do."

Wade's head jerked back with a snap. His eyes widened, his jawline went slack, and the corner of his mouth twitched.

What was that look? There was something different about his expression. An odd feeling washed over Lily.

Was Bryce right when he said Wade had feelings for her? Was she that naïve? No, that couldn't be right. Wade was like a big brother to her. No, he only wanted to protect her. He wasn't jealous, he couldn't be.

"Lily, look, I came to talk to him this morning, and to my surprise, when I got to the guesthouse after beating on the door for ten minutes, I realized he's not there."

She pushed him back out onto the front porch and closed the door behind them. "Lower your voice, Wade, Joey's still asleep."

"I only have one question for you." Wade towered over her, his face dark and menacing. "Is he here?"

Lily positioned herself in front of the door before answering. "Yes, but," When Wade shifted, she put her hand on his chest to stop him from going inside. "He slept on the couch in the den because Joey wanted him to watch some movies with him last night, and they both fell asleep." Lily tucked her hair behind her ear and sucked in a deep breath. "And, it wasn't Bryce who told everyone… it was me."

"Oh, come on, Lily. You expect me to believe that. Stop trying to protect him."

"I'm not protectin' him. If you promise to calm down, you can come in, and I'll explain everythin'."

He nodded and followed her inside.

After pouring each of them a cup of coffee, Lily sat down at the table in front of Wade and told him about the incident in the diner.

Wade pulled off his hat, laid it on the table, and ran his hand over his jawline. "Lily, why don't you call off this whole thing before it gets out of hand? Let him have all of this. You don't need this place or Martin's money. I can take care of you and Joey."

"Wade, that's sweet, but it's not your responsibility to take care of us, it's mine. I'm gonna do what I have to do to see this thing through even if it kills me."

"What if I want it to be my responsibility? I have plenty of room at my place for the both of you." Wade reached across the table and took hold of both of her hands. "You and Joey mean the world to me, I—"

The timer on the oven beeped causing Lily to jump. "The biscuits are ready." Lily rose, slowed at Wade's side, and placed her hand on his shoulder. "I appreciate your concern for me and Joey, but everythin' will be okay, I promise."

"Are you sure about that?"

No, she wasn't sure about anything anymore. However, if she could convince everyone else, then maybe, just maybe, she could convince herself.

Just as Lily pulled the pan of biscuits out of the oven, Bryce appeared in the kitchen doorway and stopped cold when he saw Wade sitting there.

Neither man spoke a word, but their expressions said it all. A chill climbed up Lily's spine as she prayed she wouldn't have to play referee again.

Bryce strolled over to the coffee pot, poured himself a cup, and leaned against the counter. "You're here early,

Haston. I guess you were right, Lily, news does travel fast around here. Are you here to congratulate us?"

"Oh, you're real funny, Fowler. Just because people think the two of you are a real couple doesn't change anything. Don't forget I know the real reason you're here."

"Do you think it really matters to me what you know or what you think you know?" Bryce blew on his coffee and glared at Wade over the rim of his cup.

"It should because I'm going to be like a bur in your saddle, boy. I'm always going to be around. Especially when I think there's a snake in the hen house."

A growl of laughter bubbled in Bryce's throat.

Wade's eyes darkened as he rose to his feet. "You think all of this is funny, don't you?"

Bryce set his cup down and pushed himself away from the counter. "No, but I do find you quite hilarious."

Both men shifted toward one another, but Lily quickly moved in between them with her hands outstretched. "No, no, no. That's enough you two. Joey will be in here any minute, and I don't want the two of your brawlin' on the kitchen floor when he shows up. Now, can we all sit down and discuss this calmly, or do I have to pull out my iron skillet?"

Wade gave Lily a curved grin and sat back down.

Bryce leaned back against the counter again and crossed his arms over his chest.

Lily breathed a sigh of relief, pushed her hair out of her face, and placed her hands on her hips. "Thank you."

"I just have one question, Lily," Wade said, tipping his head backward.

"What's that?" Lily rubbed the knot in the back of her neck.

"What are you going to tell the boys about the two of you?" Wade bobbed his head in Bryce's direction. "If you recall, he did go out with them to the bonfire the other night.. I'm sure he didn't play the soon-to-be-married role at the bonfire. Did you, Fowler?"

"I don't think you should worry yourself about what I do in my free time, Haston. Matter of fact, I don't think any of this should concern you at all. This is between Lily and me."

"Lily is my business. The sooner you realize that, the better off you'll be."

Before Bryce had a chance to respond, Joey roared into the kitchen. "Hey, Wade. Whatcha' doing here?"

Relief flooded Lily for Joey's perfectly timed interruption. This thing between Bryce and Wade was a ticking time bomb ready to explode.

"I thought I'd have breakfast with you this mornin', big guy."

Joey bounced up to Wade and tugged on his sleeve. "I got the bestest news ever. Guess what it is."

"I don't know, tell me," Wade said, pulling Joey close.

"My mom's going to get married to Bryce. I'm going to have a daddy." Joey pointed at Bryce and grinned. "Ain't it great?"

Just like that tension filled the room like a thick and heavy October fog as Wade looked from Joey up to both of them.

Lily squeezed her eyes shut, held her breath as her heart jack hammered hard against her ribs.

How was Wade going to react to this? What was he going to say? Would he lose his temper and without thinking, say something hurtful to Joey?

"I heard." Wade's voice was as tense as a wound-too-tight guitar string.

Joey reached up and put his arms around Wade's neck. "But don't worry, even if I do have a daddy, you'll always be my best friend."

Wade hugged Joey tight and pulled him onto his lap. "You'll always be my best friend, too."

"I can't wait to tell everybody at school." He covered his mouth and giggled. "They're going to be really, really surprised, won't they?"

"I guess they will be."

Joey's smile faded, and he touched Wade's face. "Aren't you happy I'm going to have a dad? You look sad."

Wade cleared his throat. "You know what, Joey? I'm happy if you're happy."

Lily smiled at Wade and mouthed, "Thank you."

"Hey, you know what? Maybe all of us can go fishin' together." Joey glanced over at Bryce. "Do you know how to fish, Bryce? If you don't, Wade's a good teacher. He always put the worms on my hooks 'cause I stuck a hook in my finger one time, and now Mom won't let me do it anymore."

He wrinkled his nose at Lily and then stretched his arms wide. "We catch big fish in the pond, don't we?"

Wade nodded. "We sure do."

"Can we, Mom? Can we go fishin'?"

"We'll talk about it later, okay? Why don't you go get dressed while I finish up with breakfast?"

"Okay." As he headed out of the kitchen, he stopped and looked up at Bryce. "I'll be back in a minute." He took a few steps toward the doorway and then ran back and wrapped his arms around Bryce's waist.

The only sound in the kitchen came from the ticking clock on the wall as the three of them watched Joey skip out of the room.

After several seconds of silence, Wade ran his hand down the stubble on his chin, stood, and picked up his hat from off the table. "I think I'll pass on breakfast."

"Wade, wait," Lily called out to him as he headed for the back door.

He paused at the door, slapped his hat against his leg, and whipped around. "I don't like you, Fowler, but for some reason Joey does. Therefore, for his sake, I'm going to tolerate you being here and cut you some slack. But if you do anything, and I mean anything, to hurt that little boy, there's not a rock in Alabama big enough for you to hide under where I can't find you." He slammed his hat on his head and grabbed the doorknob.

Without turning around, he said over his shoulder, "Lily, my offer still stands. I want you to think long and hard about what I said. Because you know, all of this is only going to get worse. You need to stop it while you still can."

CHAPTER EIGHTEEN

The following Sunday morning, Bryce quickly crossed the yard whistling as he went because he was looking forward to seeing Lily. The past week had been Joey's last week of school. So from a class party, to the all day trip to the zoo, and other school related things, Lily had been missing in action for most of the week, and he had missed her.

When he opened the screen door and entered the house, he spotted Lily coming down the hallway. His feet glued to the floor. An electrical jolt zipped through his body as his heart rate spiked. He sucked in a large, deep, savoring breath and leaned against the doorframe.

She was dressed in a sleeveless, knee length, blue and white flower-patterned dress, and she carried a pair of white sandals in one hand. Her sun-kissed skin glowed. Her long chocolate-colored hair hung loosely around her face and hugged her shoulders.

What was it about this woman that made him weak in the knees just to see her smile? Back home in New York, he could have any woman he wanted. All he had to do was turn on the charm. However, not one woman he'd ever dated made him feel on the inside the way Lily did.

Suddenly he recalled what Jason Bates, one of his engaged friends from college had told him once when Bryce had asked him why he would ever want to settle down with just one woman.

"Bryce, one day there will be a woman who will come into your life who you would spend every dime you have just to see her smile. And no one and nothing can cure that ache deep down in your stomach when you're not around her. When you close your eyes at night, she'll be the last thing you see, and she'll be the very first thing you'll think about when you open your eyes in the morning. You'll know the one when you find her because you truly don't start living until she's a part of you."

At the time, Bryce laughed it off and called him a sap. No woman could ever have that kind of power over him or ever make him feel that way. Until now.

Jason, you were right all along. Now, I understand how you felt when Hannah came into your life.

"Bryce?" Lily tilted her brows, looking at him with uncertainly on her face. "What on earth are you doin'?"

"I...ah..." Heat rushed up his neck and into his face because he'd been caught staring. Oh but she sure was something to stare at. "So, where are you off to this morning?" Pushing away from the doorframe, he strolled on into the living room.

"Church. Today is Sunday, remember?" She sat down on the sofa and began to put her sandals on.

"That's right, I forgot." He came around and sat down beside her. "You look very pretty today."

Hiking a shoulder, she tugged at the hem of her dress and said with a titter, "It's a far cry from jeans and boots, I reckon."

When she looked up into his eyes, he held her gaze. Bryce reached out and touched her cheek with the tips of his fingers, then shifted closer. "I reckon."

"Mom, can I bring my football?" Joey yelled from down the hall.

Lily scrambled to her feet and yelled back, "Yes you can, but it stays in the truck until after church."

Bryce leaned back against the sofa and quirked his brows questioningly. "Football?"

"Our church is having a family outing today at the park at one o'clock. Would you like to go with us? You don't have to go if you don't want to, I just thought—"

"I'd love to."

She bit down on her bottom lip. "Good. I'll swing back by around twelve-thirty and pick you up."

"Lily, I'd like to attend church with you and Joey this morning, too, if it's all right."

"Church? Really?" Her left eyebrow raised a fraction as a smile brushed her lips.

"Sure, why not? If we're going to jump into this head first, we might as well go for the gold."

When Bryce, Lily, and Joey walked through the threshold of the church, Sara let out a squeal, threw her arms around Bryce and Lily, and gave them a bear hug, squeezing them together. "Bryce, I'm so glad you came with Lily and Joey today."

Bryce smiled down at Sara. "It's nice to see you again, Sara."

Sara wrapped both arms around one of Bryce's and pulled him along. "You have to meet our pastor."

They stopped in front of a man who looked to be in his fifties with short-cropped salt and pepper hair. He wasn't a short man, but compared to Bryce's height, he figured him to be a couple inches shy of six foot. But the thing that stood out in Bryce's mind the most was the man's smile. He had the exuberant smile of a man who was, and one word could sum it up, happy.

Sara touched his arm. "Pastor Henry, this is Lily's fiancé, Bryce Fowler. Bryce, this is our wonderful pastor, Henry Carson."

"He's going to be my dad," Joey chimed in, grinning.

"I know, I heard." Pastor Henry laughed and patted Joey on the shoulder. He turned back to Bryce and extended his hand.

The two men shook hands.

"If y'all will excuse me, I need to speak with Sister Annie. I'll be right back." Sara bobbed her head and with a big smile, she wobbled off toward a group of women.

"I'm so pleased you decided to join us today. Sister Sara has gone on and on about you. You must have really made an impression on her," Pastor Henry said and dipped his head in the direction where Sara had hurried up to the group of women who were all talking at once.

"She left a lasting impression on me, too."

Pastor Henry chuckled. "She's unforgettable, I can say that. She's like the mother hen to all of us. Her heart is as big as the moon, and it just keeps growing."

"Pastor Henry, can I speak with you for a moment?" A woman in a denim dress took hold of the pastor's arm.

"Yes, of course. Bryce, it was nice to meet you. We'll talk later. I hope you enjoy the service this morning." Pastor Henry walked away with the woman.

"Have you already asked Pastor Henry to conduct the weddin'?" Sara asked as she walked back up and nodded toward the pastor.

Lily shrugged.

"Lily, you are planning on getting married at the church, aren't you?" Sara asked, her eyes going wide as if the idea they wouldn't be getting married in the church was the worst thing that could ever happen.

"Oh. I don't think so." Lily nervously chewed on her bottom lip. "We don't want a fuss. I think we're going to do it simple and just go to the justice of the peace."

"Oh, no! You can't do that. Sweetie, this is one of the most important days of your life. We can't have simple. No, no, no. We have to do this up right." When Sara shook her head, her whole body jiggled. "Let me plan it for you. I'll do all the work. You won't have to worry about a thing."

"Sara, I—"

"I won't take no for an answer. We'll get together one day next week and start planning y'all's weddin'." She kissed Lily's cheek. "Oh, honey. You're gonna be such a beautiful bride."

Bryce couldn't agree more.

At the park, Lily stood in a circle with some of the churchwomen, all of them giddy with excitement with wedding plans and offering their advice from color scheme to flower choices.

"What do you think, Lily? Burgundy and jade would be beautiful colors for a wedding," Mrs. Ross said.

"I don't know. What about peach and mint green?" Mrs. Stanford added.

"I like those colors. What do you think, Lily?" Sara asked.

"I…I don't know." Lily shrugged and darted glances at each of the women as dizziness swept over her. She swayed and put a hand to her head.

Bryce leaned into the circle and slipped his arm around Lily's waist. "Excuse me, ladies, but I'd like to ask Lily if she'll be my three-legged race partner." He pulled her against him. "Shall we?"

"Yes, of course. Thanks to all of you for all of your input. We can pick this up some other time if that's okay?"

"Girl, you go have some fun with your man. We can handle this." Sara gave them a nudge. "Go."

As soon as they were out of earshot of the women, Bryce said, "You looked like you needed an escape plan, so I thought I'd intervene."

Lily laid her hand on his arm and gave it a squeeze. "And I want you to know, I really appreciate it." Lily folded her hands and crushed them to her chest, batting her eyes. "My hero."

"It was my pleasure, Ma'am. I've always wanted to rescue a damsel in distress." He took a step back, bent forward, and bowed.

"Well, thank you, Sir Fowler." She curtsied.

"A prince and his princess," Mr. Stover chuckled as he shuffled by.

They both giggled like a couple of teenagers and sprinted off toward the three-legged race.

Pastor Henry stepped up on one of the picnic tables and cupped his hands to his mouth. "Everyone who is running in the race, I need you to raise your hand."

When Bryce lifted his hand, a teenage boy who was helping Pastor Henry with the event handed him a red ribbon. "Tie your legs together just above the knee."

After Bryce tied his left leg to Lily's right leg, he snaked his arm around her waist pulling her in against him. Suddenly he was aware of her in every pore of his body, her nearness, the scent of her shampoo, the heat of her skin. A shudder whipped through his body.

"Okay we're all set. Are you ready to win this thing?"

Lily lifted her face and smiled up at him and then tucked her hair behind her ear. "You betcha."

"Okay, is everybody ready?" Pastor Henry lifted the cap gun in the air.

The group cheered in unison.

"Here we go. On your mark. Get set. Go!" Pastor Henry shouted and fired the gun.

Everybody was off and running. Couples were falling to the left and right of them. One couple, the woman fell and the man was dragging her. Another couple was hopping together. Lily's squeals of laughter made Bryce's insides dance with laughter too.

"We're almost to the finish line, Bryce." Excitement bubbled out of Lily.

Only one couple was ahead of them, and Bryce was determined to win. He tightened his grip around her and lifted her slightly. "Let's win this thing, Baby."

As they crossed the finish line first, the crowd cheered.

Lily twisted into him and threw her arms around his neck. "We did it. We did it. We won!"

However, her bouncing up and down knocked him off balance, and when he began to fall, he pulled her right along with him to the ground. He cushioned her fall as she landed on top of him.

"I'm sorry. Are you okay?" hovering over him, Lily asked through her laughter as she stared down into his face. The sun reflected in her eyes making them sparkle like diamonds.

"Only a few broken ribs and a ruptured spleen but I'll be fine." Bryce jokingly grunted as if he was in pain.

When Lily laughed again, a wayward strand of hair fell down across her face. Bryce reached up and slipped it behind her ear. As he pulled his hand away, his fingers trailed down along her jawline and paused on her chin.

There was a spark of some indefinable emotions in her eyes, and a small smile of enchantment touched her lips.

"Ya'll did it, Mom. Y'all won!" Joey's voice broke the connection between them, and Lily spun over to the side and sat up.

"Yes, we did." She gave Bryce one last fleeing glance and began to quickly untie the knot of the ribbon that held the two of them together.

The next morning, when Bryce strolled into the kitchen, Lily sniggered when she saw the small lump on his forehead. She put her hand over her mouth and mumbled through her fingers. "Good morning. How are you feelin'?"

"Go ahead, have your laugh at my sufferings."

"It doesn't look that bad, cry baby." Squinting her eyes, she moved her head in close and grinned. "Well, not too bad."

"How was I to know a teenage girl had a killer Frisbee arm?"

Lily laughed so hard she snorted.

Bryce boomed with laughter. "What was that? Oh, I love it. I'm going to start calling you Miss Piggy."

"You'd better not." Lily punched him in the arm and gave him a shove.

"Miss Piggy, Miss Piggy." He started circling her and snorted like a pig close to her ear.

"Stop calling me that, knot head."

"Knot head?" He seized both of her arms and pulled her body into his. Snaking one arm around her waist, he began to tickle her in the ribs. "Come here, Miss Piggy. Let's hear that snort again."

"Stop it, stop it." Lily struggled against him trying to get free, but her resistance was weak because she enjoyed being in his arms. It felt right.

Laughter erupted out of her until another snort slipped out. Her hand flew to her mouth, and her cheeks flamed.

"I love the sound of your laugh. Snort and all." The heartrending tenderness of his gaze caused a slight tremor to prickle through Lily's body.

"I heard y'all laughin'. What's so funny?" Joey asked when he came running into the kitchen.

Lily jumped back and moved away, smoothing down her hair. "Nothing, Joey. Do you want waffles or pancakes?"

"Can I have strawberries with my waffles?" Joey crawled up onto the barstool and propped his chin on his fist.

"You sure can." Lily swallowed hard trying to make her voice sound normal. Touching her hand to her flushed face, she smiled at Joey.

Joey looked up at Bryce and pointed at his forehead. "It did leave a knot just like mama said it would."

Once again, they broke out in laughter.

"My Frisbee battle scar." He wiggled his brows and winked at Joey.

"Stop it, Bryce," Lily said, wiping her eyes with her apron. "I have to finish with breakfast."

"I didn't say anything." Bryce held up his hands. "I'm innocent."

After another couple of minutes, they were finally able to stop laughing, and Lily finished putting breakfast on the table.

"Mom, can I gather the eggs this mornin'? I promise I won't pick up the babies," Joey pleaded as he shoved the last bite of his waffle into his mouth.

"I guess so, but remember your promise, and make sure you latch the coop door when you're done." Lily reached across the table and pushed the hair out of Joey's eyes. "You're going to have to get a haircut soon."

He cut his eyes over at Bryce and grinned as he drained his milk. "I want my hair cut like Bryce's, it's cool. Then we can look alike." Jumping out of his chair, he headed toward the back door. "I'm getting' the eggs now, and I'll try not to break any of 'em either. See ya."

Lily wagged her head as Joey slammed out the back door. "That boy." She stood and began picking up the breakfast dishes.

Bryce chuckled. "He's something else. It's never a dull moment when he's around." He stood and began to help her gather up the dishes.

"You don't have to do that. Leave them be, I can get them," Lily protested.

"You cooked. The least I can do is help you clean up. I won't take no for an answer. So, you might as well surrender now."

Lily folded her arms over her chest and then nodded. "Suit yourself. I'll start rinsing these off for the dishwasher if you want to finish clearing off the table."

"Yes, Ma'am."

Just as Lily slipped the last plate into the dishwasher, Bryce eased up behind her. He put his hands on her shoulders and ran them down her arms before resting them on her hands.

A soft sigh escape her lips, causing a tingling sensation to travel up and down his spine. He buried his face in her hair and kissed the side of her head. "Do you know how beautiful you are?"

"Bryce, we have to stop this." She twisted around into him, sending an unexpected rush of exhilaration coursing through Bryce's body.

"Why?"

When she didn't answer, he gathered her closer into him, her soft moan hummed in his ears.

"Knock, knock. Can I come in?" Greg's voice echoed through the open backdoor.

Lily pulled herself out of Bryce's arms, shifted herself around him, and called out to Greg. "Of course, come on in. When have you ever had to knock?"

"Ah… well, I didn't want to interrupt anything." Greg glanced from Lily to Bryce and then back to Lily.

"Don't be silly, you didn't interrupt anythin'." Lily turned away, but not before Bryce saw her cheeks flush.

"I still can't believe you're getting married." Greg twisted his hat in between his fingers.

"We wanted to wait for awhile before we told anyone," Lily quickly said.

Greg nodded. "I've been thinking about this all week, and I guess that explains why you didn't have anything to do with the girls at the bonfire that night you went with us. I was beginning to wonder about you." He slapped Bryce on the back and let out a hearty laugh. "Especially when that hottie Rhonda Gordon was all over you and wanted you to go home with her."

"Greg, I think it's time we get to work, don't you?" Bryce pushed Greg toward the door.

Greg stretched his neck around Bryce and smiled at Lily. "Oh, you don't have to worry, Lily, he turned her down cold. He shut that girl down like flippin' the off switch on a combine harvester. And now that I know about the two of you, I'll keep an eye on Bryce from here on out." With a chuckle, Greg gave Bryce a slap on the back again. "I was just joshing with you, man. I'm sure Lily knows that, too. Ain't that right, Lily?"

Lily turned her head away, but not before Bryce saw her smile.

CHAPTER
NINETEEN

Lily's eyes flew open. Her heart pounded hard against her ribs. Her lips tingled. Her skin prickled with electricity. She sat up with a snap and quickly scanned her surroundings. It took a moment for her to realize she was in her own bedroom, alone.

"It was just a dream." Relief mingled with disappointment filled her. She collapsed back onto her pillow and pulled the covers up under her chin. "Bryce, stop haunting my dreams."

Just as she closed her eyes, the dream came rushing back like a flood.

She kicked off the covers, jerked on her jeans and a t-shirt, snatched up a nearby quilt, and slipped out of her room. Tiptoeing through the house, she went out onto the front porch and curled up on the swing.

Lily's body still trembled as she sat alone in the dark. When she closed her eyes, she could still feel the warmth of his arms around her waist. She could still feel his breath on her face, his lips on hers as he kissed her over and over again.

His kisses in her dream certainly did leave her breathless. As much as she had loved Chad, he had never made her feel the way Bryce did. She was a girl when she married Chad, but now she was a woman.

As hard as she fought it, she knew she was falling in love with Bryce. Could she go along with this ruse and keep her feelings hidden? In just a few weeks, they would stand before the minister and say their vows. Would she get lost in the delusion and be left with her heart shattered all around her once more?

She pulled her legs into her chest and propped her chin on the top of her knees. Gazing out into the stillness of the night, she watched as thousands of lightning bugs lit up the skies like glistening diamonds against the blanket of darkness, humming along with the crickets and frogs as they sang their night love songs together in harmony.

Like a candle flickering to life, the sun slowly began to light up the horizon, filling the skies with its brilliant orange, crimson, and golden colors. The early morning dew shimmered on the luscious green pasturelands, giving the impression of shards of glass shattered across the fields.

The only sound she heard was the bellowing of the cows off in the distance. She closed her eyes and breathed in deeply the scent of the crisp morning air.

"Were you out here all night?" Bryce asked as he leaped up the steps.

Her eyes jumped open, and she uncurled in one jolt. "No, not all night."

Worry coursed over his face. "What's wrong? Did you have trouble sleeping?"

"You could say that." Vivid images of her dreams danced through her mind as heat filled her cheeks. "I need some coffee." However, in her rush to get up, somehow her quilt got entangled around her feet, causing her to lose her balance.

Within seconds, Bryce leaped forward, caught her around the waist, and swept her up in his arms. He fixed his eyes on hers, and a playful smile stretched across his face, lighting up his eyes. "I've always wanted to sweep a lady off of her feet, but this is the first time I actually have."

"Very funny, now put me down." She was irritated at the thrilling current coursing through her.

"Is that any way to talk to your hero?" Bryce's eyebrows arched mischievously. His warm breath caressed her cheek.

"Hero, huh? Put me down before someone sees us." She knew she wasn't putting up much of a fight, but when it came to Bryce, her defenses were as weak as a sick calf.

"I can't carry my fiancée around in my arms?" A laugh rumbled in his throat when he set her down on her feet.

She smoothed down her clothes as if they were wrinkled, then rammed her fists on her hips. "That's not funny."

"Sorry, I couldn't resist." The smile in his eyes contained a sensuous flame that made her blood soar through her veins.

"Well, resist next time." Lily was beginning to love being in his arms, but she wasn't about to tell him that. Her dream still had her senses reeling, and every time he touched her, it sent the dream back to her mind in vivid color.

"Why? I like holding you in my arms." He moved in so close to her she could feel the heat from his body.

Her knees were weakened by the quivering of her limbs. "You're going to have to stop saying things like that."

His voice slipped into a huskier octave. "Why?"

"Because, it just isn't right, that's why." With the last of her willpower, she moved past him and reached for the screen door handle.

However, he caught her arm and whirled her around to face him. "Why isn't it right, Lily? Explain it to me. I need to know why you keep pushing me away."

"Because, we're not really in love, remember?" She swallowed the knot in her throat as sadness dropped into her stomach like a boulder. She wanted him to fall in love with her and live a happily-ever-after life together, but there was Hannah, and there was the arrangement and the fact that none of this was even real.

"I'm hurt. Is that any way to talk to your future husband?" He puffed out his bottom lip.

She shook her head and glowered at him. "You know what I mean."

"Do I?" He inched closer, crooked his finger in her belt loop, and pulled her closer to him. "I sure would like to get to know my future wife a little better."

He ran his fingers down the side of her face and left a trail of tingling sparks of electricity.

"Bryce." She tried to pull away, but he pressed her against the wall and placed both of his hands on the wall at her shoulders.

"Do you know how much I want to kiss you right now?"

His warm breath on her face made her skin prickle. She breathed in the scent of coffee and a woodsy aftershave wafting off of him. She swallowed hard. He had never been this forceful before. Fear mixed with excitement sent a charge through her body. "You need to stop." She had to force the words out of her mouth.

"Is that what you really want? Do you want me to stop?"

She didn't reply. She couldn't reply because she didn't want him to stop.

"I didn't think so." Moving in closer, he bent his head and his lips were just a breath from hers when the ringtone on Bryce's cell phone echoed through the crisp morning air.

Her heart slammed to a stop. *No.* Then she regained sanity and was thankful for the interruption.

"Whoever it is, I'll make it quick." He yanked the phone out of its case, glanced at the screen, and flipped it open. "Good morning, Hannah. You're calling early. Is everything okay?" He stepped away from Lily. "Yes, I can talk. What's up?"

Hannah.

He was still talking to her, and Lily's heart did a swan dive into Lake I-hate-him. It hurt like fire, but Lily finally had to face the fact; she wasn't any different from any other girl he was chasing. She clutched her stomach as a sudden onset of nausea coursed through her.

He held his phone against his chest. "Sorry, Lily. It's important that I take this. I shouldn't be on the phone with her long."

When he reached for her, Lily dodged his hand. "That's okay. We're finished here anyway, so you just go ahead and take all the time you need." She tried to keep the sarcasm out of her voice but didn't quite pull it off.

Bryce's head flinched back slightly, and he lifted a questioning brow.

With a shrug, she whirled around and darted into the house.

A few minutes later, she heard footsteps entering the kitchen. Her shoulders tensed, and her throat dried. How could she face him after that?

"Mornin', Lily. We thought we'd have breakfast with y'all this mornin'. If that's all right?" Greg asked as he and Kyle strolled into the kitchen.

Relief flooded her. She had been trying to figure out a way that she wouldn't have to spend any more time alone with Bryce today because her defenses were weak, and she was afraid she'd let down her guard for good if given the temptation again. Her lips still tingled with the yearning for Bryce's kiss on the porch. Now, thanks to the boys, she didn't have to worry about it.

"Of course, come on in and pull up a chair. Breakfast should be on the table in about ten minutes." Lily opened the refrigerator door and pulled out the tub of butter, eggs, and a tube of sausage. With her hands full, she closed the door with her foot.

Bryce entered the kitchen with Joey right behind him talking a mile a minute. She turned away when Bryce smiled at her.

During breakfast, while the boys were talking about the day ahead of them, Lily avoided Bryce's stares at her. Whenever he would try to pull her into the conversation, she would just nod her answer.

"Mom, can I go to work with Kyle today? I promise I won't get in the way. Can I, please?" Joey begged with a small amount of bouncing in his chair.

"Lily, it's all right with me if you don't care. He's a big help, and I'll watch out for him," Kyle said as he buttered a biscuit and smiled at Joey.

Lily nodded. "Yes, that's fine with me."

Sitting back in her chair, she let the boys talk.

"Thanks for breakfast, Lily. As always it was the best." Greg pushed his chair away from the table and rubbed his stomach. "Now, I need to go and work it off."

As Kyle was getting up from the table, he sliced a biscuit opened and slapped a sausage patty in between it. "Taking one for the road."

The boys bustled out the back door, yelling bye to Lily and wishing her a good day.

"I'll see y'all at lunch," Lily yelled back as she started gathering up the dirty dishes. Bryce eased up beside her, took hold of her elbow, and pulled her close. "What's bothering you?"

"Why would anything be bothering me?" She snatched her arm away to continue picking up the plates.

When he reached for her again, she held up one hand toward him. "Don't. Okay? Just don't."

"Bryce, are you coming?" Greg yelled back into the house.

"Yes, I'll be right there." He placed his hat on his head and looked back at Lily. "We'll talk later."

"There's no need."

After she finished cleaning the kitchen dishes, she grabbed up her hat and headed out the door to start her own chores. However, just as she stepped out onto the porch, she noticed four cars plowing down the drive.

When the cars all came to a stop, she realized it was some of the women from the church. They poured out of the cars, and to Lily it looked like one of those trick cars at the circus where dozens of clowns pile out of one tiny car.

"Hello, sweet girl." Sara waddled up to the porch with gift bags in her hands. "Where is that handsome husband-to-be of yours?"

"He's in the south pasture mending the fence. What are y'all doing here?" Lily asked as she noticed the other women getting out of their cars with gift-wrapped presents. "What's going on?"

"It's your bridal shower, silly." Lacey, Mrs. Stanford's teenage daughter, grinned through her braces.

"I want you to get your man on the phone, and tell him to get his cute little butt back here, and don't you dare tell him what's going on. I want it to be a surprise." Sara slapped Lily on the backside as she breezed past her into the house. The other women swarmed Lily with hugs and kisses as they jostled past her following Sara.

"I thought a bridal shower was just for women." Lily didn't want Bryce to come back to this. *Lord, what are you doing to me?*

"Lily, have you called him yet?" Sara's voice echoed into the air.

Kitty, Sara's daughter, laughed. "You'd better get that man of yours here pretty quick before Mom has a meltdown."

Just then, Lily spotted two more cars coming down the drive, and she closed her eyes. "Oh. This can't be happenin'."

"Girl, what are you waiting for? I'd better see you dialing that phone of yours. We have to get your bridal shower under way, and then we have more weddin' to plan." Sara moved up behind Lily and pointed at her cell phone on her hip.

"Sara, you don't have to—" Lily sighed.

"Girl, you'd better get to dialin'." Sara gave Lily a nudge.

Lily reluctantly took out her cell phone and punched in Bryce's number, holding her breath until he answered the phone.

"Hey, Lily, what's going on?" Bryce asked.

"I need you to come back to the house, please." Lily's shoulders tensed when Sara eased closer so she could hear Bryce's response.

"Lily, is everything okay?"

Sara put her index finger to her lips. How was Lily going to tell him what was going on with Sara standing right there?

"Yes, everything's fine. I'll explain it to you when you get here."

"I'll be right there."

Sara grabbed her by the arm and pulled her into the house. "Good girl. Now, come on, I want to show you the cake."

♥ ♥ ♥

Bryce's heart hammered against his ribcage. What was wrong? Lily never called him. Worse, her voice sounded edgy, and upset rang through every word. Was this anything to do with why she had given him the cold shoulder earlier?

"She didn't say what she needed?" Greg asked as he drove Bryce back to the ranch

"No, she didn't." A flicker of apprehension coursed through him.

Greg looked over and gave Bryce a reassuring smile. "I'm sure everything's okay. If it wasn't, I'm sure she would've called Wade."

"Why would she need to call Wade?" Bryce snapped, and then he immediately regretted the words and tone. "Sorry, Greg, I know what you meant. I'm just worried about Lily."

When the ranch house came into view, he noticed several cars parked in front of the house. The truck was still in motion when Bryce jumped from it and bolted toward the front door.

As he went through the door with one push, Lily met him there. "Bryce, I have to tell you—"

"Surprise!" everyone screamed and began to clap.

Sara shuffled up, wrapped her pudgy arms around both of them, and pulled them into the room. "We couldn't let the two of you get married without having a proper bridal shower for y'all. What kind of town would we be?"

Bryce looked down into Lily's flushed face. She shrugged one shoulder and mouthed the word, *Sorry.*

Relief soared through Bryce like an eagle in flight as he fought the urge to pull her into his arms and smother her face with kisses. He drew a deep breath in through his nose and pulled a shaky smile to his face. "It's okay. I'm just relieved you're all right."

Cameras flashed.

Greg edged in and whispered, "Man, you're on your own here. I'm not sticking around for this." He snorted and tipped his hat. "Good luck, buddy."

Greg made a break for the door, and within the blink of an eye, he was gone.

Coward.

"Okay, it's time to get this party started." Sara took hold of Bryce's arm. Three other women joined her. They pulled him and Lily toward a folding table which had been set up in the corner of the living room.

"What do you think of the cake? Mom made it this mornin'," a young woman in the crowd said.

Bryce looked down at the colorful cake displayed on the table. It had a small statue of a bride and groom on the top, and written in pink icing, the cake read: *Congratulations, Lily & Bryce.*

Cameras flashed again.

"You don't look very happy, Lily. Is somethin' wrong?" another young woman asked with a concerned look.

"No, I'm fine. I'm happier than a dog with a ham bone." Lily flashed the woman a smile.

Bryce was growing fond of Lily's southern colloquialisms. Even though he didn't know the meaning of most of them, he thought they were cute the way they rolled off her tongue. This woman was a true southern belle, and he wouldn't have it any other way.

After several party games, Sara finally announced it was time for the cake.

Sara held out a knife to Lily. "Okay, it's time to cut the cake. Lily, you hold the knife on the cake." She stepped in behind Bryce and pushed him against Lily. "And, Bryce, you stand behind her, wrap your arms around her, and put your hand on top of hers. That way, both of you will cut the first slice together."

Lily twisted into Bryce and whispered, "Sorry about all of this. I couldn't warn you. Sara wouldn't let me."

He buried his mouth into her hair near her ear. Strawberry shampoo wafted up his nose. But now was not the time to think about how great she smelled and what it was doing to his senses. "Don't worry about it. I get a break from work and cake, too. Who's complaining?"

"Well, what are you two waitin' for? Cut that cake already," Sara said, wiggling her camera.

Together they cut the first slice, and then Sara and another woman Bryce didn't know, took over and began slicing the cake and placing the pieces on plates.

A plump woman in a purple dress handed him and Lily a cup of punch. "This is my own special recipe. Tell me what you think."

"Thank you, Mrs. Hunter." Lily smiled sweetly. When she took a sip, her eyes widened. "It's very good."

"I knew you'd like it." She cackled and waddled away.

Bryce took a drink of the sugary syrupy liquid and puckered his lips. "Wow. If this stuff was any sweeter, the bees around here would think I was dinner."

Lily elbowed him in the side. "Be nice."

"That was being nice."

Later, Sara motioned another woman to her side. "If everyone is finished, it's time to open presents. Lily, you and Bryce have a seat on the couch, and we'll bring your presents to you."

Cameras flashed again when Lily opened the first gift. It was a large, lacey silk-covered book.

"It's an album for all of your wedding pictures. I hope you like it," the young woman, who Lily had informed him, was Sara's daughter, Kitty, said with a smile.

"It's beautiful, Kitty, thank you." Lily smiled.

Lily unwrapped several more gifts.

When she picked up a gift wrapped in bright pink floral print, Sara snatched it away. "You have to save this 'til last. It's from all of us."

After all the gifts were opened, Sara handed Lily the last one. "Okay, this one is for you. Well, now that I think of it, it's for Bryce, too."

Lily tore off the paper, gasped, and quickly slammed the top back on the box as the whole gaggle of women cackled.

Bryce leaned forward and slid closer to her. "What is it?"

"It's nothin'." Lily wouldn't make eye contact with him, but he noticed her cheeks and neck had turned a rosy red. She was embarrassed. Why?

"Come on, girl, you can't get away with that so easily. You have to show *all* your gifts." Sara picked up the box and laid it back in Lily's lap.

"Sara, I don't think this is appropriate to show to everyone," Lily softly replied.

"Honey child, everyone here is a woman, except for that man of yours, and I really do think he would appreciate this gift, too." Sara winked at Bryce. "Now, open it."

Lily slowly took a deep breath and removed the top of the box. "If I don't die of embarrassment, would you please shoot me when this is all over with? I'll provide the gun and the bullet."

She reached into the box and lifted out a black, lacey, and transparent negligee.

All the women laughed and began to clap. Whispers drifted around the room causing Lily's cheeks to glow brighter. "Could this possibly get any worse?"

"Bryce, now, we didn't forget about you either." Sara revealed a box she'd been hiding behind her back and handed it to him.

"Kill me. Just kill me now," Lily whispered.

Bryce shoulder bumped Lily, patted her leg, and chuckled. "Be brave, Lily. Be brave. Maybe it's a wallet," he teased, trying to ease the nervousness he saw in her face and the apprehension growing in his own gut.

He opened the box and pulled out a pair of black silk boxers. "Aw, thank you."

"Nice wallet," Lily murmured and quickly looked away.

"Those gifts are for your weddin' night." Sara winked and then grabbed each of them by the hand and pulled them to their feet. "I'm going to make you a scrapbook to remember this day, so all I need is one more picture to end the shower." She shoved them in front of the fireplace. "Everyone, get your cameras ready."

Sara backed away, picked up her camera, and aimed it at the two of them.

"Okay, Bryce, I want you to lay one on her, and I don't mean a peck on the cheek either. Show your woman how much you love her."

CHAPTER TWENTY

L ily was sure her heart had stopped beating. *Breathe, girl, breathe.*

Bryce looked at her long and hard as he slipped his arm around her waist, pulled her close, and whispered into her hair. "We have to put on a convincing show."

Lily couldn't say a word. There wasn't a single one anywhere in her head.

Her heart was definitely beating. It sounded like a jackhammer in her ears, and her breathing now came in short, raspy, breaths.

"Come on, boy, lay a good one on her. We need some good pictures," Sara cheered, and the other women joined in.

He placed his left hand on the side of her face and looked intently into her eyes. "I've wanted to do this for a long time, and now you can't run away."

When his mouth covered hers, an explosion went off in her head. If her heart could beat any harder, she feared it would burst right out of her chest. The room swirled around her, and every sound vanished.

When he finally pulled away, she had to grip the front of his shirt for support because she no longer trusted her legs to do the job. Never in her wildest dreams had she been kissed like that. Not even by Chad. The dream she had about him kissing her suddenly rolled through Lily's mind like a thundercloud. She remembered how that dream had affected her, and fear roiled inside her. All she could think of was, *Lord, please don't let me fall in love with him. Please.*

"If my ex-husband would have ever kissed me like that, he wouldn't be an ex," one of the women in the room said.

"My husband has never kissed me that way. I'm jealous," another one replied.

Bryce chuckled and draped his arm around Lily's shoulder. "Well then, shame on your husbands."

"You're not kiddin'. Okay, ladies, let's get this place cleaned up so these two can spend some time alone. After that kiss, I'm sure they're hankering to." Sara snickered and started to pick up the wrapping paper.

Twenty minutes later, the crowd began to dwindle, and the only ones left were Sara and Kitty.

"Well kids, we're getting out of your way now. You'd better be good to that soon-to-be little wife of yours, or you'll have to answer to me." Sara tucked her purse under her arm and gave Bryce a wink.

"Oh, you don't have to worry, Miss Sara. I'll take very good care of her." Bryce slipped his arm around Lily's waist, pulled her into him, and kissed her again.

Kitty giggled.

Lily gathered her nerves, and when she glanced up, she looked right into the eyes of Wade. His clenched jaw made the veins in his neck pulse against his skin. His barrel chest rose and fell sharply, and his fists clutched at his sides. "Lily, I need to talk to you. Now."

Bryce narrowed his eyes at Wade and tightened his arm around Lily's waist.

Sara stopped next to Wade and shook her finger. "Now, Wade, don't you keep that girl too long. I think her fiancé wants to spend some quality time with her before going back to work." Sara laughed and gave Lily a wink. "I'll see y'all later."

"Thank you for all of this, Sara," Lily said, her voice meek and her emotions shredding at her feet.

"It was my pleasure." Sara bobbed her head.

The second Sara and Kitty stepped out of the door, Wade moved toward them.

Pulling away from Bryce, Lily moaned. "I have to talk to Wade, to explain all of this."

Bryce caught her arm. "Why do you have to explain anything to him?"

"I just do."

"Lily, what's going on here?" Wade's mouth twitched as he looked past her at Bryce.

"Something you weren't invited to, Haston," Bryce jeered.

"Boy, you got a lot of nerve." Wade balled his fists, and in one swift movement, shouldered past Lily, and closed the gap between himself and Bryce.

"That's enough." Lily quickly pushed herself between the two men, placed her hands on Wade's chest, and pushed him back a few steps. "I won't have a shouting and screaming match in the middle of my living room between the two of you. C'mon, Wade, we'll talk in private. Bryce, why don't you head on back to work? We'll talk later."

Lily quickly shuffled Wade off down the hallway into Martin's office where she shut the door behind them.

"Explain to me why he was all over you in there." Wade folded his arms across his chest and huffed. "Don't you see, all of this is a game to him? The saddest part is you're his pawn, and you can't even see it."

"Wade, that's not true. He had nothing to do with this. He was just as surprised as I was when those women showed up here. They came with shower gifts, a cake, punch, and…" Her cheeks flushed when she remembered the negligee. "Anyway, everything was going fine, and then somehow it took a turn for the worst. They wanted us to—"

"I'm well aware of what they wanted, of what he wanted." Wade slammed his fist into the palm of his hand. "You need to put a stop to this charade right now! If you don't, I will."

Bitter anger rose up in the back of her throat. "How dare you come in here and demand anythin' of me."

Wade's eyes widened, and his head jerked back. "What?"

"Look, I appreciate everything you've done for me and Joey over the last several years, but I am not a child, and I'm sick and tired of you treatin' me like one. I do have a functioning brain, whether you believe it or not, and I can make intelligent decisions on my own without being treated like I'm four."

"I wasn't trying to make—"

"I know, but you do. You have to believe in me and trust the decisions I make. If I make the wrong ones, then I'm going to be the one who has to suffer the consequences. And another thing, what I do with Bryce isn't any of your business."

Wade's eyes narrowed into slits, and his nostrils flared. "What do you mean it isn't any of my business?"

"You need to stop trying to fix everythin'. Like I said before, I'm not a child. I can take care of myself."

Wade yanked off his hat and shoved his hand through his dark curls. "I can guarantee you, Lily Meyers, I don't think of you as a child. I never have. I'm only trying to protect you. Can't you see that?"

"I don't need you to protect me, Wade. I need you to trust me."

"I do trust you, but I don't trust him." Wade's features softened. "I can't stand to see him touch you, much less—"

"Is everything all right in here?" Bryce opened the door and side stepped his way into the room.

The men exchanged looks of pure disdain and distrust. "This is a private conversation if you don't mind." Wade shifted toward Bryce, but Lily grabbed him by the arm.

"You know, I think I do mind." Bryce squared his shoulders, and his chin twitched.

"Bryce, you're not helpin'." Lily sighed. "Give me a second, Wade, I—"

"You need to run along, boy, we're not finished here," Wade said. He shot Bryce a warning look, which chilled Lily to the bone.

But before she could try to defuse the situation, Bryce slid his arm around her waist. She instantly knew this had been a very, very bad idea.

"I think you are." Bryce's brows drew together in an angry frown. "No, as a matter of fact, I know you are. It's time I put you in your place, Haston. Lily's is going to be my wife, and there's not a thing you can do about it. So, get over it."

Before she could stop him, Wade lunged for Bryce and caught his chin with his fist. Bryce tumbled backward, slamming the door closed with his momentum.

"Stop it! Both of you!" Lily jumped for them, thinking her position would be the defining factor. However, this time it wasn't.

Bryce came back and hit Wade with a right hook, and Wade careened backward into the desk.

"Wade! Bryce! Stop!"

This time Wade came back, hands out, taking Bryce's throat in them, and the two of them tumbled over the coffee table, smashing right into Lily.

Fighting to stay upright, she reached out and grabbed hold of an arm, unsure of whom it belonged to even as she tumbled backward.

The three of them were tangled up tighter than a net, and the next thing Lily knew, she took an elbow to the face.

The crack of pain blurred her vision. She careened backward as she covered her face with her hands. When she pulled her hands away, she saw *blood!*

"Lily!" Just like that the fight stopped as both men yelled her name at the same time. With one motion, they leaped toward her.

No other thought came as Lily righted herself, dashed out of the room, down the hall, and into the bathroom, locking the door behind her.

"Lily, are you all right? Lily?" Wade yelled.

"Lily, Are you okay? Answer me," Bryce pleaded.

They banged.

They knocked.

They jerked on the doorknob.

Hovered over the sink, she ignored them, wet a washcloth, closed the lid on the commode, sat down, and held the cool cloth over her face. The pain was unbelievable.

"Lily. Please open the door," Wade begged.

"At least say something. If you don't open this door, I'll break it down," Bryce threatened.

The two men began to quarrel outside the door.

Their voices rattled her brain, causing the pain to magnify in her head and across her face. "Stop it!" she yelled, tired of it all. "I'm sick of this arguin'. I want both of you to go away and leave me alone. Don't you think both of you have done enough?"

"Lily, please come out," Bryce's voice softened. She could hear the concern in his voice, but she was unmoved by it.

She stood and moved back to the mirror. The bleeding had stopped, but her face was swelling, and bruising was already setting in. "Just go away."

"I'm not going anywhere until you come out of there," Bryce said.

"Me either," Wade added.

"I don't want to see either one of you right now." Lily dropped the bloody cloth into the sink, wet another one, and held it to her face again. It was cool.

"Lily, I'll sit out here all night if I have to, but I'm not going anywhere," Bryce said with certainty etching his voice.

"Neither am I."

She knew neither one of them would leave her alone until she came out of the bathroom. So, reluctantly, she finally unlocked the door and stepped out.

"Lily." Bryce sharply sucked in air the second he caught sight of her. "Are you all right?"

"I'm just peachy." She tried to push past them, but Bryce gently caught her arm, slipped his finger under her chin, and tilted her head upward.

His eyes held concern and apology. "I don't think so. We need to get you to the emergency room to make sure your nose isn't broken."

Lily shuddered from the pain even as she tried to put her brave face on. "I don't think it's broken."

Wade took her arm on the other side. "Well, you're going to the hospital, whether you want to or not, even if we have to hog-tie you and carry you out."

Lily nodded, knowing the fight just wasn't worth it.

A couple of hours later, the nurse wheeled Lily back from ex-ray and helped her back up on the hospital bed. "The doctor should be in with you any minute now. Do you need anything?"

"I don't think so."

"Well, if there's anything you need, you just get one of these young men to come fetch me, okay?" She dipped her head in the directions of Bryce and Wade, who were now standing at the foot of her bed, full of contrition and concern.

"I will. Thank you."

"How are you feeling?" Wade asked after the nurse had left the room.

"I feel like I was elbowed in the face. Oh. Wait a minute, I was." She couldn't keep the sarcasm from her voice.

Bryce took a deep breath, and Lily thought for a fleeting moment that she saw his lip quiver. "I'm so sorry, Lily. I never meant for you to get hurt."

"That goes for me, too," Wade added.

Empathy welled up in Lily when she looked at Wade and Bryce's sad, pitiful faces. Their heads hung lower than the sweeping branches of a weeping willow.

"Look, I know neither one of you meant for me to get hurt. But, please, could both of you think about this next time the two of you want to fight like little kids?"

The door opened, and the doctor walked in. "How are you feeling?"

"Okay, I guess."

"Let's take a look." He pressed on different areas of her face, asking her if it hurt. "On a scale of one to ten, where would you say you pain level is?"

"Maybe a six."

"Well the good news is your nose isn't broken. The bad news is, it's going to be painful for a few days, and you will be sporting a couple black eyes for a while. I'll write you a prescription for some pain medication, and I'll send you home with some cold compresses too. They'll relieve some of the pain and help to reduce the swelling. The nurse will bring you in something for pain in a few minutes, and then you'll be ready to go."

"Thank you."

The doctor gave her shoulder a squeeze and said tenderly, "I want you to take it easy over the next several days, too."

"I will."

"Remember the compresses and rest is the best medicine. I hope you feel better real soon." He patted her arm and nodded at Wade and Bryce on his way out of the room.

On the way home, Wade drove, Lily sat in the middle, and Bryce sat next to the door. Guilt plagued Bryce every time he remembered the sinking sick feeling that shook his entire body when he had seen the blood coming from Lily's nose the moment his elbow hit her in the face.

This was his fault, and he knew it. His jealousy toward Wade had motivated him to pick the fight that led to Lily's injury.

The medication the nurse had given Lily was taking affect on her because when he looked down, she had dozed off.

His gut twisted when he looked down at her face. The swelling around her nose was mild, but the deep purples, blacks, and blues spread across her nose and under both eyes.

Her head moved, and a wayward strand of hair fell across her face. He tenderly reached down, lifted it off her face, and slipped it behind her ear.

"I can't believe I let this happen." Bryce shook his head as he rubbed his chin and pinched up his bottom lip.

"As much as I hate to say it, don't beat yourself up too much. I have to take some blame for this, too." Wade spoke without looking at Bryce.

"It took a lot out of you to say that, didn't it?"

"More than you know."

Lily moved her head, and a soft moan escaped her lips. Bryce swallowed the knot in his throat. He knew Lily was in pain even though she was under the influence of the pain meds.

"I swore I'd always protect her and that I would never let anyone hurt her. It looks like I failed on both parts." Wade's eye twitched when he drew in a heavy breath.

Before Bryce had a chance to reply, Wade flipped on the radio. Bryce took the hint that this was the end of the conversation as far as Wade was concerned. They rode in silence on the rest of the ride home.

Twenty minutes later, when Wade pulled the truck to a stop, Bryce gently nudged Lily. "Lily, we're home."

When they climbed out of the truck, Bryce wrapped his arm around her waist to steady her.

"I can walk on my own." Lily pulled away, but when she did, she stumbled forward.

Determined not to take no for an answer, Bryce wrapped his arms around her again. "You're not as steady on your feet as you think you are."

She blinked twice, swaying even standing there. "Whoa, it must be the pain medication."

"Let's get you inside so you can rest."

Joey and Kyle were sitting on the couch, watching TV when the three of them walked into the house.

"Momma!" A terrified look swept across Joey's face when he saw Lily. He ran over to her and threw his arms around her waist. "Oh, Mom, your face looks awful. What happened to you?"

"Easy, Joey, your mother needs some tender loving care right now." Wade patted Joey on the top of the head.

"How bad does it hurt?" Joey asked, and then tears slipped over his little lashes.

"I'm okay, Joey. Please, don't cry." Lily sat down on the sofa and pulled him onto her lap. "I'm okay."

He gently touched her face. "What happened to you?"

"I, ah…" Her gaze slipped up to both of the men, standing in front of her, hands on their hips. However, just as quickly she dropped it back to Joey. "I had an accident today. But I'm okay, I promise."

Joey wrapped his arms around her neck, and his sobs grew louder. "I don't want you to have black eyes."

The boy's sobs made Bryce's insides feel like they were being ripped out. He fought the urge to sweep them both up in his arms and hold them until everything was okay.

"Joey, I need to go lie down for awhile, would you like to go with me?" Lily finally asked.

Joey nodded.

When she started to get up from the sofa, Bryce rushed to Lily's side and took hold of her arm. "Let me help you."

"I'm not helpless, Bryce. I can make it to my room on my own."

"Humor me. It's the least I can do after—"

"Bryce." She pulled on his arm and looked down at Joey. "Some things are better left unsaid. Do you understand?"

He glanced down at Joey's red and swollen face. "Yes, I understand."

"I appreciate the offer, but I think Joey can help me to my room, can't you, little man?" Lily managed a smile down at her son.

"I can take care of you, Mom, I can. I'll even sing to you if you want me to."

"You know, I think that is just what I need to make me feel better."

With that, Lily and Joey disappeared down the hallway.

Kyle picked up his hat off the coffee table, shoved it on his head, and headed toward the front door where he hesitated. "I knew the way the two of you argue and fuss all the time, somethin' like this was bound to happen, but I didn't know Lily was going to be the one who would get hurt because of it. Don't you think it's about time both of you grow up?" Without another word, he opened the door and stepped out.

Bryce and Wade stood there in silence for several minutes until Wade finally turned to leave. "I guess there's nothing else I can do here. There's still a couple of hours left of daylight. I need to get back to work." Wade glanced down the hallway and heaved a sigh. "I'll tell the boys to finish up without you. Someone needs to be here for her if she needs anything."

However, Wade just stood there, staring down the empty hallway for a few more seconds. Then without another word, he turned and walked out the door.

Bryce felt as if he'd taken a punch to the stomach at what he'd seen in Wade's eyes. He knew Wade had feelings for Lily, but he never knew how deeply they ran until now. Wade was in love with her.

Now, the question lingered in his mind. What was he going to do about it?

A week later, Lily sat at her vanity table and examined her face in the mirror. Thankfully, the bruising was finally beginning to fade. The bridge across her nose was still tender to the touch, but it wasn't painful any longer. Over a week had passed since the accident and other than the bruising, Lily was beginning to feel like her old self again.

She dabbed the liquid foundation under her eyes, and within minutes, the bruises were mostly covered.

"You look like mom again." Joey sat on the foot of Lily's bed and tilted his head from side to side. His eyes widened with amazement at the magic the make-up had achieved.

"I'm glad you approve. Do you think I'm pretty again?"

Joey crossed the room and put his arm around her neck. "You're always pretty to me even with black eyes."

"I couldn't agree more." The familiar voice tickled her ears. She glanced in the mirror and saw Bryce leaning against the frame of the doorway. His hands were shoved in the pockets of his jeans.

"Hey, Bryce," Joey said.

"Hey there, little man."

"How long have you been standin' there?" Lily asked, turning as self-consciousness reached up and grabbed her throat.

"Not long." He leisurely walked up behind her, stared at her reflection, and smiled.

"You can't see her black eyes anymore, can you?" Joey pointed at Lily's face.

"No, I can't." Bryce spoke to Joey but kept his eyes on Lily's reflection.

"You're still goin' to the fair with us, aren't you?" Joey's eyes were filled with hope.

"Yes of course, I'm going." He scooped Joey up in his arms. "I wouldn't miss spending time with you and your mom for anything."

Lily lifted her eyes again and looked at Bryce in the mirror. Why did he have to say things like that? Because when he did, it made her heart beat slow and fast at the same time.

"Well, I guess I'm ready to go." She popped her hat on her head and gave herself one last glance. What the make-up didn't cover, the hat would cast enough of a shadow to finish the job.

When she turned around, she noticed Joey didn't have any shoes on. "Joey, where are your shoes?"

"Oops, I forgot." He stuck out one foot and wiggled his bare foot.

Bryce put Joey down on the floor. "You'd better do as your mom says."

"Yeap." With that, Joey darted out of the room.

Lily started toward the door, but Bryce stepped in front of her, blocking the doorway. "I do agree with Joey, even with black eyes, you're still beautiful." He reached out to touch her cheek, but she dodged his hand.

"We need to go. Joey's waitin'." She stepped to the side and tried to get past him without making any contact, but he took hold of her elbow.

Pulling her back in front of him to see into her face, he asked, "Okay, what's going on, Lily?"

"It's not important."

"It's important to me. You're important to me. I know there was something going on, but I haven't been able to put my finger on it. You've been going out of your way to avoid me. At first, I thought it might have been because you were the one hurt in the scuffle between Haston and me, but it started before that, didn't it? What's going on, Lily, talk to me."

"You really don't know, do you?" She looked up into his eyes and shook her head. "Look, I may be old-fashion, but that's just the way I am. I'd appreciate it if you didn't try to wine and dine me when you're —"

"Mom, I got my shoes on. When are we leavin'? Are y'all ready?" Joey yelled from the other room.

"When I'm what?" Bryce's brows crumbled, and he tipped his head to the side.

"It doesn't matter." Lily looked away, tucked a strand of hair behind her ear, and then wrapped her arms around her waist.

"It does matter. It matters to me. You matter to me." When he reached for her, she held up her hands and waved him away. "There's something going on between us, Lily, and I know you feel it too."

"Look, Bryce, the only thing between us is a business arrangement. I think it's best if we just go back to the original plan and we'll be fine." She pushed past him and left him standing in the doorway with a slack jaw and his mouth agape.

Joey chattered with excitement all way on the trip to town.

"Look, Mom. Look." Joey bounced up and down as soon as he spotted the Ferris wheel. "Hurry and park the truck, Bryce. Hurry, hurry."

"Joey, be still. You can't bounce around in the truck like that when Bryce is driving," Lily scolded.

"I'm sorry, Bryce. I didn't mean to bump into you. I'm just ready to ride the rides." Joey rubbed his hands together.

A laugh bubbled in Bryce's chest. "Yeah, me, too."

"There's one. There's one." Joey pointed out at an empty parking space.

Bryce parked the truck, and the three of them walked through the fair entrance.

"Can I ride the motorcycles first?" Joey grabbed Lily's arm and pulled her toward the section with the kiddy rides.

"Yes, you can. Why don't you ride all the kiddy rides first? And Bryce and I will watch you from over there." Lily pointed at a red painted bench.

Just as they sat down, Bryce slid against Lily, leaned in, and spoke close to her ear. "Lily, I'm not going to pressure you, but I'm giving you fair warning, I'm not giving up on us. I feel something for you, and whether you deny it or not, I know you feel something for me, too."

He was so close she could feel the warmth of his breath on her neck. His nearness made her senses spin. Bryce didn't have the slightest clue about the effect he had on her. Closing her eyes, she breathed in slowly to try to calm her pounding pulse.

"But this is Joey's day, so we'll discuss it later." His lips brushed her cheek with a light kiss. Then he slid away from her and stretched his arms out across the back of the bench.

They sat in silence and watched Joey run from one ride to another.

After a few rides, Joey scampered up to them, dragging another child along, and pointing at Bryce. "See. I told you. That's him."

"What are you doing, Joey?" Lily asked.

"This is my friend, Mark. I wanted him to see I'm really going to have a daddy." Joey's face lit up with excitement as he shuffled from one foot to the other. Joey pushed his friend closer to Bryce.

"Well, hello there, Mark. Glad to meet you." Bryce held out his hand to the child.

Mark shook Bryce's hand and narrowed his eyes. "Are you really gonna be Joey's daddy?"

"Yes, I really am." Bryce didn't even flinch when he answered the little boy's question.

Joey's smile widened as joy shone on his face, and he then turned to his friend, "See, I told you so." Joey stuck out his tongue.

"Joey!" Lily wagged her finger. "You know better than that. Now apologize."

"I'm sorry, Mark." Joey's glowing happiness faded, and his bottom lip quivered.

"It's okay. I do it to my big sister all the time. Let's go ride the boats again." Mark tugged on Joey's arm.

"Mom, can we go ride the boats again?" Joey asked as the light bounced back into his eyes.

"Go on. We'll be here." Lily laughed.

Bryce leaned forward and tugged Joey to him. "Joey, what do you say, when you get off the boats, we grab a corndog? How does that sound?"

"Okay." He grabbed Mark's arm, and off the boys ran toward the rides again.

She made up her mind; she wasn't going to worry about what was going to happen when the year ended. Right now, that was a long time away. She'd worry about it when the time came.

Lily looked at Bryce out of the corner of her eye. Not only had this man made a difference in Joey's life, but he had affected hers, too. Bryce had stirred something deep inside of her. Why couldn't he feel the same way? All he wanted was someone to keep him company while he was here, because if she meant anything to him, he wouldn't have another woman on the side.

Several minutes later, Joey came running up alone. "I'm ready for my corndog now."

"You got it, boss," Bryce teased and poked Joey in the belly.

Joey squealed with delight.

With Joey in the middle, the three of them walked hand-in-hand to the food stand.

"I like lots and lots of mustard on my corndog," Joey informed Bryce when he dipped his hand in the basket, holding the mustard packets.

"What about you, Lily, do you like lots and lots of mustard, too?" Bryce asked with a grin.

"No, I think one pack will do it for me."

Just as they sat down at one of the empty tables, a voice rang out, "Well, hello there." Lily looked up to see Sara waving and making her way through a group of teenagers.

Bryce rose to his feet and extended his hand. "Nice to see you again, Sara."

"I thought you would know by now, we don't do handshakes around here, honey." She pushed past Bryce's hand and hugged him. She then turned to Lily and gave her a hug. "I'm so glad y'all came today." She squeezed Joey's shoulder. "Are you having fun, Joey?"

"Uh, mmm." Joey nodded with a mouthful of corndog.

"Looks like you sure are enjoyin' that corn dog, too."

"Yes, Ma'am, it's yummy." A drop of mustard dripped from Joey's chin.

Sara threw her head back and let out a thunderous belly laugh. "I may just have to get me one of those."

"Would you like to join us for lunch, Sara?" Lily asked as she wiped the mustard off Joey's face.

"Thank you for inviting me, but I've got to meet up with my grandkids at the Tilt-A-Whirl in about ten minutes. I just wanted to stop by for a moment and say hello. You two look so happy."

"We are." Bryce reached out, took hold of Lily's hand, and lifted it to his lips. Afterward, instead of releasing her hand, he locked his fingers in hers and slid closer.

"I remember when my Thomas and I first got married. I pray your marriage will last as long as mine has." Sara turned and patted Lily's shoulder. "I couldn't imagine my life without my Thomas."

Bryce smiled at the tenderness and affection in Sara's voice when she talked about her husband.

"Ya know, it's a blessing from God when you find that special person you want to spend the rest of your life with." Sara nodded at Bryce, and her mouth curved into a loving smile.

Bryce kissed Lily's hand. "I agree."

Lily released a nervous laugh. She swallowed hard. Just his touch sent her emotions soaring, and play-acting without starting to believe it was getting more difficult all the time. She found it hard to concentrate with all of her nerves firing at once. "How…?" She cleared her throat. "How long have you and Mr. Stover been married?"

"Next month we'll be celebrating our fortieth wedding anniversary, and the fun part is I'm still in love with the old coot." Sara's eyes twinkled.

The statement warmed Lily's heart. There was no doubt, even after so many years of marriage, Sara was still deeply in love with her husband.

"Congratulations, Sara. Maybe you could give me and Lily some tips sometime on how to keep the fires burning." Bryce raised one brow and grinned.

"From what I've seen, I don't think y'all will need anybody's advice. But I will tell you this, I want you to remember one thing." She pointed at their intertwined fingers. "When that stops, the romance ends."

Bryce raised her hand and kissed it again. "We'll remember that."

Lily blushed.

"Whelp, I gotta run, or those grandbabies of mine will wonder what happened to Mawmaw." Sara hugged them both and waddled away.

Joey shoved the last bite of the mustard-drenched corndog into his mouth, chewed a couple of times, and washed it down with his Coke. "Mom, can we ride the Ferris wheel now?"

"Sure, I'm ready when you are."

"Bryce, do you want to ride it with us?" Joey asked.

"You'd better believe it." Bryce stood and tossed his cup into the trashcan.

Joey slid in between them. He slipped his hand into Lily's and then grabbed Bryce's with the other. Together, they headed off toward the Ferris wheel.

"Look, a clown. Can I go see him?" Joey tugged on Lily's hand.

"Go on, but stay where I can see you."

"I will." Joey pulled free and made a dash toward the clown.

Lily shoulder bumped Bryce and smiled up at him. "I have to say you played the part of a devoted fiancé quite well."

He grasped her elbow, pulled her in, and whispered into her hair. "Who said I was playing?"

The next morning, the aroma of coffee stirred Lily from sleep as it drifted into her room. She rolled over and looked at the clock. It was 7:16. "Who made coffee?" She slipped out of bed, dressed, and headed toward the kitchen. A note lay on the table.

Lily,

Joey and I wanted to let you sleep in. I put on a pot of coffee, and there's pancakes and sausages in the microwave.

Bryce

"He cooked for me?" A warm glow flowed through her, making her tingle all over. Just as she poured herself a cup of coffee, the squeal of Joey's laughter echoed through the kitchen. She glanced out the window to see Joey and Bryce jumping on the trampoline.

Joey screamed with delight when Bryce bounced him up and caught him in the air. The two of them were having such a wonderful time together. It was like watching a father with his son. Lily smiled when she saw the joy beaming from her son's face.

Then they started doing wrestling moves, and Joey pinned Bryce to the mat.

Joey was right.

Bryce would be a great father.

The sad but scary truth was she wanted Bryce to be Joey's dad. She wanted to be Bryce's wife. She wanted them to be a family, a permanent family.

Lily's heart weighed heavy in her chest. Why had she allowed herself to fall in love with this man? It would be so easy to give her heart to him. However, she wasn't the only woman in his life. There was Hannah. Who was she anyway? Was she just his girlfriend, or was there something more between them?

Tell Bryce I love him. Hannah's words reverberated in her ears.

She couldn't think about any of those things right now, it was too painful. With coffee in hand, she wandered out onto the front porch and sat down on the swing. As she swung lightly, she noticed her flowers looked somewhat wilted. Hoisting herself out of the swing, she hopped off the porch, grabbed the hose, and began watering the flowers.

"Whatcha doin'?" She heard Joey's voice behind her.

"I'm givin' the flowers a drink. What are you doin'?"

Joey slipped his hand in Bryce's and smiled up at him. "We've been jumping on the trampoline. It was so much fun, wasn't it?"

"You bet it was. I may not be able to get out of bed in the morning, but I enjoyed it." Bryce winked at her.

"I'm glad the two of you had fun. Joey, do you want me to spray you down with the water hose? You're all sweaty." Pointing the hose at Joey, she waited for the response she knew she would get.

"Yes, yes, yes." Joey jumped up and down, clapping his hands.

Lily squeezed the handle and water gushed out. "Here you go."

After a few seconds, Joey was drenched and giggling.

Lily cut her eyes over at Bryce and gave him an impish grin. "As a matter of fact, you look awful sweaty, too."

"I'd rather shower the old fashion way, thank you." He held up one hand and waved her off.

"Are you sure? I don't mind coolin' you off. I don't mind at all."

"Don't even think about it."

"Why? It's just a little water." She gave the sprayer a quick squeeze and sprinkled him with water and then pointed the nozzle directly at him.

"Lily." He held up one hand and waved a warning as he took a step toward her. "Don't do it."

"Wet him, Mom, wet him," Joey howled.

"Hey, whose side are you on, anyway?" Bryce grinned at Joey.

Joey laughed and squealed some more. "Get him, Mom!"

"Lily, put the hose down slowly and walked away. Just walk away, and no one will get hurt." Bryce inched toward her with his hands extended, looking as though he getting ready to pounce at any moment.

She hiked a brow. "I don't think so."

He leaped forward, but not before she squeezed the nozzle and the water came out full blast. Bryce fought through the stream of water while Lily screamed trying to dodge him.

Bryce wrapped one arm around her waist and grabbed the hose with his other hand. "Got ya."

"No!" Lily screamed. "Joey, turn off the water. Turn it off! Do it now. Hurry!"

"Don't do it, Joey," Bryce yelled. "We men have to stick together."

Bryce turned the nozzle on her and let it blast.

"No, no, stop," she screamed, trying to free herself from his grasp.

The ground around them was soaked with water. Fighting to regain control of the hose, Lily felt her feet slipping beneath her, and she grabbed onto Bryce to stay upright. However, when his feet began to slip too, she knew they were in trouble. The next thing Lily knew they were both on the ground, still struggling over the hose.

Finally, the water stopped.

Lily laid there exhausted, laughing, and trying to catch her breath. Bryce propped up over her and pushed her wet hair out of her face. "I don't think I've ever had so much fun cooling off." He looked down at her as his smile reached his eyes.

"Me either."

Bryce's Adam's apple bobbed up and down as he swallowed, and his smile turned serious. "I've never wanted to kiss anyone anymore than I want to kiss you right now. If only you knew what you do to me."

She wanted his kiss, too.

Lily opened her mouth to speak just as Joey screeched, "It's okay, Mom, I'll help you."

Joey jumped on Bryce's back and wrapped his arms and legs around him.

"Oh no! Help me, somebody! Get this octopus off of me," Bryce shouted, and then he rolled Joey to the side and started to tickle him.

Lily scrambled to get to her feet. "Okay, Joey, I think it's time to surrender." She looked down at her wet, muddy clothes and laughed. "I think we may need to go shower and get ready for church."

Bryce propped himself up on his elbows and smiled up at her causing a pleasant shiver to crawl up her spine. Even covered in mud, he was still a fine-looking man. His blue eyes sparkled in the summer sun, and his crooked smile lit up his face.

"Are you going with us this mornin'?"

"Yes, Ma'am, I sure am. I really enjoy Pastor Henry's sermons. After church, why don't the three of us go into town for lunch? Would you like to do that?"

"That would be nice." Heat radiated in her chest and traveled throughout her body. They were beginning to feel like a real family.

When they crossed the threshold of the church, Sara came waddling down the aisle. "Good mornin'." She enfolded Bryce and Lily in a tight squeeze.

"Good morning to you too, Sara. You look lovely today," Bryce said.

"You cute little sweet talker you." She pinched Bryce's cheek, and Lily saw his face redden.

"Lily, are you going to sing for us this mornin'?" Sara asked. "We haven't heard you sing in a while. We sure enough miss it."

Pastor Henry popped his head around Sara's shoulder and nodded. "I agree with Sister Sara, it's been much too long since we've heard you sing." Pastor Henry gripped Bryce's hand and gave it a hardy shake. "It's good to have you with us again this morning." He turned his focus to Lily. "So, how about it? Are you going to sing for us?"

Heat flushed her face. "Not this mornin'."

"Lily girl, you have to sing. Bryce, tell her," Sara pleaded.

Bryce tilted his head and wrinkled his brow. "I didn't know you could sing."

"You've never heard her?" Disbelief etched Sara's face. "You don't know what you're missin." She turned to face Lily again and gave her arm a gentle shake. "Lily, you have to sing now, if not for us, at least for your man."

"I think she isn't going to take no for an answer. Besides, I'd love to hear you sing." Bryce slid his hand under her elbow and gave it a gentle squeeze.

"Come on, Mom. Please sing," Joey pleaded as he tugged on her dress, looking up at her with his big brown puppy dog eyes.

"I think you're outnumbered, Lily." Pastor Henry grinned.

"It looks like you're right. Okay, I'll sing this mornin'." Her stomach tightened in one big knot at the thought of singing in front of Bryce.

Why? She had sung in front of a hundred people before. So why was her heart slamming into her ribcage?

After Lily sang her rendition of *My Redeemer Lives* with her knees feeling like wet noodles, she left the podium and took her seat again next to Bryce.

As soon as she was settled into her seat, he reached over, gripped her hand, leaned in close, and whispered into her ear. "Wow that was the most beautiful song I've ever heard."

Were those tears in his eyes? No, they couldn't have been. It probably was just a yawn or something.

"I know, it's one of my favorites," Lily swallowed the lump in her throat and whispered back.

"No, what I meant was, you're the one who made it beautiful. You never cease to amaze me, Lily. You make me love you more and more every day." He kissed her cheek and pulled away but still held her hand.

What? Did he just say he loves me?

Her heart slammed against her ribs as she tried to steady her breathing and give her attention to Pastor Henry. After several minutes of failing miserably to do so, her focus gravitated back to Bryce. She observed him as he intently listened to Pastor Henry's message.

Questions flooded her mind. Could she trust her heart to love again? Could she trust him? What about Hannah?

She glanced down at her hand in his, and a smile prickled on her lips. This felt right.

For the first time in years, Bryce had accomplished something no one else had ever been able to do. He made her believe she could love and be loved again.

Joy filled her soul as a tear slipped down her cheek.

Bryce turned, and concern filled his eyes. He gently wiped away the tear on her cheek with his thumb. "What's wrong?"

"Nothing's wrong. As a matter of fact, everythin' is just right."

After church, they decided to pick up a family pack of chicken from *The Chicken Shack* and eat lunch in the park.

Clouds began to move in, and Lily heard the rumble of a distant thunder. A rain shower would put a damper on their day, she thought. "It looks like we may get some rain."

"I'm finished with my chicken, Mom. Can Bryce push me on the swings before it rains, please?" Joey asked, wiping grease off his mouth.

"I think you need to ask Bryce that question, don't you?" Lily said, handing him another napkin.

"Bryce, will you push me on the swings before it starts rainin'?" Joey crawled up on his knees on the bench.

"Let's go. Lily, do you want me to push you on the swings, too?" Bryce smiled and waggled his eyebrows.

"I think I'll pass. You two go on. I'll get everythin' packed up here."

Several minutes later, Lily looked up and saw Bryce, Joey, Joey's friend Nathan, and Nathan's mother Beth, heading in her direction.

"Hey, Lily, I heard the good news." Beth smiled and turned her eyes toward Bryce. "I'm so happy for you." With that, she gave Lily a quick hug. "Wow, he sure is a cutie," Beth whispered in Lily's ear and giggled.

"I know," Lily replied, with a sly grin.

A raindrop hit her on the cheek as the two women pulled away.

"I came to ask you if Joey can come spend the night with Nathan." Beth smiled at the hyperactive boys.

"Mom, can I go to Nathan's? Please, I'll be good. I promise." Joey tugged on Lily's arm.

"Well, if you promise to be good, I guess it will be okay." Both boys squealed.

"Thanks, Mom. I promise to be good." Joey hugged her around the waist.

The raindrops increased.

"Thanks, Lily. I'll bring him home around noon tomorrow. Once again, congratulations. Let's go, boys, before the bottom drops out of the sky." Beth hurried to her car with both boys on her heels.

Bryce watched Joey all the way to the car, and when Joey waved bye, he smiled and waved back. "You know, I already miss him, and he's not even out of the parking lot yet."

Lily's head jerked upward. Her pulse quickened in her throat. That was something a father would say.

He lightly laid his hand on the small of her back. "Are you ready to head back to the ranch before the heavier rain gets here?"

She couldn't wait to spend more alone time with him. But before she could really enjoy herself, she had one question that simply couldn't wait any longer. Even if she received a heartbreaking answer, she had to know.

Lifting her eyes to meet his, she swallowed hard, and asked, "Bryce, who's Hannah?"

He crimped his brows. "Hannah?"

"I know it isn't any of my business, but I have to know who she is. I know I told you when you first got here that you could see other women if you wanted to. Is she someone in New York, or did you meet her here? How long have you been seeing her?"

"Whoa, whoa, whoa, wait a minute." He waved his hands at her. "Let me understand this. Is that why you've been pushing me away? You thought me and Hannah were…" Bryce shook his head, took hold of both of her arms, and drew her close. "Lily, Hannah is my best friend's wife. Over the last few weeks, I've been helping her plan a surprise birthday party for Jason. What made you think I was seeing her?"

Relief and joy rushed through her like a wildfire on a windy day. "When she called that day, she wanted me to tell you she loved you. Your world is so different from mine. I guess when you were in New York, you probably dated more than one girl at a time. You as much told me so yourself, and then there's our arrangement..."

"First of all, forget about our arrangement, and yes, back home, I never had a steady relationship with just one girl, but it's different now, I'm different now. I'm not that man any longer."

"Why?" Lily held her breath and bit down on her bottom lip.

"Because of you. No other woman has ever come close to touching my heart the way you do. I wake up in the morning with you on my mind. I go to bed at night with you on my mind. And, woman, you're even in my dreams."

She'd gone this far, she needed to be honest with him even though it pained her to admit it. "Bryce, everyone I've ever loved has left me one way or the other, except for Joey. How do I know you're not going to leave me too?"

He drew her into his arms. "I promise you, I'm not going anywhere. When I see my future, I see you right there with me."

Suddenly a crash of thunder rippled across the sky, and then heaven opened up and released its rain.

Standing in the torrential downpour, she linked her arms around his neck and laced her fingers in his rain-soaked hair and whispered, "Kiss me."

His smile broke through the rain streaming down his face as he skirted his arm around her waist and pulled her against his body. "My pleasure."

Her lips tingled for his kiss. Her heart rattled in her chest. Her body shivered with anticipation when he leaned in slowly and captured her lips with his. Warmth radiated throughout her. For a moment, time stood still as they were lost in each other's arms as his lips moved against hers in perfect harmony.

Moments later, when he released her lips, her breath lingered in her throat. The only word that came to mind was... *Breathless.*

Bryce was right. Lily knew in that instant that she could no more control her deep feelings for him than she could keep the sky from pouring out its heavy rain. She was a goner for sure. That both frightened her and exhilarated her.

CHAPTER
TWENTY-THREE

Over the next few weeks, Bryce and Lily's relationship deepened. Bryce began to believe his grandfather had known exactly what he was doing when he came up with his outlandish scheme to bring him and Lily together.

He no longer cared about the inheritance. He was rich enough just having Lily and Joey in his life. Now, the only thing left to do was to make it permanent.

Bryce sat on the front porch steps, fumbling with the small black velvet box in his hand as he watched the early morning sun burst above the horizon. He surveyed his grandfather's land. Lily's land. His land. Their land.

Cows bellowing in the distance, the hum of bumblebees, birds singing their songs to welcome the morning, the fragrance of the early morning dew, all filled his senses with wonder and awe.

As he stared at the unopened box, a chuckle escaped his throat and drifted away in the breeze. He thought about how his life had changed over the past three months.

After thinking back over his life, he had come to the shocking conclusion that he had always been a self-absorbed, arrogant, egotistical kind of man. He went after what he wanted with full vigor, with no regard for who might get hurt along the way.

Guilt twisted in his chest when he recalled some of the things he'd done.

He shook the memories out of his head when he spotted a sapphire colored bird as it flew in and out of the barn. Each time on his departure, he had a piece of straw in his beak. Bryce sat in awe as he watched this small creature work relentlessly on his task, building a home for his family.

Bryce smiled, amazed at how much enjoyment he'd received out of something so insignificant. He remembered how deafening the silence had been when he'd first arrived, but now he relished it, took pleasure in it even. Just like his grandfather, he could call this place home. It didn't matter where he lived. He would live in a cave if it meant being near her.

Bryce had never experienced true, fulfilling happiness before. A gentle quake shook his body when images of the dark-haired, dark-eyed girl with the contagious smile consumed his thoughts.

What had started out as a strong attraction had turned into something much, much more. He loved her. He needed her. He wanted to spend the rest of his life with her.

The squeaking sound of the screen door snagged his attention.

"Good morning. You're up early." The female voice behind him caused a rippling effect in his abdomen. His heart leaped when he turned and saw Lily standing in the doorway, holding two cups of coffee.

Her hair hung loose and hugged her shoulders with its long curls. She wore a sleeveless, lilac-colored sundress.

He quickly slipped the box back into his pocket. "Good morning to you, too."

"I thought you might like this." She pushed the screen door fully open with her knee and glided across the porch in her bare feet. "Would you mind if I join you?"

"You didn't even have to ask." With a sweeping motion of his hand, he invited her to sit and took one of the cups from her as she lowered herself down next to him.

Lily's eyes brightened as they moved over the pastures. "I love this time of morning. I've sat here many times with Martin and watched the sunrise. Isn't it the most breathtakin' thing you've ever seen?"

Bryce didn't take his eyes off her lovely face. "Yes, I have to agree. Breathtaking is the word I'd use, too."

She twisted around and met his gaze. "What are you doin'?"

"I'm just admiring the view." Breathtaking she was. He lost all awareness of his surroundings because everything else paled compared to her.

"But you're looking at…" Her cheeks flushed as she turned her face up, and a soft and lovely curve touched her lips.

"That's such a lovely shade of pink on you."

"Stop it." As she shook her head, a warm, light breeze stirred her hair causing a loose strand to fall across her face.

Without hesitation, he reached out, twined the strand around his finger, and tucked it behind her ear. Then he trailed the back of his fingers down her cheek. "Do I have to? I like seeing you blush."

"You're hopeless."

"You make me that way."

"Sorry, I'll try to change." She wrinkled her nose and gave him a teasing smile.

He seized her hand, locked his fingers in hers, and rubbed her hand in between both of his. "Oh no you don't, I like you just the way you are."

She slid closer and snuggled into him. Her touch was like electricity on his skin, her closeness caused his pulse to soar, and the scent of her strawberry shampoo pleasantly filled his senses. He closed his eyes and savored the moment.

If he was going to do it, this was the time. He swallowed the lump in his throat and spoke softly into her hair, "Lily, I have something for you."

"What?" Contentment filled her voice. She raised her head and met his gaze. The silver flecks in her dark eyes sparkled against the sunlight causing a rippling wave in his chest.

He stroked the side of her face with his fingers. "I don't want to marry you anymore because I have to. I want to marry you because I want to. I may not be the first man you've ever loved, but I want to be the last."

Her long eyelashes fluttered like butterfly wings. "Wh—what?"

He pulled the box from his pocket and slowly opened it. He got down on one knee in front of her. "I love you, Lily Meyers. Will you do me the honor of being my forever wife?"

Lily sat motionless for what seemed like an eternity.

"Say something." Bryce's eyes searched her face. Every muscle in his body twitched as he held his breath while he waited for a response.

"Yes, I say yes." She held out her trembling hand.

With a wave of relief, Bryce's heart started beating normally again. He slipped the ring onto her finger and pulled her to her feet and into his arms.

"I think we should seal the deal with a kiss."

She smiled and wrapped both of her arms around his neck. "I couldn't agree more."

"Lily." He breathed her name as his lips captured hers. A bolt of pure adrenaline shook his entire body when a soft moan bubbled in her throat. "You are so beautiful. If only you knew what you do to my head." He kissed her tender lips again. "And my heart. I love you."

"I love you, too." Lily whispered.

Suddenly Champ thundered up, jumped up against both of them with such force, he knocked them to the ground.

While they were down, the dog pounced on them and a licking frenzy began.

"Champ, no, no." Lily's laughter echoed in the mountain air.

"Down." Bryce pushed on Champ. "Come on, boy, down." But every time he opened his mouth with a command, he was silenced with a drooling tongue.

"What are y'all doin'?" Joey bolted out the front door and down the steps.

Bryce grabbed Joey around the waist and pulled him in. "Your mom and I don't want to have all the fun. Say good morning to Joey, Champ."

Champ's focus turned to Joey, and the dog happily greeted him with sloppy kisses.

"Yuck, doggy drool." Joey giggled, turning is head from side to side to avoid being lapped up.

Champ's attention was drawn away to the truck coming down the drive. He licked Joey one more time and dashed off barking toward the truck. Joey jumped up and ran off after the dog.

With one look, Bryce moaned. "Wade. Great."

Lily gripped Bryce's arm. "Listen, I don't want you to say anything to him about this." She held up her hand and wiggled her fingers. "I need to be the one who tells him about us. I think it will be best comin' from me. Let's not add any more fuel to the fire between the two of you. Give me a few minutes with him before comin' in."

"Are you sure about this? You know he isn't going to like it. If he loses his temper, I'll—" Bryce balled his fist at his sides as his shoulders stiffened.

Lily was his true-to-life fiancée now, and there was no way under God's blue sky that Wade was ever going to put his hands or his arms on her again. Recalling the times Wade would wrap his arms around Lily and kiss her on the cheek or on the head, Bryce knew Wade would do it just to get under his skin, and it always worked. However, all of that was going to stop today, he was going to make sure of it.

"I can handle Wade. We just need to get this out in the open as quickly as possible." The sun sparkled in her eyes, making Bryce's stomach flip-flop.

The delicate touch of her fingers on his arm made all of the anger and tension that had built up inside of him melt away. "And then we can plan our real wedding."

She turned away, threw her hand up with a wave, and yelled when Wade stepped out of his truck. "Mornin', Wade. Are you having breakfast with us this mornin'?"

"Yeap, be up in a sec," he shouted, reaching in the truck to grab his hat.

She gave him a thumbs-up. "I guess I need to go start breakfast."

Bryce snagged her arm when she turned to go up the steps and drew her close. "Hey, do you think later we can finish what we started before Champ interrupted us?"

"It's possible."

"Can I get that in writing?"

She giggled. "You're impossible. Would you please keep Joey out here with you and give me a few minutes alone with Wade? The sooner I do this the better off we'll all be."

"I'll do anything you ask me to. What's the southern aphorism I'm looking for? Oh yes," he snapped his fingers. "I think I just might be hen-pecked."

She laughed, bounded up the steps, and disappeared into the house.

Bryce was picking up their coffee cups when Wade came up behind him. "The two of you sure did look awfully chummy. Is there anything I should know?" Wade's gravelly voice from behind him raked over Bryce's nerves, but he stoically held his temper and his tongue.

Over the last couple of weeks, the two men had stayed clear of one another, but they both knew where each one stood, and neither was willing to give an inch.

Bryce turned and dumped out the coffee from one of the cups onto the lawn. "I think I've already made it perfectly clear, Wade, anything that goes on between me and Lily isn't really any of your business."

"Hey," Wade grabbed Bryce's arm and jerked him around. "Your day in the sun is almost over, city boy. Haven't you been wondering why I've been laying so low over the last couple of weeks? Well." His twisted grin made Bryce flinch. "Lily's gonna soon find out exactly who you are and what you're up to. But, I don't want you to worry yourself none because I'll be the one who will be here holding Lily's hand and helping her pick up the pieces long after you're gone."

Bryce jerked his arm away and stepped nose-to-nose with Wade. "I'm not going anywhere, Haston, so you'd better learn to deal with it now. As a matter fact, I'm about to make Trinity my permanent home, and there's nothing you can do about it."

Wade laughed with a snort, stepped past Bryce, turned, and walked backward toward the door. "I wouldn't be so sure about that. You never know when something unexpected can come along and turn your world upside down. You know, I think I'm in the mood for some of Lily's home-cooked biscuits this mornin'. My advice? You'd better enjoy them while you can." He gave a short laugh, began to whistle a tune, and walked inside the house.

Bryce gritted his teeth as he raked his hand through his hair. Wade was up to something. He could feel it in his bones, but the problem was he had no idea what. He shook off the uneasy feeling in his gut.

"Are you ready to go eat breakfast?" Joey asked when he bounced up the steps with Champ on his heels.

"Let's talk for a few minutes before going in."

"Okay, what do you want to talk about?" He jumped up in the porch swing.

"Have you lost your mind?" Wade's angry voice rushed through the open screen door. "No! I won't let you do this, Lily. If you don't put a stop to it, then I will."

Joey jumped up to run in the house, but Bryce stopped him and picked him up in his arms. "Whoa, hold up there."

Wade charged out the door, slamming it against the wall so hard it caused some of the paint to crumble off. He took a step toward Bryce but then looked at Joey.

"I'll stop you if it's the last thing I ever do." With that, he stormed out across the yard toward his truck.

Lily ran out the door and down the steps. She had to make him understand. She just had to. "Wade, please, try to understand."

289

However, smack in the middle of the driveway, Wade spun around on his heels and held up his hand for her to stop. Like an obedient child, she froze in her steps.

"Understand what, Lily? I understand you're making the biggest mistake of your life, and you're just too blind to see it." Stomping over, Wade jerked open his truck door and looked back at them once more. "But, I'm gonna show you. I will prove to you just what kind of man he really is."

Lily's bottom lip quivered when Wade spun around in the driveway and drove off, his tires kicking up a huge dust cloud.

"What's wrong with Wade? Where's he going?" Joey asked with tears in his eyes as Lily came back up on the porch.

"He's okay, Joey. He just needs some time to cool off." Lily rubbed the chill out of her arms. "I'm sure he'll be back in a little while. C'mon, let's get breakfast goin'."

As they walked into the house, Bryce wrapped his arm around Lily's waist, hugging her close. "Are you okay?"

"I didn't want to hurt him, but he needed to know." Worry wrinkles creased her forehead as she chewed on her fingernail.

"I'm not worried about Wade. I want to know if you're all right."

She turned into him, slipped her arms up around his neck, and planted a light kiss on his lips. "I'm better than all right. You've made my life perfect."

Over the next few days, Lily tried to mend the damage done to her friendship with Wade, but he refused to have any contact with her at all.

She missed him, but she finally decided it was best to give him some time. He would eventually come around. Wouldn't he?

A week later, after Sunday morning service, Bryce and Lily sat on the front porch and watched Joey throw a stick for Champ to retrieve. "Why don't we pack a picnic lunch and go fishing down at the lake? Since Joey is starting back to school tomorrow, it will be a great way to end his summer break. I can't believe it's already the fourth of August."

"That's a great idea. Joey would love that. We'll go in the truck instead of horseback so we can carry some folding chairs; the ground gets pretty hard after a while."

He leaned over, kissed her cheek, and then whispered in her ear. "I'll grab Joey, and we'll get the fishing gear together if you want to go ahead and pack us a lunch."

"Deal." Lily got up, tilted her head toward him, and gave him one of the sweetest smiles he'd ever seen. It was the kind of smile that made his heart do funny things in his chest, and then she slipped into the house.

Bryce breathed in her perfume that still lingered in the air, and thrill chills zipped up and down his arms. He rubbed his arms, breathed in a sigh of contentment, and stood. "Hey, Joey, you want to go fishing with your mom and me?"

Joey dropped the stick and sprinted to the porch. Champ was jumping around behind him still wanting to play. "Yes, yes, yes, I'd love to go fishin'."

"You want to help me get the fishing gear together?"

"C'mon I'll show you where it's at."

They gathered up all the fishing rods, tossed them over into the bed of the truck, and headed inside.

"Mom, I told Bryce he could use Grampy's tackle box, but I can't find it. Do you know where it is?" Joey picked up a slice of ham and shoved it into his mouth.

"I think it's in the top of his closet. Bryce, I'm up to my elbows in sandwiches here. Would you mind going to check and see if it's there?" Lily pointed the mayonnaise-covered knife toward the hallway. "And, Joey, would you run and get the blue cooler off the back porch?"

"Sure, I'll go check." Bryce nodded, stealing a slice of ham for himself. Lily gave him a gentle shove. Her laugh delighted his senses as he trotted out of the kitchen.

Bryce opened the door to his grandfather's room and stepped inside. The room was dimly lit and smelled like pipe tobacco smoke. He picked up a framed photograph from the bedside table. It was his grandfather holding a smiling Joey in his lap. "You loved them, didn't you? And you knew I would love them too." He placed the frame back on the stand.

As he rummaged through the closet, he spotted what he thought might be the tackle box on the top shelf. When he began to pull it down, his elbow caught another box and knocked it off the shelf, spilling its contents on the floor.

He bent down and began putting the papers and other items back in the box. When he picked up a stack of letters tied together with a ribbon, his heart stopped.

Sweat splattered his forehead, and he dropped to his knees.

CHAPTER
TWENTY-FOUR

"Mom, what's taking Bryce so long? Do you want me to go check on him?" Joey asked, fidgeting.

Lily glanced at the rooster clock on the wall. Bryce had been in Martin's room for at least twenty minutes. An odd feeling played in the pit of her stomach. Something didn't feel right, and she needed to find out what was wrong. Making her voice sound light, she patted Joey's shoulder. "No, I'll go. I'm sure he just got sidetracked. Would you run into my room, get one of the big quilts out of my trunk, and take it to the truck for me? We're gonna need one to sit on for our picnic."

"Okay, but tell him to hurry. I'm ready to go fishin'."

"I will. Now scoot." As soon as he was gone, Lily traipsed down the hallway to Martin's door. She still hated going in there. "Bryce?" Lily eased the door open and stepped into the room. Looking around, she found Bryce sitting on the floor reading something. His shoulders were slumped, and when he raised his head, his slack expression caused a tightening in her heart.

"Bryce, what's wrong?" She rushed over, knelt down in front of him, and squeezed his arm. "What's wrong? Are you okay?"

"You see this stack of letters?" He pointed at the pile of letters on the floor in front of him.

"Yes, what are they?"

"When my grandfather first left, I received one letter from him. One." He held up his index finger, pain illuminating his eyes. "And these are the letters I wrote back to him. I wrote my grandfather almost every day for months after he left. Do you see this stack of letters?" Bryce pointed at another pile of letters with a shaky finger.

"Yes."

He shoved his hand through his hair and took a deep breath. "These are the letters he wrote back to me."

The pain in his face caused a deep ache inside of Lily. She softly touched his arm and moved in closer to him. "I don't understand, Bryce."

He picked up the stack and handed it to her. "Read what it says on the front of every one of the envelopes."

Lily took the letters, and her eyes skimmed over the top one. She was beginning to understand now. As she flipped through them, *Return to Sender* was hand-written on every single one. "Oh, Bryce, I'm so sorry."

"I would ask my mother every day if I got any letters from him, and she would always tell me no. I grew to hate him because I thought he didn't love me enough to answer any of my letters." He pointed to the hand-written, *Return to Sender*. "That's her handwriting, Lily. My grandfather answered every single one of my letters, and she sent all of them back to him."

A pang shot through her heart like a bullet out of a gun. She shook her head in disbelief.

"In this letter, Grandfather explains the reason he left New York. He had been under such extreme stress and suffered a heart attack that almost took his life. His doctor told him if he didn't get out from underneath the stress, the next heart attack would kill him. A distant cousin of his owned this ranch and offered to sell it to him. Grandfather begged the family to move with him, and they all refused, even my grandmother."

He pressed his palms against his eyes and let his head fall back against the wall. "All this time, my mother let me suffer, thinking my grandfather didn't care anything about me, and the whole time she knew the truth. My grandfather died not knowing. He died thinking I didn't care about him."

The bedroom door creaked, and Joey inched inside. His eyes widened when he spotted them. Easing up beside them, he laid his hand on Bryce's shoulder. "Bryce, are you okay?"

Bryce wiped his eyes and pulled Joey down onto his lap. "I'm just fine, buddy. Are we ready to go fishing? Maybe we'll catch our supper today."

"I want to catch a catfish this long." Joey stretched out his arms.

"Well, then let's go and see what we can do about that."

Bryce lifted Joey to his feet, pushed himself up, and held his hand down to Lily. She slipped her hand in his, and he pulled her to her feet.

"I bet I can beat y'all to the truck." Joey raced out the door.

Lily grabbed Bryce's arm when he moved past her. "We don't have to go fishin' today, Bryce. I know all of this is heartbreakin' for you, if you need some time to—"

"No, I think I need to get some fresh air to process all of this. Besides, I promised Joey we'd go fishing, and I'm not going to break my promise."

After lunch, Bryce and Lily sat on the bank of the lake with their fishing lines in the water. Joey splashed around in the water with Champ.

Bryce had not said any more about the letters, but she could see his mind was a million miles away.

"Do you want to talk about it? I can lend you a shoulder and an ear if you need 'em."

A smile pulled at the corner of his mouth. "Thank you, but I think I'll be all right."

"Are you going to talk to your mother about what you've found out?"

"No, she'll just try and lie her way out of it like she always does when it suits her, but now I know the truth for myself and that's all that matters."

"Maybe she had a reason to do what she did."

"You're always trying to find the good in people, aren't you? I assure you whatever reason she had, it was a selfish one." Pain and anger washed over his face.

How could a mother do such a horrible thing to her son? Lily wondered but kept the thought to herself. "When was the last time you talked to her?"

"The last time I spoke to her was couple of weeks after I arrived. Sid had a consultation with one of his many lawyers, and they informed him there wasn't anything he could do to change Grandfather's will."

Thank you, Lord. Lily silently whispered a prayer of thanks. She'd prayed many times she wouldn't have to deal with those cruel and vicious people ever again.

"Mother was livid about the whole ordeal, so she told me I wouldn't hear from her again until I received my inheritance and came to my senses about…" His cheeks turned red, and his gaze slipped away from her face and fell to the ground.

"Me." Lily finished his sentence.

He reached over, took hold of her hand, and pulled it to his chest. "I have come to my senses about you. You're the best thing that's ever happened to me. As long as I have you and Joey in my life, nothing or no one else matters."

Lily gave him a reassuring smile, but it saddened her heart to see the hurt in his eyes. She took hold of his hand. "Bryce, if you'll put all of this in God's hands, He will work it out for you, I promise."

Tears filled Bryce's eyes. "Will you pray with me?"

"Yes of course."

They bowed their heads and prayed together.

Later, Lily stretched out on the quilt and watched Bryce and Joey fish. The realization that they were going to be a real family filled her with joy and excitement.

"Bryce, you got a bite! You got a bite!" Joey yelled and came running out of the water.

Bryce snatched up his pole and began reeling the line in. "What do I do now?"

"Keep reeling it. It must be a big one. It sure is puttin' up a fight." Joey leaped up and down. "Reel it, reel it, don't let it get away."

Lily watched Bryce trying to pull the fish in. The more he reeled, the closer he came to the edge of the bank.

"Bryce, you're gonna fall in the—"

Splash!

Bryce went off into the water, and Joey went right in behind him. Lily ran and peered over the edge and then burst out laughing when she saw Bryce soaked to the bone and standing in waist deep water, still holding the fishing rod.

He grinned up at her, lifted the rod in the air, and dangling on the end of the line was a large-mouth bass.

"Look, Mom! Can you believe it? He caught it."

"Bryce, you know if you catch 'em you get to clean 'em for supper." Lily giggled.

His brows shot up. He cut his eyes over at the flopping fish and looked back at her. "Do you think we can have chicken for supper?"

Bryce sat on his bed with all of his grandfather's letters scattered around him. His grandfather had loved him. It was apparent in every word written on each page.

He found one letter his grandfather had written to his mother, Sherry Ann. Apparently, she had opened and read where his grandfather had asked if she would allow Bryce to come and live with him for a while in Alabama. She wrote the word *NO* in red marker across the top of the letter, taped it back closed, and scribbled *Return to Sender* across the front of the envelope.

Bryce battled with trying to understand why his mother had been so cruel. Had she refused to let Bryce go to his grandfather's because she didn't want her son to leave? Or did she refuse because she wanted to be spiteful to her father? He chose to give her the benefit of the doubt. He wanted to believe it was the love she had for him that caused her to do what she did.

Surprisingly, Bryce felt a peace about the whole ordeal. Now, he had concrete evidence that his grandfather loved him and knowing that took away all the bitterness and anger he had felt toward his grandfather for almost half of his life. As far as his mother, what she did was horrible, but she was still his mother, and he loved her and forgave her.

Why cause unwanted heartache over something that had happened fifteen years ago? It was time to let go of the past and take hold of his future.

He packed all of the letters back in the box and slid it under his bed.

He felt that peace that passes all understanding that Pastor Henry had preached about earlier that morning. Bryce had never been a religious man, but the feeling inside of him made him close his eyes and whisper a prayer of thanks to the Father up above.

The following Saturday morning, Bryce stepped out onto the front porch, stretched, and breathed in the fresh air. He looked out across the yard and saw Joey sitting on the ground beside his bicycle. The little guy looked upset.

Bryce crossed the yard and flopped down on the ground beside Joey. "What's wrong, little man?"

He hugged his legs and plopped his chin on the top of them. "I wished I could ride my bike without the trainin' wheels, but I don't know how."

"Do you want to try it? If you do, I can take the wheels off for you."

"I don't know. I'm afraid I'll fall."

"I'll be there right beside you to make sure that won't happen."

Joey's face brightened, and he smiled. "Ya mean it? You'll help me?"

"Sure I will. What do you say? You want to try it?"

"Yes." Joey sprang to his feet, grabbed Bryce's arm, and tugged him to his feet. "Let's do it. Let's do it now."

"Let's get some tools from the barn." Bryce headed toward the barn with Joey following in his tracks.

After he found the tools he needed, he returned to the bike and removed the training wheels.

"Are you ready?" Bryce asked as he steadied the bike for Joey to climb on.

"You won't let me fall, right?"

"I promise, I'll be right here to catch you if you fall."

Joey looked past Bryce and waved. "Hey, Mom. Look, Bryce is gonna teach me to ride my bike."

"I can see that. Are you sure you're ready, Joey?" Lily tucked her hair behind her ear and wrapped her arms around her waist.

Bryce had grown fond of the way Lily would slip her hair behind her ear when she was nervous or upset. He flashed her a reassuring smile. "Don't worry, Lily. I'll stay right by his side. I won't let anything happen to our son."

Lily nodded and sat down on the swing. "Okay."

Thirty minutes later, Bryce noticed Joey was controlling the bike on his own. He took a deep breath, let go of the bike seat, and watched Joey as he pedaled his bike all on his own.

"You're doing it, Joey. You're riding your bike on your own," Bryce yelled.

Joey turned the bike in a big circle, pedaled back, and then stopped it on his own. "Mom, did you see me? Did you see me ride my bike on my own?"

"I sure did."

"I'm so proud of you, Joey." Bryce bent down and stretched out his arms.

Joey jumped off the bike, sprinted toward Bryce, ran into his arms, and wrapped his arms around his neck. "I did it, Daddy. I did it."

Bryce's heart swelled as he swallowed the knot in his throat. "Yes, you did."

Joey wiggled out of Bryce's arms. "I'm gonna do it again."

Lily eased up beside Bryce, slipped her hand in his, and leaned against him. "You know Joey has been right all along."

"Right? Right about what?" He pulled back slightly and stared into her face.

"You are a great dad."

CHAPTER
TWENTY-FIVE

"If I didn't know any better, I'd think you just got engaged, Lily. You seem happier now than you did when we first started planning your wedding," Kitty said as she elbowed her in the arm. "I sure hope when I meet Mr. Right, I'm as happy as you are."

"She's in love, Kitty," Sara said and pulled her car into a parking spot in front of Daphne's Bridal. "I still can't believe the weddin' is only a little over a week away."

Lily's face warmed just thinking about Bryce. "I want to thank both of you again for helping me pick out my wedding gown."

"Sweety-Girl, you don't have to thank us. We should be thankin' you for lettin' us be a part of plannin' your weddin'." Sara looped her plump arm through Lily's.

Like a herd of ducks rushing to get into the water, the three of them scurried toward the door of the boutique and stepped inside the large room.

Lily's eyes widened at the racks and racks of white and even off-white wedding gowns and the brightly colored bridesmaid dresses hanging throughout the store. She had no idea where to begin.

But Sara sure did. She waddled around the store as fast as she could and grabbed several dresses and all but shoved them in Lily's face. Kitty had her arms full of them, too.

"Now, you just go on and try these on, honey. And don't you be takin' them off until you let us see you in 'em, ya hear? Now scoot." Sara and Kitty loaded Lily's arms with the dresses.

The saleswoman hurried to her side, apologized for not greeting her sooner, relieved her of her burden, and then led her to the nearest changing room.

"What do y'all think about this one?" Lily asked when she stepped out of the dressing room in the fourth dress she'd modeled. "I think this is the one."

"Oh, Lily. You're beautiful." Kitty touched her hand to her chest.

Sara dabbed her eyes with a tissue. "I agree with ya. You don't have to try on any more. That one is you."

Lily gazed at herself in the mirror and took a deep, calming breath. Her hands tingled when she ran her fingers over the silk and tiny pearls on the waist of the wedding gown. She wondered if she should pinch herself to see if all of this was real.

She was happy. Truly happy. Bryce's face flooded her mind, and a warm feeling radiated through her chest, vibrating her insides. She couldn't wait to wear this dress and to say her I do's. A smile crossed her face. "I'll take this one,"

Lily said to the saleswoman when she came back into the room.

"Excellent choice. Your groom is one very lucky man."

No, the saleswoman had it all wrong...*she* was the lucky one.

Later at home, Lily unzipped the bag and lifted out her wedding gown. She held it against her body and looked at herself in the mirror again. "Hello, soon-to-be Mrs. Bryce Fowler," she said to her own reflection, and the words made her lips tingle. She smiled and heaved a happy, contented sigh.

The grandfather clock downstairs chimed, alerting Lily of the time. "It's almost time for Joey to get home from school. I need to get my head out of the clouds and get his snack ready."

She carefully placed the gown back in its bag, hung it in the closet, and skipped down the stairs. It was as if she was walking on air.

Happiness filled her heart. Life was perfect. She pinched herself to make sure she wasn't dreaming. "Nope, it's not a dream. Thanks to you, Mr. Bryce Fowler."

Just as she reached the last step, the phone rang. "Hello?" She almost sang into the phone.

"Is this Lily Meyers?"

"Yes it is."

"Miss Meyers, this is Sherry Ann Fowler, Bryce's mother."

A sickening feeling started in the pit of Lily's stomach and traveled upward.

"Bryce isn't here at the moment. Can I take a message?"

"I don't want to speak to my son. I wanted to speak to you." The coldness in the woman's voice made Lily want to slam the phone down and run and hide.

Get a grip, Lily. You're not a child. Lily's legs shuddered. "Me?"

"What other reason would I have for calling this number? If I'd wanted to speak with Bryce, I would call his cell phone like I always do." Sherry Ann's snarly voice made Lily's skin crawl like she was covered in spiders.

"Yes, Ma'am, what can I do for you?"

"Miss Meyers, you may have fooled my father and convinced him to leave half of everything to you, but I can assure you, you haven't fooled my son. He's a very clever young man if you haven't already noticed, and he'll do whatever it takes, and I do mean whatever it takes, to receive what is rightfully his. I just thought you needed to know. I've seen a long trail of broken hearts following my son, and it would be such a shame for you to be one of them."

"Mrs. Fowler, I don't mean you any disrespect, but I'm not worried. Bryce is a good man with a good heart, and I love him, and I know he loves me, too."

"Loves you? Oh, please. Do you actually believe Bryce would be in love with someone like you? A farm girl? He's just in it for the money and nothing else."

"I don't have to listen to this. Good-bye, Mrs. Fowler."

"Wait, did he tell you who Hannah really is?"

Lily's hand froze in mid-air, and then she pulled the receiver back to her ear. "Yes, he did. He said Hannah was his friend's wife."

"Really? Ha! Well, if that were true, I don't believe Bryce would have been dating her for the last three years, do you?"

Panic like she'd never known before welled in her throat. Fighting back tears, Lily swallowed hard and found her voice. "What? That can't be true."

"Are you really that naïve? He lied to you, honey. He's been lying to you the entire time he's been there. The ring you're wearing for example, it isn't real. He just had to convince you it was real just long enough to make sure that Wade fellow didn't get in his way. He told me he thought Wade might be in love with you, so he had to do whatever he had to do, to keep him away from you. Shall I go on?"

"Why are you telling me all this?" The tears burned in her eyes like gasoline.

"Because I thought if you knew the truth, after the wedding, you would take your son and leave. Everything there rightfully belongs to Bryce anyway, and I want to make sure he gets it all. Don't stand in my son's way, Miss Meyers, or you and your son will be the ones who will suffer the consequences."

Click.

Lily stared at the receiver like it was an evil creature draining the life out of her. Didn't Bryce say he hadn't spoken to his mother since he arrived? So, how did she know about Hannah? The ring? Wade?

Lily's world came crashing down around her when the reality of Sherry Ann's word sank into her brain. The only way that evil woman would have known any of this was if Bryce had told her himself.

"He lied. He lied to me." She crumbled to the floor as bitter sobs wracked her body.

"I can't believe we finished up early today. I think I'm gonna go get my girl and take her into town for dinner," Greg said as they loaded up the truck to head back to the ranch.

"I think I'm going to spend some alone time with my girl too." Bryce grinned as he slammed the tailgate.

"I still can't believe the two of you are getting married. I guess the old saying 'love at first sight' was meant for you and Lily. I really am happy for you, man."

Bryce reached out and gripped Greg's shoulder. "Greg, I want to ask you something."

"What's that?"

"Well, I feel like we've become friends over the last few weeks, and I'd like to ask you to stand up with me at my wedding. Greg, would you consider being my best man?"

"Your best man? Why, I'd be right honored. Absolutely. I've never been a best man before. Cool." The men shook hands and gave each other a quick man-hug.

When they arrived at the ranch, Bryce excitedly leaped up on the porch. He was looking forward to spending some time with Lily. To see her smile. To hear her laugh. To smell the sweet fragrance of her perfume.

"Lily, I have something to tell…" His heart stopped when he saw her in a heap on the floor with the tears streaming down her face. "Lily?" He rushed to her, and when he touched her arm, she jerked away.

"Don't touch me! Don't you ever touch me again." Her face was swollen and red. It appeared she'd been crying for a while.

"Lily, what's wrong? What's happened?"

She glared at him with burning, reproachful eyes. Her lips thinned with anger. "Like you don't know. How could I have been so blind?" Pulling herself up from the floor, her body swayed when she got to her feet.

He thought she might fall so he reached for her again, but she shoved him back. "Don't! Wade was right all along about you. Get out!"

"Lily, what are you talking about?" His mind reeled with confusion as he watched his happily-ever-after slipping away. The hatred he saw in her eyes ripped his heart in two. "Lily, talk to me. I'm not going anywhere until you tell me what's going on."

"Fine, if you won't leave, then I will."

She shoved past him and started toward the front door, but he grabbed her. "Oh no, you don't. Not until you talk to me."

"Let go of me." Lily's nostrils flared with fury.

"No." He took hold of both of her arms and tightened his grip. "Talk to me."

"Okay, if you want to know, your little secret's out now. Your mother called me today. She told me everything. Bryce, I trusted you. I trusted you with my heart. I guess money really is the root of all evil. How could you be so cruel?" Lily threw the words at him like stones, each one hitting their mark.

Panic rushed through him because he knew if his mother was in the middle of this, it wasn't good. "Lily, what exactly did my mother say to you? I haven't spoken to her in—"

"Don't lie to me! I know you've been talking to her." She jerked both arms free from his grip and pushed him away.

Her words cut deep into his heart. A sudden coldness hit him at his very core. "No, I haven't spoken to her in weeks. Lily, please you have to listen to me. My mother can't be trusted, you know that." He took a step toward her, but she held up a hand.

She clenched her jaw and narrowed her eyes into slits. "Well, isn't that the pot callin' the kettle black." She turned and grabbed her bag off the hook.

"Lily, please. We need to sit down and talk about this."

Whipping back around, she shook her head. "I have to get out of here. I can't be around you right now."

What had his mother done? What had she said to Lily?

"Lily, you have to believe me."

"Believe you? I did once, but not anymore." She jerked open the door, and without turning, said over her shoulder, "I don't know when I'll be back. Don't call me because I won't answer."

He stared at the door for a long time after Lily left. What was he going to do now? His world had just walked out the door with his heart in her hand.

Bryce paced the floor. It was ten o'clock, and Lily still had not returned. He'd called her cell phone, but no answer. He'd stepped on the porch and looked down the road in hopes of seeing headlights. Only darkness stared back at him.

"Lily, where are you?" he whispered into the warm night air.

What had his mother said to Lily? He'd tried calling his mother too for some answers, but he wasn't at all surprised that she didn't answer her phone. After the first few calls, she must have shut her phone off because his calls now went straight to her voice mail.

"Mother, what have you done?" was all he said on her voice mail in his last attempt to contact her.

He needed answers because the pain he'd seen in Lily's eyes devastated his heart. He shoved his hand through his hair. He had to fix this, but how?

The next morning, Bryce stretched, rolled over in bed and looked at the alarm clock. It was 6:35. He'd dozed off somewhere around four-thirty. Jumping up, he jerked aside the curtains and breathed a sigh of relief when he saw her truck parked in front of the house.

Bryce quickly dressed and jerked on his boots. It only took him seconds to cross the yard. Just as he reached the steps, Wade came out of the house and pulled the door closed behind him.

"Is she here?"

"I don't think she wants to see you. She's still pretty upset, and it looks like she's been crying all night." Wade pulled off his hat, pushed his hand through his hair, and looked back at the door. "I've never seen her like this before."

"I have to see her, Wade. I have to talk to her."

"She asked me to give this to you." Wade held out Lily's ring.

Bryce's hand shook when he reached out and took the ring from Wade With no strength left in him, he dropped down onto the swing.

"Well, I need to get to work." Wade started down the steps.

"Wade, I know we have made it obvious there is no kind of friendship between us, but I'm asking you, did she say anything to you? I don't understand what happened."

Wade turned and looked right at Bryce. "It's not my place. If Lily wants you to know, she'll be the one to tell you."

"Please, Wade. I feel like my heart's been ripped out of my chest. I'll do whatever I have to do to make this right."

Wade didn't reply for a long time but just stood there, one foot down off the top step, twisting his hat between his fingers. "You know when I first met Lily, I thought she was the sweetest little thing this side of the Mississippi. She was so good to Martin, and I could see the way he acted toward her, she was like a daughter to him. I'd never met anyone like her before, and then about a year ago I realized I had fallen in love with her."

Bryce didn't reply.

"But as heartbreaking as it was, I soon realized she didn't feel the same way about me. Then one day she told me I was the closest friend she'd ever had and that she loved me like a brother." Wade chuckled, but there was no humor in it. "After that I never told her how I felt. I figured as long as I got to be around her, hopefully one day she would begin to feel the same way about me. Then you come along." He twisted on the step and looked Bryce in the eyes. "She's never looked at me the way she would look at you. It wasn't long before I knew she was falling in love with you. I thought I was doing what was best, I was protecting her, but to see her like this." The moment stretched into two, and then the cowboy shook his head. "I can't do it. I just can't do it."

Confusion zipped through Bryce's mind. "What are you talking about? What can't you do?"

Wade stepped back up and towered over Bryce in the swing. "I thought I had you all figured out, Fowler, but maybe, just maybe I misjudged you. So right here, I need to know how you really feel about Lily. Do you really love her, or are you only here for the money? And this time, I want the truth."

Bryce thought through the answer from beginning to end. Saying it, admitting it nearly tore him in two. "When I first got here, I won't lie, yes, it was all about the money, but then Lily changed my whole world. To answer your question, I'd give up all the money, the ranch, everything, just to have her in my life. Yes, Wade, the truth is, I love Lily more than my own life."

The cowboy's nod was long and sad. "Then I've got to make this right." He snatched Bryce up by the front of his shirt. "Come on, you're coming with me."

"What? What are you doing?" Wide-eyed and stumbling, Bryce half followed, half tripped his way with Wade up to and through the door. He considered telling the man that he was capable of walking, but with the mood Wade was in, he wasn't sure that was healthy.

"Just shut up, and come on."

When they reached Lily's bedroom door, Wade knocked and then said louder than maybe he needed to, "Lily, I hope you're decent because I'm coming in."

When they stepped into the room, Lily sat up quickly in the bed. "Wade, I told you I didn't want to see him. Get out! Both of you."

"Now, Lily, you're going to listen to me whether you want to or not. All of this isn't Bryce's fault, it's mine." Wade hung his head then raised it as he finally let go of Bryce.

"Your fault? What are you talking about?" Lily sniffled, wiped her eyes with a tissue, and gazed at Wade in confusion.

He took a deep breath, walked over to where Lily sat on the edge of the bed, and stood in front of her. "I did this, Lily. I did. It was all me. I thought I was protecting you, but I was wrong. I was so wrong."

"You're not making any sense. How could any of this possibly be your fault?"

A harried expression crossed Wade's face as his shoulders slumped. He dragged in a deep breath, and pain flickered in his eyes. "I'm the one who called Bryce's mother."

"What?" Lily and Bryce bellowed simultaneously.

"I had to stop what was going on between the two of you. I found my opportunity when I saw Bryce had left his phone in the work truck. I remember how you told me his family was dead set against all of this, so I found his mother's number and together we cooked up a plan. I told her about Hannah calling, and we just went from there."

Lily jerked her head up and glared at Wade. "Why? Why would you do such an awful thing? I thought you were my friend."

Wade pulled off his hat and spun it in his hands. His shoulders slumped forward as remorse shadowed his face. "I thought I was protecting you. I thought he was only here for the money and was using you to get it. I didn't realize until today that he really is in love with you. I'm sorry, Lily, I never meant to hurt you. That's the last thing I wanted to do."

"But you did!" Lily almost screamed, and then she turned away from Wade. Finally, she focused her gaze on Bryce. "So it isn't true about Hannah then?"

"Hannah? What about Hannah?" Bryce asked, dropping his balled fists to his waist not altogether sure he didn't want to throw Wade right through the closed window on the other side of the room.

"Your mother said you lied to me, that Hannah had been your girlfriend for the last three years." Lily didn't really look at Bryce instead she covered her face with her hands. "She lied to me, didn't she? Oh. I'm so sorry, Bryce. I didn't believe you, but she was so convincing. What have I done?"

Understanding flooded through Bryce as he crossed the room, sat next to Lily, and gathered her into his arms. "It's okay, Baby. Please don't cry anymore. Please."

"I'm so sorry, Lily." Wade's voice was low and gravelly.

Lily pulled away from Bryce and looked up at Wade. Choking back a sob she said, "What you did was cruel, and I don't think I can ever forgive you for what you've done."

"I understand." Wade turned to leave the room, stopped at the door, and said over his shoulder, "Bryce, I trust you to do a better job in taking care of her than I ever did."

Bryce stood. "Lily, I'll be right back. I need to speak to Wade."

Lily grabbed his arm as fear rolled across her face. "Bryce, don't."

From the expression on Lily's face, he realized Lily must have thought he was going after Wade for a fight. "It's okay, honey. All I'm going to do is talk to him, nothing more. I promise." Bryce kissed her on the top of the head and hurriedly followed Wade out into the hallway.

"Wade, hold on a minute." Bryce darted down the hallway and caught up with the man at the front door.

Wade stopped with his hand on the door handle. His shoulders slumped forward as he turned to face Bryce. "What do you want, Fowler?"

"I have something I want to say to you. I have to admit what you did was a terrible thing, but somehow I understand why you did it. I know it took a lot for you to make it right. You risked everything, and for that I'm grateful." Bryce held out his hand.

Wade paused for a moment but then took Bryce's hand. "I never meant to hurt her."

"I know. I'll talk to Lily and try to make her understand why you did what you did. I know Lily cares about you, and she needs you in her life, too."

"Why would you do that for me after what I've done?"

"Because, I know Lily cares about you and you for her. Besides, if we're going to be working together, don't you think it's time we bury the hatchet as Lily would say?" He offered his hand to Wade again.

"Yeah." Wade chuckled and slapped his hand into Bryce's. "I think I can live with that."

Bryce nodded as Wade walked out the door. When he turned around to go back to Lily's room, she was standing right behind him. She smiled and rushed into his arms. "I'm so sorry I didn't believe you. Can you ever forgive me?"

"I don't blame you. I love you, Lily, and I want to spend the rest of my life with you." He slipped his finger under her chin, lifted her face, and tenderly kissed her.

"I love you, Bryce."

He drew the ring out of his pocket and held it up. "I think this belongs to you."

"I think you're right." Lily held out her hand, and Bryce slipped the ring onto her finger again. Then he pulled her into his arms and covered her lips with his. Love poured from her kisses into him. He had once told her that his kisses would leave her breathless. Well, if anyone was breathless here, it was him. His country girl sure could kiss. And this city-slicker-turned-country-cowboy would spend the rest of his life letting her.

EPILOGUE

When the wedding march began to play, Lily looped her arm through Wade's as he began to escort her down the aisle toward her groom. A warm feeling flooded her heart when she smiled up at him. She was so thankful they had been able to repair their friendship after what he had done because over the years he had become so important in her and Joey's lives and she didn't want to lose that.

Lily glanced over at Bryce's parents who sat in the second pew of the church.

The day after Wade's confession, Bryce had flown back to New York and had a long sit-down, heart-to-heart conversation with his parents. He confronted his mother about her role in what her and Wade had cooked up. Afterward, his mother wanted to do her best to try and mend her relationship with Bryce and to get to know Lily and Joey.

Lily knew it would take some time and effort but she was willing to work hard at it so they could all be a real family. Bryce's father had even insisted on paying for their honeymoon. God was putting all the pieces of their lives into place.

Wade placed her hand in Bryce's and kissed her on the cheek. "You look beautiful, Lily. Bryce is a very blessed man."

"Thank you, Wade." Her cheeks warmed, and she tiptoed to return a kiss on Wade's cheek.

After the "I do's," Pastor Henry smiled at Bryce and said, "You may now kiss your bride."

Lily tilted her head to accept Bryce's kiss. He drew her into his strong arms, and instead of giving her a short kiss like she thought he would, he kissed her long and sweet until her legs were as limp as bailing twine.

Pastor Henry cleared his throat.

Bryce raised his head and thankfully kept his arms around Lily. If he hadn't, the floor would've swallowed her up. She looked up at his handsome face, and he winked. *Oh you,* she wanted to pop him on the arm but wouldn't in front of all these people. He knew what his kisses had done to her. Well, he didn't look none-too steady either. Her kiss had affected him the same way his had her. She smiled, and a knowing look passed between them.

Pastor Henry turned them around to face family and friends. "Church, I'd like to introduce you to Mr. and Mrs. Bryce Fowler."

Everyone in the church rose to their feet and applauded.

"Bryce and Lily would like to invite everyone to join them in the fellowship hall for the reception," Pastor Henry announced.

When they started down the aisle, Bryce stopped and picked up Joey in his arms. "This is your wedding too, isn't it, Joey?"

"It sure is, Daddy."

At the end of the reception, Mr. Hopper, Martin's lawyer, came up, shook Bryce's hand, and kissed Lily on the cheek. "Congratulations, to the both of you."

"Thank you, Sir." Bryce smiled down at Lily.

"Martin was right all along. He already knew this would happen even before the two of you met. I don't know why I'm so surprised." Mr. Hopper nodded with a grin.

"Surprised? Surprised about what?" Lily asked.

"Well, I have a confession to make. There isn't another DVD." Mr. Hopper shrugged with a blush.

Lily and Bryce looked at each other and then back at Mr. Hopper.

"What? Mr. Hopper, what are you talking about?" Bryce asked.

"You're not making any sense. I'm confused," Lily added with a shrug.

"Martin was convinced that once the two of you met, you would in fact fall in love with each other, and by the time the wedding rolled around, it would be a real marriage, not an arranged one. So everything goes to both of you now. He never devised a will to divide anything."

"What if he had been wrong?" Bryce asked.

"Was he?" Mr. Hopper lifted a brow.

Bryce pulled Lily's hand to his lips and kissed it. "No, no, he wasn't."

"That's what I thought." Mr. Hopper winked and walked away.

Bryce turned to Lily, pulled her close into his arms, and whispered against her ear. "Well, Mrs. Fowler, are you ready to start our marriage of convenience?"

"This isn't any marriage of convenience, mister. It's the real deal."

"It sure is." They both laughed, and then melted into each other's arms.

About the Author
Debra Lynn Collins

I was born and raised in Georgia, but I moved to Alabama after my husband and I were married in 1981. I consider myself a Georgiabamian. I adore the south, I couldn't imagine myself living anywhere else.

God blessed me with four wonderful children, and as of right now seven grandchildren.

Through the years I've tried my hand at many, many other crafts. I enjoy quilting, making candles, soap, and jewelry. I also scrapbook, do woodworking, and cake decorating. Oh, and did I mention, I LOVE TO COOK!

My writing journey...I started writing romance stories at the early age of 13. I still remember vividly the night I wrote my first story. I had watched a movie with my sister that night, and I didn't like the way the movie ended. So I slipped away into my bedroom, grabbed a pen and paper and wrote the ending the way I wanted it. Before I knew it, I saw the sun peeking through the curtains and realized I'd been up all night, writing...and that was the beginning of my writing journey.

I'm a Contemporary Christian Romance Writer...There's just something about those***Heart Pounding***Pulse Racing***Makes You Weak in the Knees***Happily-Ever-After***Once in a Lifetime***Love Stories!

I do believe in those fairy tales romances because I'm living mine with my wonderful husband, Steve. He is my hero, best friend, and he still makes my heart skip a beat when he just holds my hand.

♥ ♥ ♥

The reason I write the stories I write... I believe everyone yearns for that happily ever-after, fairy tale romance.

Although my characters may suffer tragedy, loss, or past broken relationships, they ALWAYS find an everlasting love in the end. Love always conquers all!!

I write Christian romances, because I can tell my stories without compromising my convictions.

Visit my website: http://www.debralynncollins.com/
Facebook: https://www.facebook.com/debralynncollins
Or email me at: debracollins@tds.net

I'd love to hear from you!